Many thanks to the beautiful towns of Baraboo and Spring Green.
They have been an inspiration.
Baraboo is the origin of the marvelous Ringling Brothers Circus, and Spring
Green has one of the greatest museums in the world:

House on the Rock.

Jackie Bennett

THE BARABOO MCGUFFIN

AUSTIN MACAULEY PUBLISHERS™

LONDON * CAMBRIDGE * NEW YORK * SHARJAH

Though the Ringling Brothers and *House on the Rock* are part of this fictive novel, this is not a work of historical fiction. The stories and events that reference them are fully made up. Names, characters, businesses, places, events, locales, and incidents are either the products of the author's imagination or used in a fictitious manner. Any resemblance to actual persons, living or dead, or actual events is purely coincidental.

Ordering Information
Quantity sales: Special discounts are available on quantity purchases by corporations, associations, and others. For details, contact the publisher at the address below.

Publisher's Cataloguing-in-Publication data
Bennett, Jackie
The Baraboo McGuffin

ISBN 9798886931334 Paperback
ISBN 9798886931341 ePub e-book

Library of Congress Control Number: 2023908929

www.austinmacauley.com/us

First Published 2024
Austin Macauley Publishers LLC
40 Wall Street, 33rd Floor, Suite 3302
New York, NY 10005
USA

mail-usa@austinmacauley.com
+1 (646) 5125767

Perhaps the mission of those who love mankind is to make people laugh at the truth, to make truth laugh, because the only truth lies in learning to free ourselves from insane passion for the truth.

– Umberto Eco

The McGuffin? It's the object of every quest.

                    Hitchcock? No. Anonymous

Part I
Departure

Chapter One

Where had it come from, that doodle on Mr. Bononosetta's desk – not *on* the desk, but on the blank white paper there – a doodle that looked like a whale, but perhaps was not a whale, a doodle that looked like this:

Well, we know where it came from. It came from Mr. Bononosetta himself, of course, or through him, anyway, for who can trace the springs and hatches of a doodle to…where? The mind? The toilet training or the *TV Guide*? A loving universe, perhaps? But enough and good enough to say that Mr. Bononosetta made that mark – a whale? Very like a whale. You can see the eye yourself. Perhaps a whale then, and that would make some sense, for who was this Mr. Bononosetta but a fish out of water, or a landsman dreaming of the sea, or, in any case, a high school English teacher dreaming of a novel – living in a novel! – *Moby-Dick*.

But that's ridiculous. Nothing lives in novels except for certain types of saprophytic fungi, look them up and you will find this for yourself. No, Mr. Bononosetta did not live *in* a novel. Still, perhaps he did live *through* one – Ishmael's novel, *Moby Dick*.

Now all of us remember *Moby Dick*. We have seen a film of it or read it in abridgement, or we have had a certain kind of teacher prescribe it for us like a dose of cod liver oil that the teachers would be loath to take themselves. We know at least who Ahab is and how he lost his leg to Moby Dick, and how he chased that great white whale right around the globe to get it back. Most of us know that Ahab failed and that the whole thing ends in shipwreck, and some of us even know enough to think that maybe it is not Ahab who is truly at the center of that book, nor even Moby Dick himself, but instead the rather mild Ishmael, the storyteller, who tells the tale because he alone survives to tell it, buoyed up in the coffin of his bosom friend, his Queequeg, noble savage, son of kings. It was this tale our English teacher loved.

It was this tale that he had read perhaps a thousand times. It's true. He had. He had studied *Moby Dick* and Moby Dick. He had considered the whiteness of that old white whale from every angle of the page. He had held Ahab's gold doubloon at length, and hovered over the blue Descartian vortices, deep ocean whirlpools, just as Ishmael had. Sometimes it seemed he had even fallen in.

But these are *Moby Dick* things – the gold doubloon, the vortices. The reader of this tale need hardly be concerned with things like that. Still, Mr. Bononosetta was more than just concerned. He was obsessed with *Moby Dick*. He lived within this book, and sometimes, though he knew he was not Ishmael, he called himself Ishmaelean and amused himself with correspondences – was not Ishmael something like a teacher? Did not he too dream of the sea? True, Mr. Bononosetta had never actually gone to sea as Ishmael had, nor seen the great leviathan in its savage element – the raging waters, the sea and sky contending, the damnéd fury of the white-capped waves – no he had not seen all that. Still, he *had* seen something once: a killer whale –an orca – performing acrobatics in a grand amusement park's aquarium, and though the killer seemed quite friendly (no leg-biter, that, balancing a leggy blond upon his great black brow), it had thrilled him nonetheless. He could easily imagine Moby Dick.

And yet he was not Ishmael. When it came to questing, Mr. Bononosetta had heard the call to quest, but he had stayed at home to study it, tracing the quest for truth back and forth through a trail of dusty books, seeking a metaphoric dragon as all questing knights must do. And there was something sad in that for Katie White (you will meet her for yourself in just a minute), and for Mr. Bononosetta something maybe sadder still. True, perhaps, that to leap from one book to another is itself a certain kind of quest, and true again that no one could expect him to ship himself upon the seas of high adventure. Whaling was, one must admit, a dying industry. Still, if only he could have shut the books just once and gotten up upon his legs, and hung a sign "Gone Questing" on his chalkboard much as Ishmael would have done if he had taught, and then gone out and sought the dragon-whale – and yet here he sat, by night among his volumes, and by day in high school classrooms, out of his depths.

In school, the problem was his students; he could not fathom them. After all, Mr. Bononosetta was not merely a literary man but a man who studied literature, and like all humans of his kind, he could not quite figure out why the world around him did not know the obscure things that he knew. Why, for example, couldn't his students discern the footprints of the Jungian subconscious in a simple fairytale? Why hadn't they read Foucault and Paul deMann? Why didn't they even know if Shakespeare's plays should be considered Freudian or Marxist?

These were great mysteries for Mr. Bononosetta, and there were other, stranger things: the scrawl the students ciphered onto desks, for instance, and the way they only did their questing for their mirrors and their lipsticks in their book bags – why for these? Why not in books? If they shunned their books because they had what he did not – that is, the will and the ambition to "get up on their legs" and do great things – well, that he would have forgiven, and would have understood. But as it was, he could not fathom them. They were kids who drove fast cars to nowhere special and laughed at all the roadmaps – they were not an audience interested in the quest.

Well, he did not understand them. They all said that they were not questers, and who could blame them? They were young, after all, school was a bore. Why sacrifice their morning hours? Printed words swimming on a page (like white whales, he would have told them, like hieroglyphics on the brow of the leviathan) – well, who had time for that?

Mr. Bononosetta sighed, picked up his pen and dangled it just above what he'd begun. It was June, the last day of school. Above his head the dust of chalk swirled in upon itself in the overheated light. Katie White, he thought, at least Katie White – and then, just as the pen descended, there she was. "What's that, Mr. Bononosetta? Is it a whale?"

"Katie!" Mr. Bononosetta looked up startled.

"Mr. Bononosetta!"

Katie was scoffing at him, the way a person scoffs when they love the thing they scoff at, the intonation of her voice a perfect imitation of his own.

"What? I thought I was alone."

"*Alone dwell the kings of the sea*, Mr. Bononosetta. As for you, you have your whale." Katie looked down at the doodle again. "It is a whale, isn't it?"

Mr. Bononosetta smiled up at the girl standing before him, clear of eye, long of leg, and – even on this last day of the term with classes done and nothing left for her but graduation – armed as always for the battle, a pen in one hand, a notebook in the other. She was, perhaps, the one exception among his students that proved the general rule: Katie White read everything and anything. And more than that: Katie White was just the sort, he thought, to embark upon a quest.

"Well," she demanded, sitting down. "Is it a whale?"

"A whale? Nothing like a whale," he said, "nothing like at all. It's a doodle. Don't you ever doodle?"

And Katie told him that she didn't. No time, she said, a waste of time – and then, as if she'd read his thoughts, or as if to make her favorite teacher smile – "Would Sir Lancelot have doodled," she demanded, "on his way to slay a dragon? Consider me Sir Lancelot," she said, half laughing, "as summer starts and high school ends, I'm ready for a quest. Although of course, now Harry – and then she told how Harry doodled, or how at least he used to, Harry Jinx "– but that was only natural," Katie said, "a boy like that, characters from comic books, the same two doodled characters, sitting, standing, playing baseball, the same stupid expression on their face."

So Katie said, and leaning forward, tapping her pen against the desk, twirling it round between her fingers, above the first, beneath the next, from forefinger to pinky and then back up again, she returned to her Sir Lancelot, and demanded answers. "Did he ever slay a dragon? Because St. George did, didn't he? And Sir Gawain too? So then why not Sir Lancelot? Same hero, no? Just a different face?" Her father had said no, but she said yes, but she couldn't find it in a book, and though Mr. Bononosetta interrupted just enough to suggest that really, her father being who he was, he really ought to know (Mr. Bononosetta keeping both eyes fixed upon the pen). She interrupted back again. "No," she said, "not really, he isn't always right," and then went on and told him of her summer plans.

"I'm packing Harry Jinx up. I'm taking him away."

"Harry? Isn't he a little…"

"A little what? We always do it. His parents and my mother travel together while Harry and I stay somewhere on our own. We leave right after graduation."

"You and Harry? Where?"

"Anywhere. Nowhere. When we were kids, it was camp. We hated it. And Harry. Boy oh boy. And once we went to New Hampshire, and then last year it was Cape Cod. We stayed with Harry's aunt. Harry doodled quite a bit and waded in the breakers, and I made sure he didn't drown."

"That's all?" Mr. Bononosetta narrowed his eyes. "At Cape Cod I mean?"

"What, whales?" Katie laughed a little. "No. No whales. No Moby Dick. Harry Jinx gets sick on boats. We couldn't even take the whale-watch tour."

Then Katie told Mr. Bononosetta all about Cape Cod and then New Hampshire, about Harry, her father, a book of beasts she had recently acquired, all the while her right eye squinting slightly. Katie knew about the squint. People had remarked on it all her life, told her that she looked like a carpenter about to measure something, or an astronomer at his telescope, the way that one eye squinted, and maybe it was something she had inherited, but lately she preferred to see it as a sign of some sort, a mark, like her last name might be a mark, or like the seven toes of Cuchulain or the purple pimpernel. Heroes destined for a certain greatness were always marked in such a way. Even now she was thinking of precisely this when suddenly, just as she began to lay out for Mr. Bononosetta the current summer plans, he interrupted.

"Wisconsin?"

"Yep. Wisconsin. Ever been there? My father's girlfriend's uncle's cousins – two of them actually, twins – have some kind of farm or something… Blunderbee outside a town called Baraboo."

And then (and Katie White would swear to this later, over and over again, to Harry Jinx, who of course did not believe it) something happened. Mr. Bononosetta's eyes began to glint! And when he spoke, there was thunder in his voice.

"SHIPPED THEN, ARE YOU?" he boomed, leaning forward, both hands on the desk. "Are you shipped?"

"Shipped?" Katie sat back just a little in her seat. "In Wisconsin?"

"Yes, yes, your names are down for it then? – Thunder and blast, girl. Have you signed the articles? Signed them? Was there anything down there about your souls? About Harry Jinx's soul?"

Katie's eyes went wide. Thunder and blast? Had he really said thunder and blast? There was something vaguely *Moby Dickish* in it, she thought, and she remembered Elijah, a prophet of a certain type who warns Ishmael not to quest upon the Pequod with that crazy Ahab. So, thought Katie, Mr. Bononosetta has become Elijah! – and although you and I might say at most that Mr. Bononosetta was only imitating Elijah, that books are books and Mr. Bononosetta was Mr. Bononosetta, and certainly no more an Elijah than an Ishmael, even if he was "shabbily appareled in a faded jacket" as Elijah was (for what teacher is not?) – although you and I may be sure that Mr. Bononosetta was indeed no Elijah – yet for Katie, well, she was enthralled.

She stood up and leaned in closer. "Is this some kind of –"

"You are thinking of Elijah? But perhaps I am more suited to be a Joachim."

"Joachim…?"

And then, seeming more himself, but only slightly, Mr. Bononosetta let out a single note: HA!, such as men in books will do, as if to show her that that allusion to her soul was nothing but a game, that he was just pretending, playing prophet to her questing Ishmael (or her Lancelot, had not she mentioned Lancelot herself?) – a joke, a vast joke, Wisconsin and its cheddar cheese and dairy maids, hardly a place for questing – how hilarious – except that in that single HA his breath came hot and dry as flames.

Katie stepped back. She was about to say something, anything, when he spoke again.

"But – and mind you this, Katie White," he said, his voice nearly a whisper, "Wisconsin may seem like just a place for cheddar cheese, but cheddar cheese or no, the whale is there. And see you do not lose your soul to him, for souls are easy things to lose when the whale has made its final turn and four gaunt horses fly above your head!"

And then it was over. Katie shook his hand with both of hers, squinted, and then left. She had been given a hint, she told herself. All she had to do was look it up.

Chapter Two

Harry Jinx. Well, you know Harry Jinx. You have heard his name already in Chapter One, and maybe you have met him before that too, sometimes taller, sometimes shorter, sometimes with glasses and sometimes without – do with him what you will and he will still be Harry Jinx of Jinx Stinx playground fame – though he did not stink, it was just something they said when he was younger. Children in a playground will say all kinds of things about a boy like Harry, a boy in whom there is something glazed about the face, something stuck midway between selfishness and fear. But he was not so odd really, and really not so selfish, just a boy growing up, any boy at all who is a little clumsy and prefers the mindless replication of things he knows to new games or new frontiers. You see him? Good. Untie his shoes now – this is crucial, you shall see why later on, and in any case, if his shoes were not untied, then his mother could not always be shouting, "Harry, for God's sake, tie your shoe."

She should have said both shoes.

And so, there sat Harry Jinx on the stoop of Katie White's house barely an hour after the Katie White – Mr. Bononosetta foreshadowing scene of Chapter One, knowing not a thing about it, and yet ready enough to play the noble squire at Katie's side, for he was half in love with her. Perhaps he would be Queequeg to her questing Ishmael, or even Sancho Panza to her Don Quixote. But they are different sorts of sidekicks, are they not? A Queequeg and a Sancho Panza? But Harry Jinx knew none of that – questing books were not the sorts of books that he would read.

"Hey, Harry Jinx, your shoe's untied." And Katie didn't even stop, sailed right on up the steps and through the door, and went inside.

Harry waited. It was always this way. Katie didn't like him – or at least she didn't like him any more than she liked her mother's basset hound (also named Harry, and whether they had done it on purpose he would never know for sure), which meant that he was merely worthy of the human equivalent of an occasional scratch behind the left ear, or a toe nudged up beneath his belly, which he imagined she was nudging on the basset hound, even now as she stood before the freezer trying to decide between the creamsicle and the chocolate ice cream pop. Inside, she chose chocolate. Outside, Harry tied his shoe and thought about Wisconsin. Cape Cod was one thing. Anyone could see the reason for Cape Cod. But Wisconsin? Who goes to Wisconsin?

"Who goes to Wisconsin, anyway?" he called in through the door.

"We do." And that was it. She vanished into the darker recesses of the house, to her bedroom maybe – he trembled just to think of it. She had let him see her bedroom only once, when he was ten and she was thirteen– but that was four years ago, and he hadn't been there since.

Harry sighed and gave his lace a final tug. No point staying here, he thought. Down the steps went Harry Jinx and out the front gate, stopping only once when something on the pavement caught his eye. He stooped, examined it, and picked it up. It was a small thing. We shall hear more about it later.

Meanwhile, upstairs sat Katie White cross-legged at the center of her bed, lights out, shades down, a candle lit, scanning the books upon her shelf and looking for a link or clue to Mr. Bononosetta's prophesy.

When she was younger, Katie had believed in the magic of mere things: crystal balls, and eye of newt, and drugstore horoscopes decorated with moons and stars and the round face of a cat. She had believed, as witches do, in the secret linkings of one thing to the next – the link of an elixir made of lionheart to the rising courage of a man, for instance, or the pin inside the voodoo doll to the pain inside an enemy who clutched his sides and fell down dead. And did not the planets move in telling ways? And could not even a big bald head be tufted when sprinkled with the essence of a fuzzy peach? These links were everywhere, Katie had thought when she was younger. Someone might have made them up, but she never thought that someone had simply made them up. Links were everywhere, and hidden, and it became her task to use her skills at divination to find the linking threads that lurk beneath the surface of the visible, in talismans and tea leaves, the entrails of an eagle, and the pathway of the stars. Thus Katie believed, and she had acted on belief. She had cast spells and sat with Harry at the Ouija board. She had practiced divination with tossed-out chicken bones. She had read Harry's sweating palm. Find the links, she thought, between the one thing and the next and then another, and at the end one must find God.

But Katie was much older now; the universe, she had discovered, did not respond to incantations of that kind, and even by the flipping of her tarot cards God had refused to speak. But if the universe were indeed strung out along a cable, then how to pull the string? Katie had desired magic and then despaired of it, but desire is desire; desperate, she had transferred her desires to her books and sought for links between their many universes, believing they would all add up to truth. So then Katie, now, was a kind of story witch.

Of course, Katie did not see it quite that way. The phrase "story witch" would never have occurred to her – as far as she was concerned (and in spite of the candles she sometimes chose to read by) she had left magic far behind. Reading stories and summing up the meaning of all the books she read – this had nothing to do with magic. She did believe, however, that there were links and patterns across the books she read, and that perhaps writers were inspired by powers higher than their own. After all didn't writers sometimes say they'd been inspired by powers higher than their own? And if God inspires artists, then how much of a leap is it to think He might have woven a single holy grail between the texts? Holy grails are the things that questers quest, and that wasn't magic, Katie reasoned; it was common sense.

And now: *Four gaunt horses*, she muttered to herself, *four gaunt horses and a whale* These words of Mr. Bononosetta had been spoken in the real world, not the world of fiction, Katie thought. But these words could also be a kind of bridge, a magic key of sorts, as if he had unlocked and opened up a door and then invited Katie to cross the threshold between the ordinary world she lived in, and the world she loved and dreamed of, the paragraphs of fiction and the cantos of romance. After all, the real Mr. Bononosetta had also proffered a warning out of fiction – "Anything down there about your souls?" he had asked her, in words from *Moby-Dick.* So then, surely the door had opened, and should she dare to cross the threshold, she would be plunged into the landscape of a quest, yellow brick roads and vast Akian seas, from Thebes to Canterbury and La Mancha and beyond, through a labyrinth of written labyrinths, where she would find the answer to the single, overwhelming question, *Who am I?*

Katie longed to go.

But if the door was opened, just where was it, and where was the threshold she might cross?

Walking home from school that day, Katie thought that before she plunged into a fictive world, she had to find some objective link between the real-life

Mr. Bononosetta who tapped his lectern and bored his students, and the prophet he had become from a work of fiction he had read. And that link, she reasoned with a coolness that impressed her, would not be found in *Moby-Dick,* or in any other fictive work, but rather somewhere between novels and real life, somewhere in that twilight world where real life becomes written life or where (as Mr. Bononosetta had said in class one day) the written whales of fiction meet the living whales of facts. And where did such a meeting happen? Where did written words meet up with life? Well, in nonfiction books, of course, in reference works and history books, and maybe even occultish books aimed right at cultish teenagers, like the ones that lined her bottom shelf. *Illuminati, Templar Knights, and Lennon* one was called; *Order out of Chaos, Collections and Calliope* was another.

And so, when she got home, she scanned the shelf, skipped these two, and chose the first book of her quest, this vaguely lovely teenager's guide to prophets and apocalyptic writings, *A History of the End of the World.* After all, she thought, four gaunt horses are part of the biblical apocalypse: Death, Famine, War, and Conquest.

Whales made no appearance in the index. Nor did Wisconsin, nor Elijah – but how about this Joachim? There were three whole pages devoted to an old Sicilian monk, and when Katie turned to them, she discovered that Joachim was a prophet just like Elijah was a prophet, though in this case it was not the fictional Ishmael that Joachim harangued, but four medieval popes and several emperors whom he entertained and  terrified with his predictions about the coming End.

Born in about 1135 and called by some the most influential European up until Karl Marx, Joachim had penned three major works and a few more minor ones, and during the intervening centuries at least a dozen more had borne his name – hoaxes every single one. This information appeared in a brief biography on page seventy-seven of the book, and along with the biography, the editors had also provided a rather whimsical cartoon of the bemused

Joachim seated at his desk, one hand wrapped around his pen and the other cupping at his ear as if he had just heard the call to dinner, or more likely, Katie thought, had heard the voice of God. That's what it is, she thought, God dictating some true thing about apocalypse that the old monk had now embellished on his own and jotted down.

The jottings became a treatise, and the treatise seemed to be the usual stuff: monsters, circles, alphas, omegas – a monk with too much time on his hands, Katie's father would have said (we shall meet him soon enough) – and, in the excerpt included on page seventy-eight, even a seven-headed dragon with his attendant kings, false prophets and an Antichrist or two. Here, for the reader's edification, is an excerpt of the excerpt Katie read:

In that time the seventh head of the dragon will also arise, the king who is called Antichrist and a multitude of false prophets with him…He will arise from the West and will come to the aid of the king who will be at the head of the pagans. He will perform great signs before him and his army…The Lord will shorten those days for the sake of the elect…

Hmmm, thought Katie, a seven-headed dragon. That seems significant. According to the editors, seven was a magic number for this Joachim, along with two and three, and this intrigued Katie, but though she read the passage three times over, she could find no link between Mr. Bononosetta and this prophet, Joachim. True, Mr. Bononosetta (though he had never even been to Italy) was almost as Sicilian as this monk. His parents were Sicilian, or his parents' parents, and he had, now that she came to think of it, sometimes in his darker moments – when, for example, not a single student could (or as he suspected, would) name the author of *Catcher in the Rye* – he would speak Silican to his bewildered students who could only suspect that they were being cursed in a language they did not understand. So, yes, there was that connection to Joachim. Still, thought Katie, a mere allusion to a common ancestry was not the stuff to hang a quest on. That link was almost incidental. There must be something more. Katie read the passage one more time, and then turned back to look again at the picture of the monk.

And then, suddenly, there it was, the link, so obvious, so everywhere that she could not believe she had not seen it right way. It wound its way throughout the picture's fluted frame and curved along the windows behind the seated monk. It trellised right across his desk. It snaked along the rim of the chalice on the desk. It even slithered up the monk himself, it was his line of lip, the slant of his left eyebrow – it was there, the shadow of the Mr. Bononosetta's doodle, a very leitmotif of swimming whales in the illuminating cartoon of this prophet, Joachim.

Katie was astounded.

And then, like thunder after lighting, something else occurred to her: the significance of her beloved teacher's name. She had always known that Bononosetta had its Latin roots in "good," just as *bon* in French means good and *benne* in some other spoken tongue. But now she also remembered that Mr. Bononosetta's given name was Jack, a name so queerly close to Joachim that it set her teeth on edge. Mr. Bononosetta, she now realized, was not simply some impersonator of the old Sicilian monk; rather, he was this Joachim in one form or another, and in his goodness he was sending her on an apocalyptic quest. Just what that meant – apocalyptic quest – she wasn't sure, but she knew he could be trusted to do right by her; his virtue was written right there in his name.

But I see the reader protests. Names are only names, the reader says, and besides, how could Mr. Bononosetta have known she would open this book, and find this picture? What possible connection could this picture have with whales (do you see any whales?), or with his warning about being shipped and losing souls? What possible connection, for that matter, to Wisconsin?

What possible connection indeed. None, perhaps, for the teller of this tale, or for the reader of it, but for Katie, well, Katie leaned back against her headboard and smiled into the dark. Things were linking up somehow, some kind of magic was at work. Like Percival, Katie White would seek a holy grail (and never mind the fate of that poor knight). This whale-doodle connection between Mr. Bononosetta and the book-bound Joachim was a beginning. Mr. Bononosetta had unlocked a door, Katie decided. The door was open; she would go.

A knock upon another door, and time for dinner. Katie put her book back on the shelf, snuffed the candle out, shook off the dust of mystery descending and descended herself the thirteen steps to dinner, to see what mystery waited for her there.

Forty miles away, meanwhile, in the drab heart of New York City, Professor Harold White said good-bye to his ex-wife, hung up the phone, and turned to his bookshelves. It was an instinctive thing, this turning from his wife to his bookshelves, and it was in fact this turning that had led halfway to their divorce. In this particular case, however, he turned there not so much to escape the ex-Mrs. White, as to find something for Katie. His ex-wife had called to remind him that she would be travelling with the Jinxes this summer as she always did, that Katie would be spending the summer in Wisconsin with Harry Jinx, and that he, Harold White, would be caring for the family's basset hound. Thus, Professor White, ever thoughtful (or, at least, always thinking), had turned to his shelves to find for Katie White a summer book.

Professor White was a New York City intellectual, all beard and stomach, tweed and pipe, and he taught obscure courses like *George Gasgoine and the Allegory of Knowing* at Columbia University. He was a literary critic, an Eminence, a Grand Wizard who wrote books about books – and more, wrote books about books about books, critiquing the literary critics, so that if feminism were the current cant, he did not churn out a book about the women of *Moby-Dick,* as one of his colleagues had (a ridiculous book in any case, the only females in *Moby-Dick* being an innkeeper and a sister of charity, with these two comprising so little of the novel's bulk that they were like fleas on that Leviathan), but churned out instead a book about the critic who wrote that book. He commented on the commentators, glossed the glossers like a flea upon a flea, weighing flea souls, electing some and damning others. And because he was glib, and because he could sometimes write without resorting to the esoteric twaddle of his colleagues, his voice was heard beyond the ivory towers that he haunted: he had once been profiled in a very popular New York magazine, for example, and his name came up at publishing parties and gallery openings where perhaps no one had actually read his books, but they had read articles about his books, and could even let a glibbish phrase of his role off their teflon tongues.

Now this man brought Katie up, and over the years he had inoculated her against ignorance in much the same way that Hawthorne's Rappaccini had inoculated his own daughter against evil, except that he did not feed her poison out of vials, but rather stories out of books. It was he who had given her the complete works of Matthew Arnold, for example, as well as those of Aristophanes, Luigi Pirandello, and Laurence Sterne. And he had given her other things as well: *Mimeticism Made Easy* at nine; *Phenomenology and Ontology: Probing Questions in the Sphynxtic Postulations of Intent,* at ten ("What's ontology?" Harry Jinx had asked her. "Something like proctology only worse," she muttered, and he didn't dare to ask her any more); then essential essays by the world-renowned George Lukas and Lionel Trilling; and finally, at thirteen – an impressionable age in girls, some say – Northrop Frye's *Anatomy of Criticism*, in which this critic-hero slew the story-minotaur and wrote an exposition of its bones.

Fear not, good reader, you need not care about such things. Critics, glossers, fleas on fleas and such – they have naught to do with us. We only mention them for Katie's sake, because Katie had to read them, and because she had been impressed by Northrop Frye. The bones beneath one story, Frye had theorized were much like the bones beneath the others. Frye had found connections, patterns, a way to link up stories, and such a feat is likely to work powerful magic on the psyche of a story witch. Even now, more than four years since she first had read him, Katie still rattled off an occasional Fryish disquisition to the bewildered Harry Jinx.

Still, that was only Katie, and Katie's father had himself abandoned Frye some time ago for greener fields, for deconstructed fields in fact, *deconstruction* being the latest turf where academic battles were fought and won and lost. No patterns anymore in literature. No common bones. The pendulum had swung the other way. Indeed, it was a book on deconstruction, along with a deconstructed book, that he gave his daughter when the Whites arrived two days later (Harry in tow, both Harrys, both boy and basset hound), Professor White having adjudged, perhaps too rashly, that Katie was prepared to deconstruct.

"…three bowls of water a day," his ex-wife was saying about one Harry while Katie parleyed with the other by the door. "It has to be three bowls, and it has to be the red bowl, otherwise he starts to fuss. Harold, are you listening or are you playing with your pipe?"

"Hmmm? Of course I'm listening. You said Harry fusses." Professor White put down his pipe and glanced toward Harry at the door. Strange boy. What did Katie see in him anyway? "Harry fusses?"

"Of course Harry fusses, if you bothered to pay attention to our basset hound once in a while, you'd see he fusses quite a lot. Why else would he drool? And don't forget the eye drops. He's nearly blind."

Ah. The dog. She meant the dog. Harry the dog was blind? "Poor thing," he murmured, leaning down to pat the old dog on its head. "Yes, there's a good…Katie? Kate, I have a gift for you."

"A gift?" Katie abandoned the human Harry by the door and stepped into the room. "I asked Mr. Bononosetta about Lancelot, I'm still not sure – Is it a book?" Katie glanced at the package her father was holding and then looked him – as she always did – directly in the eye.

"A book? Of course a book!" Professor White thrust the package into her hands. "Two books actually…a…something to jam against mouse holes and throw at rats, as someone said…Lichten-something…?"

"Lichtenberg." Katie looked down at the books. "You wrapped them?"

"Of course I wrapped them! Well, actually, Ellie must have wrapped them." Right, Ellie, Katie thought. The earnest young blonde. That's what her mother used to say before the divorce whenever Katie asked – your father's off in the city sleeping with an earnest young blonde – or brunette sometimes, or occasionally a redhead, graduate students one and all, and Katie didn't really mind them (even if it did seem odd to her, the way that every single one of them described themselves as poets). But still, she wished that Ellie had left the gift alone.

Katie tore the wrapping off.

"Wow!" she said. "Trithemius! King of the occult."

"You've heard of him? Hmm…" Professor White pushed his glasses into his face, the way he always did when he thought he might be bested.

Of course she had heard of him. Katie owned all three volumes of *The Stegonographia* by Trithemius and during the days she was deep into her witch phase, she had poured over these volumes on countless moonlit evenings, especially the third volume, indexed by the pope, and puzzled over by hell-raisers and witches for at least five-hundred years. A book of spells, they said. Not that she believed that anymore, of course. Still, what a great gift for a quest. Katie thanked her father profusely. "I never knew you liked Trithemius…"

"Yes, well…it's not exactly Trithemius, Katie. *Trithemius Decomposed* by someone else. You're not familiar with the other one I hope?"

Katie looked at the title of the second book. "*On Grammatology*?"

"Yes! *On Grammatology*! By Derrida."

"I've never heard of it."

"Katie, you will love it." Professor White beamed and patted Katie on the head. "It cuts everything to pieces. You'll love them both, and you know, I really think you're ready for them too."

But later, in the car on the way home, Katie wasn't so sure. Derrida looked harmless, but the cover of *Trithemius Decomposed* was black, and the title stood out in such startling relief. In Italian class she had read the third canto of

Dante…What was it he had written on the gates of hell? *Abandon hope all ye who enter here*? She'd bring the book, but she wouldn't read it yet.

Chapter Three

It was a hot blast of wind that followed them out of New York, an easterly in a land where easterlies were rare, an easterly that stirred up flies and tied the tongues of weathermen in knots, blew dust into the puzzled eyes of farmers and gave barren birth to a host of bland apocalyptic visions all along the airwaves, one station to the next. Sitting in the front seat between his mother and father, Harry turned the dial on the radio back and forth stringing one voice into the next until Katie thought she heard them blend into a single, linked cabal. *Ozone Holes and Aliens*, one talk show host declared, and – as Harry spun the dial to the right – *The Virgin lurking in a hotdog roll…polar bears in the desert*, and *a grand aligned conspiracy among the stars of Hollywood*. Monstrous, Katie thought, monstrous wonders and monstrous accusations directed to our internal seven-headed monsters that are our longing and our fear.

Followed by the wind? More. They were pursued. That's what Katie thought sitting beside her mother in the back seat of Mr. Jinx's Chevrolet. The wind had pursued them 700 miles across New Jersey, Pennsylvania, Ohio, Indiana, and Illinois, and they had fled before it, not stopping at the visitor centers, hardly stopping even to eat except at roadside rest stops where, stumbling from the car into the hot oppressiveness of it all, they'd buy candy from vending machines, stretch, and use the restrooms, and then struggle back to the safety of the comforting interior of the Chevrolet and cross another dead expanse. "Nothing to see in these parts," Mr. Jinx insisted when his wife wondered if maybe they should get off the Interstate and wander along the corn-stalked by-ways stretched out to right and left. "Nothing to see…" and maybe he was right, but that wasn't what kept him from stopping the car. It was the wind. None of them spoke of it, but all of them knew.

In fact, they hardly spoke of anything. A deep lethargy had come over everyone but Katie; there was an excess of yawning, and sometimes Katie noticed that Mrs. Jinx's lips would stretch tight across her teeth so that she looked like something washed up in a desert. Katie was unnerved.

"What are the roots that clutch?" she demanded softly. "This, this heap of broken…something…"

"What?"

"What's that Katie? What's that?" Mr. Jinx was momentarily roused, or maybe anxious. He was a science teacher, Mr. Jinx, but he had studied poetry in college.

"Nothing," Katie said. And then, *"The Wasteland. T.S. Eliot"*

"What?"

"Nothing…It was nothing…"

"Nothing?"

"Nothing, Mr. Jinx. It was nothing."

But then, a few minutes later, "Better merely to say, Mr. Jinx, that the time is out of joint."

Blandly, without a shadow of thinking to ruffle up his forehead, Mr. Jinx smiled into the rear-view mirror and pushed the car to eighty-one.

Pursued. The night before – their first night out – they had found rooms in western Ohio, and when they emerged into the parking lot in the morning, a fine dust had blown over the car – but oddly only theirs. "It must have been the angle," said Mrs. White – but Katie could discern fine tongues of fire drawn into the dust, a rooster and towers too, and then at breakfast in a diner, a man, alone at the booth across the way had tapped the edges of his forehead and then gone to pay the bill, looking back at them three times – three times! – before he finally left, rode out on a skelter of noise, driving his motorcycle straight into the wind.

"Gone off to tell someone about us," Katie murmured to Harry on the way out, but Harry was yawning, his hands deep in his pockets, as if he hadn't heard. The fact of the matter was that Harry Jinx was avoiding his beloved. He loved her, yes, of course he loved her, there could be no doubt of that, but she had been acting strangely – strangely even for her. First, there had been this business about questers ("Jesters?" he had said, the night before they left. "No. Questers, Harry Jinx. Questers with a *q*."). Katie said she was an archetypal quester – a hero on a journey to the center of herself. She explained it all to him, and she accompanied her explanation with passages xeroxed out of books for his perusal: something about a knight fighting a windmill; something about how questers find their father ("But your father's in New York," he said. And

Katie answered, "Forget about my father."), and then something else, about the three archetypal aspects of a quest: departure, initiation, and finally return. "Not to mention," Katie added, "something small and physical that sometimes happens. For example, ...*the finger pricked by spindle* or *the knick on Gawain's neck.*"

None of it meant a thing to him, of course, and now there was this business with the books. It had come out the first night of the journey – come through the motel wall actually where, while he and his family sat on one side in their room (his mother giggling, her fist up at her mouth, a hotel glass against the plaster wall), Katie and her mother argued terrifically in the room next door. It seemed Katie's suitcase contained nothing except for books: *The History of the End...? The Book of Beasts...?* and plenty more – her travelling library Katie called it, the bare essentials for a quest – these books, and only two changes of underwear and socks, some glue-on moons, a candle, nothing else.

"What is all this," they heard from Katie's mother, vaguely, through the wall. "You're going to Wisconsin, not a fucking séance!"

And in the morning, there wasn't a single word about it to the Jinx's. Katie looked clean enough it was true (even if she was wearing yesterday's clothes), – but even Harry had to admit there was something queer in all of it – best to love her from a distance, especially with this other thing going on.

Hmmm. This other thing.

"Ma. Hand me that newspaper again."

It was the afternoon of their second day out, and they had been heading west through the anonymous landscape of interstate 80 since early morning. Mrs. Jinx was half asleep, but at the sound of her son's voice, she reached mechanically for the crumpled paper at her feet, handed it to him, and let her head roll forward once again, leaving him to scan, for perhaps the tenth time, the article about the Sag Harbor Whaling Museum. According to the article, the museum had been looted by what were apparently teenage pranksters – graffiti on the scrimshaw, obscenely placed harpoons, toilet paper strewn like a bower on the old whale skeleton that hung from the ceiling, a real mess, the article said, but none of it too serious, except that these pranksters had taken a coin that was on loan to the museum.

The article claimed that the coin was probably of very little value on the underground numismatic market, but that its owner, one Annabel Higgins, attached great sentimental value to it, it being said to have been in her great-grandfather's pocket when his whaling ship set sail one winter night in 1850, with high hopes of high adventure and blubber-founded fortune – which hopes, like most, were not borne out, this ship having been stove to by a whale, and thus this great-grandfather along with his coin fell to the bottom of the sea…*full fathoms five…those were pearls that were his eyes…*until enterprising divers funded by Mrs. Higgins plucked out those pearls more than one century later, and this coin too – supposedly – from right beneath the old man's ribs. The divers then presented it to Mrs. Higgins in a red-ribbon ceremony in "recognition and thanks for the sums she had contributed for the salvaging adventure," said sum undisclosed. The story seemed interesting enough, but the coin itself was, nonetheless and in spite of the ceremony, considered counterfeit. And then she gave it to Snug Harbor's Whaling Museum, and it was stolen. "Real or not, I want it back," snapped Mrs. Higgins, ninety-six years old now. Reward. Ten thousand dollars.

Ten thousand dollars was a lot of money – enough to buy Katie a whole new wardrobe. Harry folded up the newspaper and felt along his pocket for the outline of the coin – was it even a coin? – that he had found near Katie's stoop on the final day of school. It seemed incredible to him that it might belong to this Mrs. Higgins. The description included in the article seemed to fit the coin inside his pocket, but why should a coin that disappeared from a museum at the east end of Long Island show up at Katie's house, at least fifty miles west? It shouldn't, Harry reasoned, so it wouldn't – which was convenient enough since Harry had no intention of giving the coin back, even if the reward were twenty thousand dollars (which it wasn't), even if the newspaper had printed a picture of it from which he could be sure (which it hadn't), even if they threatened him with jail. It was a strange thing, and Harry didn't know quite what to make of it, but he felt an odd attachment to the coin, so that he was forever putting his hand inside his pocket to make sure that it was there. The coin was mysterious somehow, and more real than real things are, in the same way that pots and pans and bits of bone seem realer when we see them in the half-light of museum interiors, behind a wall of glass. More real, and yet more distant. The coin was just like that.

Harry did not like mystery. At the funeral of his grandfather that past winter he had been horrified to peer even those six feet beneath the surface of the ground, in the hole where his grandfather would be buried. The final loss of this companion who had collected clocks and cheated him at chess (one autumn afternoon, his grandfather snuck his queen back on the board and when Harry made a protest, the old man had declared that in chess the player must be a King who does exactly as he pleases, never a pawn, or, God forbid, a hop-scotch knight) – this loss of his grandfather had been a mystery that Harry simply did not wish to riddle out. Death was a mystery for Harry Jinx. Thus, he had only stood there dumbly beside the open grave trying not to look or hear or think. Still, something had insisted. It was as if his own grandfather whispered in his ear, forcing him to understand that between those flawless walls of the dug-out earth lay the inevitable endpoint of his own existence.

And he remembered too what Katie always said: life was a labyrinth and men ran through it just like mice looking for the cheese, turning left or right or hiding at some dead end, but it didn't matter because everyone wound up at the same place once the maze was run and the lives were dead. But Harry had not wanted to think about any of this, any more than he had wanted to imagine his grandfather dead or rising up, cheating death the way he had cheated Harry at the chess game.

But he did think that his grandfather was a king.

In any case, Harry did not like mystery, and mystery alone could never bind him to the coin. Yet something bound him, nonetheless, and mysterious or otherwise, the coin was his, he reasoned and he would not give it back.

And he would not tell Katie about it either. What was it she had said exactly, that last night before they left? That she lacked a magic sword? A ring? A ruby slipper? – looking him right in the eye, squinting, saying how all heroes at the moment of departure usually get that kind of help. "But I haven't been given that yet, Harry Jinx," she said. "Have you?" And then she winked. Of course, Harry didn't believe in magic swords and ruby slippers, but he knew she did, and that if he told her of the coin, she would claim the coin was something of that sort. Therefore, he did not tell her because he did not want to feed her craziness, and there was something more to it than that. Perhaps the coin could give him a little power over her. That would be rare, but with the coin he knew a little thing, and she did not.

"I've been given nothing, Katie," Harry said that night. "And if I had, I wouldn't tell you anyway! Just joking!" And then he laughed and laughed. So then, Katie White was on her own.

That's how it is with heroes anyway, thought Katie, staring briefly at his back inside the Chevrolet, noticing for the hundredth time how he was too big for the seat between his parents in the front, how his knees came nearly to his ears, the way a spider monkey's might. Who volunteered to go with Theseus when he slew the Minotaur? she asked herself.

No one. Oh, sure, they'd followed later, follow where Theseus had led them, and then turn the beast into a barbecue no doubt, and a few bones for the dog, but in the quest itself, the hero Theseus was alone, and if Tanto kept the Lone Ranger company, if Sancho Panza kept Don Quixote amused, still only the hero fought the windmill. There was no communion there. Katie shook her head as if to clear it of self-pity. No time for that, she thought. They were pursued by that hot blast of wind. As the car sped through the gathering dark of Illinois, Katie reached into her backpack on the floor in front of her, and pulled out *The Book of Beasts*.

A book of beasts, or bestiary, is a scientific sort of book that treats exclusively on beasts. Katie's book had been compiled during those darker ages when its creators were more likely to have heard of certain creatures than to have actually seen them, and that meant that the creatures were under none of those dull constraints imposed by modern man because of frequent observation of the real and living thing. Thus we learn in this midieval book that the elephant "has no desire to copulate" that his feet are cloven as a goat's, and that he lives 300 years. The twelfth-century monks who had described these elephants along with many other common beasts, had also told of stranger marvels – phoenixes and unicorns, for example (for to a man who has not seen an elephant, why might not a unicorn exist?) and the Latin text described them with extravagant illuminations, though in Katie's version – translated into modern English and bound in paperback – these illuminations had been converted to the rudiments of sketch. Still, to Katie, there seemed to be much matter here that might fit nicely with her quest. The title page alone, with two brief quotations, gave ample food for thought.

THE BOOK OF

B E A S T S

BEING

A TRANSLATION FROM

A

LATIN BESTIARY

OF THE TWELFTH CENTURY

MADE AND EDITED BY

T.H. WHITE

*Ancient traditions, when tested by the severe processes of modern
investigation, commonly enough fade away into mere dreams: but
it is singular how often the dream turns out to have been a half-
waking one, presaging a reality.* – T.H. HUXLEY

*And as dutifull Children let us cover the Nakednesse of our Fathers
with the Cloke of a favourable
Interpretation.* – A. ROSS

The first quotation did not seem significant (though Katie, always looking for connections did wonder about the mysteriously repeated initials – *T.H.* – of editor and epigramist). But the second by one by A. Ross intrigued her. '*And as dutifull Children,* it said, *let us cover the Nakednesse of our Fathers with the Cloke of a favourable Interpretation.*' Well, thought Katie. That was clear enough. Ross was cautioning us not to laugh at the foolish things our fathers do. Katie knew the epigram alluded to Noah and his sons, neither of whom had so much as snickered, let alone guffawed when they came upon old Noah drunk and naked in his tent. "Of course he's drunk," Shem must have said to Ham while the old man brayed out bawdy ditties. "After all, God spoke to him, and now here he is shipwrecked on a mountaintop, his creatures fled, the same old tale forever on his tongue." And, upon such favorable interpretation of Noah's drunken folly, Shem wrapped a cloak around the old man's shoulders and then took himself quite soberly to bed.

31

Of course this T.H. White, the editor who had placed Ross's warning beneath the title of his book, was not concerned with Noah. Instead, for him, those fathers whose folly was laid bare were instead the creators of the medieval book of beasts that was now translated. The book described, for example, the Bonnacon as a beast who "when he turns to run away…emits a fart with the contents of his large intestine which covers three acres," and sets all the trees to flame. *Laugh not at these medieval fathers*, implied the compassionate T.H. White through his epigramist Ross. *Cover such nakednesse, and do not call it folly; interpret seeming folly with a kindnesse if you can.*

T. H. White had nothing to fear; Katie was not laughing. On the other hand, however, Katie had always pictured herself as someone who was more likely to expose a naked folly than to cover it, like the little boy who shouted out, "The emperor has no clothes!" All heroes see themselves like that. Was this epigram then a warning meant especially for her? And were those who remained devoted to the emperor likely to say that the emperor's non-existent clothes were marvelous things – of good cut and glorious weave – were *they* the heroes then, and not the little boy who dared to name the monstrous folly, the monstrous *nakednesse*? Ponderous thoughts indeed for Katie White (and this A. Ross with his strange spellings would take some looking into), but this was only the title page, after all, and there was much, much more within.

There was that Bonnacon for example, whose very flatulence, she speculated, could have been the hot blast of wind that they might even now be fleeing in the Chevrolet – but she dismissed this as too unlikely and offensive for a classic quest. There was also the vervex, a sheep with "maggots in his noddle" (not unlike Mrs. Jinx, she thought), the Monoceros, the Perdix ("a cunning, disgusting bird") and various serpents, monkeys, and hybrids of all kinds.

But it was the whales Katie searched for most of all, and anything resembling a whale (for had not Mr. Bononosetta said, "The whale is there, Katie, and see you don't lose your soul to him…"?) and it was to page 178 she turned most often, the page she slowly came to realize, that illustrated the object of her quest, the McGuffin.

Page 178 contained a combination of picture and text, and it was the picture that Katie noticed first. Like most of the other illustrations throughout the volume, it was a simple sketch in black and white, but unlike those others it did not delineate the full shape of the beast. Instead, the illustrator had portrayed only the creature's tale, as if, Katie thought, the face itself were too awful for the average reader to contemplate, or too transcendent for the average illustrator to draw. The illustrator had buried the head and front parts of this first beast in the mouth and gullet of a second so that the creature looked as if it were being swallowed by something even larger than itself. But Katie was not fooled. Katie assumed this second beast was mere fantasy, something dreamed up as a way to cover the ambiguity of the object of her quest, or else – and this second thought thrilled her – something devised by author, illustrator, and editor to hide the creature from her, to throw her off the track. If that were the case, she thought, it hadn't worked.

Katie stared at the monster, vaguely tracing its serpent tail as it wound throughout the text. True, she thought reading the copy over, this McGuffin was a hydrodragon. According to the text, the name was Hydra Dragon, but Katie preferred hydrodragon and used that word instead. A hydrodragon was not technically a whale. It did, however, live in water, and it also had many heads (Joachim, you will recall, had mentioned seven heads). A hydrodragon was a kind of dragon, and dragons had been the objects of a hundred thousand quests. Furthermore, the hydrodragon was to be found especially in rivers (there was a river named Hydra somewhere on the globe), and it seemed to Katie far more likely to find a water dragon in the rivers of Wisconsin than a full-blown whale in oceans that the state just didn't have.

Katie turned down the corner of the page, closed the book and squinted out at the passing landscape. She had been granted, she believed, her first glimpse of the Holy Grail McGuffin, and it would take a dragon form.

Of course, certain sophisticated readers of this tale may refuse to think that such a dragon cum McGuffin might actually exist, but Katie herself was far beyond such childish denial. Katie was a quester after all, and all questers believe in just such things. And surely, if we are honest with ourselves, even those of us who do not believe in dragons will admit that there may be things in nature that give birth to dragon stories and endow these mythic beasts with their power to enthrall. Might not earthquakes be dragons, for example, or volcanoes, or the spiny back of rocks and trees along a mountain ridge? Or, alternatively, couldn't a dragon be a metaphor for humankind's rapacious, sinning self? She need only find it then – find the hydrodragon, find it with only the vaguest understanding of what it was, uncertain that she would know it if she saw it, uncertain how she would act if in the end she did recognize this thing – find it somehow, to complete the quest and discover who she was. And now that the wind pursued them and drew flames and roosters and towers in the dust, now that the weathermen did not know what to say, now that indeed the time was out of joint – it was her quest to save some ravaged kingdom up ahead.

Part II
Initiation

Chapter Four

The kingdom of Wisconsin is a green one. Think of a storybook, the way the hills roll soft across the page. Golden roads wind through these hills, and they are dotted with red barns, and cows all black and white against a sky just blue. Color is true here, and voices too: birds sing along the picket fences accompanying a traveler with his pack, and by a post a rooster crows so mightily it almost sounds like speech.

A traveler pauses. We see that he is very old. He leans upon a wooden staff we cannot possibly imagine him without. He goes, of course, to Baraboo. Up ahead he almost hears calliopes and circus brass, he thinks…but, no, that's still a long way off. He consults a hand-drawn map, adjusts his sack and continues on his way.

It was into this Wisconsin (onto this very road, in fact) that Katie and her companions finally arrived. The wind had stopped, or at least had stayed behind them (laying waste to cornfields, Katie thought), and a slight pink breeze just barely dusted with the smell of cotton candy drifted through the air. Softly, gently, the wind that had oppressed them so in Chapter Three abated now and Mrs. Jinx, mildly awake and singing, asserted gently that she was a little teapot short and stout. Katie's nostrils quivered. Talking teapots! she thought. As if that's what this is all about. We are however – and here she bit a bottom lip, quite horrified – immersed in pleasantness. Katie's mother, who had been slumped against the door for hours, sat up now, rubbed her eyes, and looked around.

"We're almost there?" she asked.

"In the twinkling of an eye,
We shall be there by and by"

squeaked Mrs. Jinx, giggling at her own cleverness, making Katie's mother giggle too. Katie squinted at Mrs. Jinx's back and consoled herself with the reminder that at least Mrs. Jinx would be out of the picture soon – her, Mr. Jinx, and even Katie's mother, a mother Katie liked well enough, but who really had no business on a quest. Who, Katie wondered, would ever take their mother on a quest? No one, except maybe Harry Jinx, singing with his mother now, cracking notes with great abandon right and left. Three years of puberty, Katie thought, and still not through it yet.

Down the road they went, and up, the hills rolling, the sun sparkling, a single, white, iconic cloud suspended in the sky. Katie stared out the window. *White sheep, white sheep, on a blue hill,* she murmured, letting the words of a childhood nursery rhyme roll lazily out of some long-forgotten corner of her mind, and then, suddenly and with great force, shoving them back in again. Vigilance, she remonstrated. Even here, in pleasant green Wisconsin there may be McGuffins. She looked out the window expectantly, but saw nothing but the old man with a pack who did not interest her, and so she turned away, leaned forward and whispered into Harry's ear. "Hey. Harry. Are you ready? Soon the fun begins!" – to which Harry, slightly embarrassed at having been so intimately whispered to as he sat right next to his own mother, leaned himself forward to get away, looking back only once over his shoulder, his eyebrows drawn together in an attempt – and a ridiculous attempt, Katie thought – to look austere. So they sat, just like that, Katie leaning forward in the back, and Harry leaning forward up ahead until they finally arrived at the white clapboard house with the green shutters, the yellow sunflowers, and the shady porch trellised with sweet peas and surrounded by six low shrubs that looked like rue.

"Rue!" said Mrs. White, once the car had rolled to a stop and they had gotten out, admired the barn, and climbed the steps to the front door of the house. "Odd choice – gloomy choice! – for such a pleasant place. Isn't there…isn't there…there's something in *Hamlet* about rue, isn't there, Katie?" But Katie hadn't noticed the shrubs, and in fact she wasn't listening. She was knocking on the door, silently amazed by the ponderous knocker – solid brass and shaped just like a whale – and then the door opened, and they were admitted by their hosts to Blunderbee.

Blunderbee Farm was in the chubby little fists of two brothers hatched from one egg some sixty years ago (much more than that, the first one would have said; the other claimed far less), brothers who stood no higher than the doorknob, with the knocker – if they tried to reach it – too far out of reach. They seemed identical: identical in dress at least (pink shirts and blue suspenders for today), and identical also in the way their hairlines had receded exactly half-way up their heads. In fact, so far as Katie and the other travelers could tell, the twins were identical in every way, moving with the same stiff motions, smiling the same pale smiles, and wrinkling their broad brows at precisely the same moment and at the same bland jokes and minor consternations. According to the twins however, these superficial similarities, and even their absolute coincidence of dress, did not in any way betray a deeper parallel identity. They were, they insisted at dinner that night (in unison, finishing each other's sentences as they spoke) entirely opposite, and in fact they claimed that this oppositeness of character had so worked upon them that even if they had begun life looking quite the same, anyone with a keen eye could see that now they looked entirely different, a few trivial resemblances being all that remained of a sameness that had once been so acute that fifty years earlier (one said it was thirty, another sixty-five), they had fooled Mistress Midden on the math tests and kissed each other's girls behind the barn.

"Well, that was then –"

"And then is now –"

"And now we are –"

"Oh, altogether different."

Katie was immediately suspicious. She knew all about this twin thing from literature. It was an often-used motif, and she had read up on it that very afternoon in fact, after she and Harry had settled into two oddly tilted rooms just beneath the eaves, rooms separated only by a thin plaster wall and opening onto a common landing. The twins had led them there, huffing up the twisting steps, insisting on carrying the luggage even though it was bigger than themselves, and then each opening a different door with a little bow. Staring in, Katie had thought immediately of a poem she had read in Mr. Bononosetta's class about a carpenter, which began *Nothing is plumb, level or square,* and ended with some kind of martyrdom. Still, even she had to admit there was a certain charm to the room. It was brightly painted for one thing, and the bed was just a little too large, the chair just a little too small. True, none of the walls met at proper angles, but they were stenciled here and there with moons and stars, a cat, a fiddle, and – along the tilting eaves – the gaily painted creatures of the sort one finds on carousels. Harry's room too was stenciled, but with things more typical for boys – cars and airplanes and fantastical contraptions of all kinds – though they were set against a background that was strangely, even embarrassingly, pink.

Once alone, Harry had spent the afternoon testing out his summer mattress and staring at the stencils, but Katie had unpacked her books and gotten down to work. She had known that her father had arranged for her and Harry to stay with twins here in Wisconsin, but the full implications of that arrangement had not occurred to her until they actually knocked upon the door and the twins appeared. Twins are a storyteller's trick, and that afternoon, thumbing through dog-eared copies of various treatises on archetypes (including one by her favorite critic, Northrop Frye), she reviewed what she already knew, reading about how sometimes storytellers would split a character in two, just as someone had split Jack and Jill, for instance, or Jekyll and Hyde, or, as in *The Wizard of Oz*, the good witch and the bad. This pattern was sometimes called doubling and storytellers used it to explore internal and universal oppositions with a certain clarity – to ravel out the dark side of a human being without the interference of the light, or to distill the force of action from a less ambitious will. Quite often, one twin embodied evil and the other goodness. In any case, twins could pose a ticklish problem for a hero on a quest.

She'd have to watch these two.

"Different?" Mrs. Jinx was saying now at dinner. "You two are different? I'm sure I can't see how."

She's worried, Katie thought, she's squirming like a woolly vervex at the sheering shed at the thought of leaving little Harry in their hands. So much for talking teapots. Two dwarves, she's thinking, they might be capable of anything.

"Dwarves, Mrs. Jinx?" said one of the twins.

"What? I didn't say…"

"Not dwarves, oh no."

"Not midgets either."

"Though we are rather small."

"And we did work for the circus."

"Circus! Well, that's something anyway!" (This was a hearty Mr. Jinx, trying heartily to join the conversation.)

"Didn't you know?"

"Baraboo's a circus town, the winter –"

"Grounds, that is the winter grounds."

"What are you, then…?" asked Mrs. Jinx. "I mean if you're not midgets."

"We prefer to think it is a matter of perspective."

"The…how can we put it?"

"The perspective's very strange somehow in Baraboo."

"Now, somewhere else…"

"Of course, we never *have* been somewhere else."

"Just Baraboo. The circus spent its winters here. We were the ones who cared for sickly beasts –"

"When the circus left to do the summer tour."

"And which of you…did what?" asked Mrs. Jinx, still bent on telling them apart and hoping, as it seemed to Katie, that by these indirections she would find directions out.

"Did what?"

"At the circus, what were the different things you did?"

"Oh, well, and as for that,"

"We did everything together."

"Of course, we didn't like the elephants"

"No. The elephants they had were rather odd –"

"But we loved when the she-goats were in heat, we –"

"She goats? At a circus? But…" (and this was Mrs. Jinx again, clutching one hand lightly to her throat), "What was it that you did with she-goats?"

"No matter now."

"All long ago…"

"And far away."

"Now, as to this other thing,"

"Yes, the matter of our differences."

"Can't you tell?"

"He took all the math tests."

"And I kissed all the girls."

"Oh, yes, we're completely different."

"Don't let the bow-ties fool you."

"Now who'd like another bowl of apple soup?"

That night, well after sunset, Harry knocked at Katie's door.

"Katie, can I come in?"

"Go away."

"Kate, there's mice in my room."

"Three blind ones?"

"What?"

"Did you bring your *Mother Goose*?"

"What?"

"Nothing. Go away."

"C'mon, Kate, open up the door."

"You've been avoiding me, Harry Jinx, and now three blind mice come along to frighten you, and all of a sudden…" Katie got up and let him in. "It wasn't even locked. All you had to do was push a little."

Harry stepped into Katie's room and looked around. "So what are you doing?"

"Nothing. Pouring over maps."

"What, with a candle? Don't you want the light on?"

"No, Harry. I don't want the light on." Katie sat down at her desk again and squinted at the maps. "Some things are best by candlelight."

"Like reading maps?"

"Like reading maps. What's in your pocket?"

"What's in my pocket? Nothing's in my pocket why should anything be in my pocket?"

"Lately, you always have your hand inside your pocket. It's not that frog again, is it? That frog you kept in your pocket when you were eight years old? It's not –"

"There's nothing! Here, here's my hand, okay?" Harry thrust both hands in front of her and turned them over quickly. "Satisfied? Boy oh boy." Katie shrugged and turned back to the maps. "Boy oh boy," Harry repeated, and then, "Some twins."

"Hmmm…?"

"I said, some twins," repeated Harry Jinx.

"Some quest. Funny, isn't it, the way the quest is working out?"

"A regular riot. We're spending the summer with a couple of crazies, and –" Katie turned away from the maps, leaned back, and looked past Harry at the eaves above his head, as if she were working out something important.

"Thing is," she finally said, "The backdrop's wrong." The signs and portents of the quest that she had pursued had indicated a different sort of setting altogether. "Remember, there were roosters, flames and towers in that dust on the car? I…I anticipated cliffs and castles, once we got here, Harry, or a wasteland maybe, or a deep ravine – or at least the modern metaphorical equivalent of an enchanted isle in the middle of a mist-enshrouded lake…and now…"

Harry waited. What kind of map was she looking at anyway, he wondered. It looked like something from a pirate ship a thousand years ago. "Well?" he finally said, getting impatient. "What do you mean by the backdrop?"

"Well, it's obvious, isn't it, I mean there you are with three blind mice –"

"I didn't say there were three of them. And I didn't say they were blind."

"Go back and check then. Listen, Harry, I think this is my first test."

"Well, you're in luck then" said Harry sitting down on the bed, trying to change the subject. "Because you always get a hundred on your tests. Though what that's got to do with three blind mice –"

"Jesus, Harry, didn't you even read those notes I gave you? The ones from Northrop Frye? In the archetype of romance – an archetype is a pattern, Harry, you know, the way stories follow certain patterns, the way they all link up. Anyway, look. In the archetype of the quest romance, in the first stage (*agon*, according to the Greeks), after the departure there have to be some preliminary trials, like, you've got to fight some minor dragon, or save someone, you know, like a second-rate princess, or a black knight –"

"You save a black night?"

"No, no, you fight him, or, maybe – here's the situation – you get distracted in a castle of mirrors, the *Castle of Delusions*, say, or a field of poppies, like in *Wizard of Oz*. You go there, and the quest just disappears. Temporarily. It's a dream world, Harry. It's temptation. Like Red Crosse."

"Mmmm. Exactly. I was thinking of Red Crosse."

"Red Crosse, he's a knight, Harry. Don't you know anything? He's from *The Fairie Queene* by Edmund Spenser, 1590, I believe. Red Crosse goes into this castle, and the quest seems to disappear, and all he finds there is the beautiful Duessa. Duessa is really lovely, Harry, she's everything you want and all she wants is you. So there you are with Duessa getting your sword oiled, and you think, 'What the hell, let someone else kill that McGuffin – it probably doesn't even exist.' I mean, really, Harry, do you think there could be a Holy-Grail McGuffin here, in Baraboo? Or does it feel as if we've left the quest altogether and we're in a children's storybook? We are in the castle of a storybook, Harry Jinx…sure, three blind mice, maybe Turkey-Lurkey, but no way you're gonna find a Holy Grail-McGuffin."

"How about that Duessa then? Because I mean as long as there's no McGuffin, I might as well –"

"No, you're…look, Harry, you're not getting it. That's the point. You think there's no McGuffin here, you think you're in a storybook, or with Duessa, and everything is coming up sweetness, and you can just relax. But it's really quest romance. You know what Duessa looked like when she took her nightgown off?"

Harry didn't dare to make a guess.

"Remember, she was lovely, Harry, blond and blue, everything you want – and then she took her nightgown off and there was snakeskin underneath."

"Jesus Christ. Snakeskin? What, like that Mrs. Hanlohan next door, the one that's only got six teeth?"

"Forget the teeth. Snakeskin, Harry. Snakeskin. She was a monster."

> *Her wrizled skin as rough, as maple rind,*
> *So scabby was, that would have loathed all womankind.*

"Wrizled?"

"She even had a fox's tail. Beneath the fair illusion lurks a monster, Harry Jinx."

"The McGuffin hidden in a storybook."

"See that? You're not so stupid. Things aren't what they seem, and you must admit…don't you feel it? Something strange? The twins, for instance. You said yourself the twins seemed odd."

Hmmm… Harry thought about the twins. "What's a McGuffin, anyway?"

"It's a water dragon. It's what we're looking for."

Later on that night, Harry lay in his bed unable to sleep. Moonlight streamed in through the windows (casements, Katie had called them, in the spirit of the quest) illuminating the tilting eaves above his head, and beneath his bed he thought he heard the mice, perhaps plotting some blind and ghastly scurry across his midsection should he dare to fall asleep. But it wasn't the mice that kept him up, or even the moonlight; it was something the twins had said after Katie had left the dinner table, her three bowls of roasted apple soup consumed along with a hearty helping of goat brains in ginger sauce ("How could you *eat* that," he had asked her later). As dinner ended, the twins had invited Katie to admire the nearing sunset ("Pink as roses! We guarantee, it,

Kate, and it makes the whole world smell so sweet!"), but she had waved them off and headed straight upstairs without Harry, leaving him to fidget at the table on his own. Then his mother – still suspicious of what unseemly entertainment these two dwarves might have planned for her baby boy, still trying to tell one twin from the other – demanded suddenly, "But you're not answering! Which of you is which?"

The twins were startled, nearly frightened it almost seemed to Harry. One bit his nails, the other fiddled with his napkin, someone murmured something about hellcats, and then, quite timidly…

"Oh, well…"

"You see…"

"Really, it's quite simple."

"Simple, yes."

"You simply…"

"Well, there *are* our names…"

"Though that won't help, since they both begin with *J*."

"But still, it's easy."

"Look…"

"He throws away…"

"And I collect."

Mrs. Jinx gave up, sat back, and threw her napkin with disgust upon the table.

"Collect?" Harry spoke for the first time since sitting down to eat.

The one twin nodded gratefully, the other proudly beamed at him across the table.

"Oh yes, we collect,"

"Collect just everything."

"Calliopes,"

"Toy ships,"

"And shoes,"

"And sealing wax? And cabbages and kings? Ha!" Mr. Jinx rapped the table once, triumphantly, and sat back in his chair.

The twins looked doubtful.

"Well…no…we have no kings."

"But coins!"

"Oh yes, and coins have kings!"

"Unless they come from some republic…"

"You collect coins?" Harry stammered out, his hand on the coin in his pocket, his mouth freezing on the final sound, half smile, half grimace, waiting to hear what he didn't want to hear.

"Oh yes."

"More coins than kites."

"Or ships or shoes."

"Coins really are our specialty."

"We have an…interest, you might say."

"In coins."

"You have an interest too?"

The twins were staring at him. "Who me? Oh, no! I was just saying…"

"Come, Harry."

"Come, come, come."

"You might as well say."

"A young boy takes an interest after all –"

"What say you, Harry?"

Harry said nothing. He merely looked from one parent to the other, got up, and bolted to his room.

A few minutes later, his mother arrived to complain about his rudeness and wring her hands about the twins. Perhaps Harry would rather stay with her, she said. After all, they would be driving out to the Black Hills of South Dakota "…you know, Harry…the wild, wild west?" – Mrs. Jinx shaped her hands into two colt pistols and pretended to shoot him – and they would be stopping to see Aunt Betty in Sioux Falls. "You remember, Harry. Aunt Bessie with the lisp?"

"And Kate? What about Kate? You know Kate won't go."

"Well, Katie could stay here." She paused and then continued. "Really, Harry, all those books. There's something odd about Katie, and it gets odder every year."

And that was it. Whatever doubts Harry had had about his Katie and her books and roosters, flames and towers in the dust, they were his own affair, and not his mother's. After all, all soldiers grumble sometimes. That doesn't mean they won't defend their king. Like a soldier to his king, then – or a loyal squire to his errant knight – Harry had, perhaps unconsciously, sworn allegiance to Katie, and he would protect her with whatever little courage he might have. And, as all great battles are pitched not so much out of hate for the thing we fight, but rather out of sudden love for the thing we would defend, so Harry, by his mother's intimations was stunned back into love.

"Well, Harry?" Harry's mother leaned above him, smiling smoothly. "What do you say?"

"No," he said. "I'll stay here…with Kate."

A wound. Perhaps a fatal one. His mother turned away without one kiss and walked on out, and in the morning when the car drove off, she could hardly bring herself to say good-bye.

But that would be tomorrow. For now Harry lay awake in the moonlight clutching at the coin and feeling a curious sympathy with old Mrs. Higgins from Sag Harbor and her desperation to get the old thing back. Was it possible, he wondered, that the twins knew about the coin? That they knew about Mrs. Higgins and her great-grandfather, the robbery at Sag Harbor, and the coin that he had found? Ridiculous. They had seemed intensely interested in coins, but Harry could not possibly believe in a world where things hooked up: him with the coin, and the twins with Mrs. Higgins way back east. It was too horrible to imagine – only machines hooked up like that, he thought, like the machines painted on the walls of his room here, or like the old clocks his grandfather collected, calling them the "wonders of creation." "See?" he'd say to Harry, showing him the shifting gears "Isn't it a miracle? All these different pieces fit together and make a single time." But Harry, though he loved his grandfather, had never liked the clocks.

The mechanics of it all had made him shiver.

Still, what if it were all true? What if the coin he had found really was the coin from the Sag Harbor Whaling Museum, and what if the twins knew he had it, and wanted it for some reason of their own? But why should he give it to them then? And that's where Harry's sympathy with Mrs. Higgins entered in. Because Harry knew that even though the twins frightened him – more even than those clocks – he would not yield up the coin, and even before, in Katie's room where he had gone straight from his mother thinking he would tell Katie everything, including his mother's treachery – even *then,* he had remained silent when she asked about his pocket.

The coin, he told himself, was only his.

Night deepened. Somewhere in its fleeting clutches Harry fell asleep and dreamed, perhaps of coins, perhaps of clocks or airplanes, or else maybe only such dreams as boys will dream on summer nights in far off story lands.

Chapter Five

The next morning the grown-ups left right after breakfast, Mrs. Jinx looking piqued, and Mrs. White looking peaked, the latter having experienced on the previous evening not only the primrose sunset that the twins had promised, but a brandy of the twins own making with even more beguiling hues than the sunset – so beguiling, in fact that Mrs. White had sipped at it all night long and almost into morning, in the library with the twins (Mr. Jinx having followed his wife reluctantly to bed), before a crackling fire, deep inside a leather chair. She had listened while the twins told circus stories (though later she would not recall a single one) and sucked on cherry-colored pipes – she listened, sipped, listened some more, and sipped a little more so that when the stories finally ended, she was not quite sure just how they ended, though there seemed to be something vaguely unsavory…but for the life of her she could not remember what. Now, standing in the driveway, she shook that off and gave her daughter, whom she loved, one final kiss.

"You'll be okay?"

"Of course I'll be okay."

Good enough. Mrs. White collapsed into the backseat of the car behind the Jinxes and in another minute, they were gone.

"Thank God," Katie said more to herself than Harry as she watched them drive away. "Now we can get started." It was time to look for clues.

"Hey kids! Check the barn!"

"What?" Katie looked around. It was the twins shouting across to them as they emerged from the house and headed for a small green station wagon of the sort one sees in center circus rings all crammed with clowns.

"The *barn*," one of them repeated.

"If it's clues you're looking for –"

"But I didn't say –"

"Oh, the barn's the place."

"Nothing you can't find inside a barn. If there's nothing there, there's nothing anywhere."

"Unless it's in the tower."

The tower? Had someone said the tower?

"Enjoy yourselves!"

"Wait!" Katie yelled, running halfway back. "What was that about a tower?"

But the twins merely pointed vaguely to the west, folded themselves into their station wagon and slowly drove away. To where, they didn't say.

Had they really said the tower? There had been towers in the dust that had settled on the car on the way to Blunderbee, and she had mentioned towers to Harry just last night. And now the twins…Katie scanned the landscape to the west, but didn't see anything she might construe into a tower. Maybe they hadn't said tower at all, she thought, maybe they had just said town. "Harry," she said. "We're going to the barn."

"The barn?"

"The barn. To look for clues that further our quest. Tie your shoes and follow me.

Harry looked down. "My sneakers," he muttered to her retreating back. "My sneakers, not my shoes," – but why did she have to be like that? Wasn't it bad enough that he had hardly slept, and that the twins had served them – what was it? – squabcakes for breakfast in a "bath of dill and maple sauce." Katie had eaten six of them, but with food like that, was it any wonder that he forgot to tie his laces? He ate no squabcakes. He tied his laces up and hurried to catch up with Katie before she disappeared inside the barn.

There was nothing unusual about the barn so far as Harry could see – it was just a red barn with a Dutch roof and a cool interior that smelled vaguely of leather – but Katie White was not to be deterred. She stood in the aisle, arms akimbo, her head swiveling back and forth as she took in the stalls, the straw-strewn corners and the loft, seeking something, counting the beams beneath the rooftop, adding and dividing and coming up with numbers that, as she told Harry, "didn't seem to fit."

"Fit what?"

"I don't know. Climb that ladder, check the haystacks in the loft."

Harry trudged up the ladder. "Looks like hay," he said.

"Any needles?"

"What, like pine needles?"

"Needles, Harry. Needles in the haystack. Never mind."

Harry grumbled. Katie tipped the empty milk cans, and shook a set of ancient sleigh bells hanging from a nail upon the wall. "Isn't that lovely…" she murmured, tilting her head toward the jingle that they made. Harry climbed back down the ladder, and she shook the bells again. "Isn't that a lovely sound?"

Harry shrugged. "I guess. Where are the cows?"

"Hmmm?" Katie straightened up. "I don't know. Gone off to decorate the emerald hillsides, one would think, as is the way of all their ilk." She swept aside a small pile of hay with her foot and leaned down to examine the floorboards underneath. "So," she said, "you are or looking for the clues, aren't you?"

Harry peered into the milk cans and then joined Katie on the floor. "Kate," he finally admitted, "I really don't know what to look for."

"Oh. Anything. The trail of the McGuffin."

"Is there…anything to go on?"

"Sure there is. Whales for one thing. Whales seem to figure prominently in this quest – did you notice that brass knocker? And then there's Joachim, of course, and towers…flames…"

"Flames?"

"Like I saw drawn in the dust."

"How about a rooster?"

"Rooster?"

"Yeah, a rooster. Look."

Katie turned and saw a big red rooster silhouetted in the doorway through which they'd come, pacing back and forth and lost, to all appearances, in the throes of a decision. *Maybe*, the rooster seemed to say as he turned about, *and maybe not*, and every time he reached the midpoint of his circuit, he paused to cast an eye up at the intruders, head cocked, beak half-opened, something rising in his throat apparently – and then, perhaps deciding not to bother them, he took up the pace again.

"I'd swear he was about to speak," Katie whispered, leaning down, extending her right hand and rubbing the fingers together in a gesture of friendship. "Hey, Cock-a-doodle-do, hey, Cock-a –"

"HEY!" said Harry. "Don't you touch that rooster if you know what's good for you!"

Harry froze. The rooster flapped away. Katie took immediate control. She stood and whirled around, one hand flying to her hip as if she were about to draw a sword, and thundered out, "Who goes there?" – and then saw what went there: something big – a giant! – framed by the further doorway and made even bigger by the light that spilled its shadow through the barn. "Who goes there?" she repeated, even louder. And then, scratching her head, "Who the hell are you?"

"Who *goes* there?" scoffed the giant. "Jack goes there, that's who. And that's a mighty touchy rooster, and the twins are even touchier. You lay one finger on that rooster, you're gonna lose it either way."

Harry moved closer to Katie and slipped the coin into his fist.

"Well, Mr. Jack," replied Katie, undaunted, "I am Katie of the Eastern Kingdom, and if you think the twins –"

"Which one of you collects the coins?" Jack demanded, ignoring what she said, and coming two steps closer. He had an axe in one hand, Harry saw, and a leg of mutton dangling from the other.

"Coins?" Katie was intrigued. "What's that, a riddle?" She knew that sometimes questers had to answer riddles. "I search for what's of value, if that's what you mean."

Oh Jesus, Harry thought.

"You have it?" asked the giant.

"No. I'm searching."

Jack the giant twisted up his eyebrows and scratched at his chin absentmindedly with the axe, as if he were trying to figure something out. "Humph," he finally mumbled (and it really was a *humph*), "That's not what the twins told me. They said –"

"Well the twins were mistaken, weren't they? In fact, I doubt those twins know a single thing about my quest!"

"Your quest? Ha!" The giant laughed. Harry felt the floor and roof beams shake.

"And what, Mr. Jack, is so funny about a quest?" Katie demanded.

"Funny?" The laughter stopped and Jack looked serious. "Nothing's funny I guess. Was your father a king? Why, once upon a time…"

He paused, and Katie moved in closer, squinting, pricking up her ears. "Well?" she almost whispered. "What happened once upon a time?"

"Oh, some other time." The giant turned away. "There are bikes there, just outside the door if you want them. Jack's got work to do." And off he lumbered, but just before he disappeared through the far door, he paused briefly at the threshold, casting his shadow halfway down the barn. "But mind you, now," he rumbled, "you let that rooster be!"

And he was gone.

"My God," Harry whispered, once they were alone. "Did you see that? I think he had a leg of mutton in his hand."

"Of course he had a leg of mutton in his hand." Katie turned back to look for the rooster, but he had disappeared. "All giants do in storyland. Haven't you seen the pictures?"

Harry didn't answer. Annoyed, suspecting insubordination, Katie turned back to explain.

"Look, Harry, haven't you read *Jack and the Beanstalk?*"

"That was *that* Jack? The kid who sold his mother's cow for little bag of beans? Boy, if that was Jack, I'd hate to see the giant…"

"*That*, Harry Jinx, was Jack *and* the giant. Not really, of course. Didn't the twins say they used to work for the circus? And that the circus wintered here? So Jack was part of the sideshow or something, but somehow, he got that story into his head, and he's become the whole damned thing. Who knows, maybe it was part of his act or something, you know, like *Ladies and Gents! Fee, Fi, Fo, Fum!* then drum rolls."

"They do that in the circus?" Harry was appalled.

"I don't know, but maybe the story is why he's asking for the coin. In the story, Jack bought those beans with a coin, remember? and his mother was unhappy. It's all about guilt Harry Jinx, guilt over spending his mother's coin, disappointing the mother and all, in fact, the whole story's very Freudian. I mean…the kid, look, you sublimate a child's desire to sleep with his mother and what do you get? A great big beanstalk. It's a symbol, get it? Major phallus, Harry. Check your Jung."

Harry had no intention of checking his Jung. He didn't even know what that meant. "Jack sold a cow for the beans, not a coin. And why would anyone want to sleep with his own mother?" he finally asked.

Katie shrugged. "To fulfill the archetype, I guess. Just look at Oedipus. He killed his father and then married his mother. But it would be something different here. In some versions of the *Jack and the Beanstalk* story, Jack is avenging his father's murder when he goes to kill the giant – it's a form of quest-romance, but it's also possible that in an Oedipal sense, the giant *is* the father…"

Harry was lost. Katie was not making too much sense. "Is there a rooster in the story too?"

Katie paused to consider. "No, but there is a hen that lays golden eggs; Jack steals it at the end, so maybe that's a metaphor for his mother-love, stealing the hen and all her eggs right out from under the giant's nose like that. But who knows…maybe with our Jack, the rooster is the hen. …Maybe he's transformed the hen into a cock…"

Harry blushed. Why did they have to use a word like that for roosters, anyway? It had always embarrassed him, whether he saw it in his mother's birding book or sprawled right across the front page of the newspaper, as he had seen it once when the local police had raided a cockfighting ring. *Informant Fingers Cock Ring*, it had said, and then in smaller letters, *Cops Grab Cocks* – and now, to hear it roll off Katie's tongue like that, and in such unseemly connections. Harry changed the subject.

"Wanna go biking?" he asked.

"Of course, analyzing the Freudian implications of a fairytale is child's play," Katie continued, ignoring his question but heading toward the bicycles nonetheless. "The real question is what does all this have to do with the quest? How do the giant and the rooster link up to the whale, the flames, and all the rest?"

Harry didn't answer. They left the barn and found the bikes, and as Katie straddled the larger one, she turned to him again. "Harry, back there, did he say tower?"

"Who? The giant? I didn't –"

"No, not Jack. The twin. I think he said to check for clues in the tower."

"The twins? I don't know, I wasn't listening. Which way are we going, anyway?"

Katie checked her tires, squeezed the brakes. "West, of course. The town of Baraboo is west, and west is where they pointed. Now maybe they said *tower* and maybe they said *town*, but either way, west seems the way to go." And then, without so much as an are-you-ready, Katie peddled off.

Harry watched her go. She peddled even on the downhills, Harry knew, and if he didn't hurry, she'd be gone. He turned to look at the remaining bike and sighed. It was a woman's bike, a mixtie, but alone now, and remembering the giant lurking near the barn, fear outpaced humiliation: he climbed on and charged right after her as quickly as he could. And, it wasn't just the giant's size that bothered him, nor the leg of mutton, nor even the axe. What rattled

Harry was that business with the coins, that *Which one of you collects the coins,* and as he peddled out of the driveway those words and Jack's enormous shadow, filled his mind. Why, he wondered as he struggled up the hills in vain hopes of catching up with Katie – why was everyone talking about coins all of a sudden– the newspaper article about Sag Harbor and Mrs. Higgins, the twins last night, and now this crazy giant with an axe. Probably, there was nothing at all to it. Probably people were talking about coins all the time, and he'd just never noticed it – this was America after all – but even if that was true, why all that talk about collecting? Surely that wasn't something you heard of everyday. Of course, it seemed impossible to him that anyone could know – or even care – about what he had found at the foot of Katie's stoop that day. Still, he couldn't shake the feeling that someone did know about his coin, and was behaving sinister and relentless – Harry tried to peddle faster up the hill.

That didn't last. The hills were steep and once Blunderbee Farm had receded behind him, the fear too receded just a little, and now the postcard pastures of the surrounding countryside opened up before him, and he allowed the bland enchantment of the day to pull him in. Why struggle up one road and then the next, he wondered, when the hillsides are so green? Along a steepish incline, Harry stopped.

Katie had been right: Wisconsin was like storyland. The cows did decorate the emerald hills, and everything – the sun, the sky, the apple orchard to his left – was exactly what he had seen in countless picture books that his mother had read to him when he was very young. In the middle distance lay a deep blue pond, and as he watched a yellow duck glide back and forth across it, he was comforted somehow; there was something so perfect about it, and perfect too about the slight smoke that climbed out of the chimney at the farmhouse just beyond. Why he wondered, would anyone ever want to go questing for some troublesome McGuffin when everything was so pleasant where they were? It's ridiculous, he told himself, and just as ridiculous to think that anyone in Wisconsin could want my little coin. Thus, happy enough for the moment that the coin was in his pocket, Harry Jinx stood enchanted by the farmer's house, the apple trees, the little yellow duck. And, when he finally resumed his ride, it was only because he sensed that greater charms might lay ahead in Baraboo.

Chapter Six

Baraboo had once been the wintering grounds of the Ringling Brother's Circus, the five Ringlings being natives of the town and representing in the amalgam of their various natures (showman, artist, manager, athlete, clown) one force so suited to success that Fortune, which eludes the grasp of most men, could not escape the clutches of these five. Fortune ran, but they ran faster; she led them down blind alleys, came up behind them and whispered bad advice into their ears; she hid herself in various improbable disguises, and then escaped when they thought that they had clutched her, but in the end they found her hiding in the circus, and what had started as a small affair (perhaps two elephants, one dog, a giant and a horse) became a circus with a train of circus wagons about 100 strong. It truly was, as the brothers had always claimed, *The Greatest Show on Earth.*

This show traveled, and its arrival at towns up and down the great Midwest must have seemed something like a miracle to the people living there. On a dry afternoon in August in Topeka (or else Lincoln, Kansas City, or Des Moines), a drum would roll. Posters would appear in storefront windows all along main street, and iron mallets would ring like church bells against the stakes that would support the tent, the clamor of it drifting from the fairgrounds to the barber shop and then further, calling the faithful to the canvas temple rising just outside the town. From town the citizens saw it, and in the outlying fields of corn and wheat, the farmers, sick to death of worrying about the fretting summer sky, the locusts, and the heat, dropped their picks and hoes, packed up their families, and came to see the circus and marvel for themselves.

Yes. They saw. The tent was rising. The train on which it had arrived – which had come at night and which now lay sprawled along the railroad tracks like some great serpent sleeping off a supper that had been swallowed live (and in fact the train could be heard to rumble, kick, and even sometimes trumpet from within) – this serpent-train soon woke, and soon from every yawning portal came the beasts and things of miracle that are the circus, the beasts all seeming vaguely shocked, like Jonah's coming forth from the belly of the whale.

Tapirs appeared, and emus, orangutans and seals. Even the horses and the elephants seemed shocked, even the unicorn that came one year – all these and more stepped off the train and stared quite wide-eyed at the crowd, and the crowd stared back in equal shock with something like a whisper on its lips, moving forward, gently, one hand extended in a kind of supplication, one hand almost touching the horn of nature's handiwork – until the exotic circus men who until that moment had lounged against the serpent's iron flanks, now herded off the crowd, rolled the circus wagons from the flatbeds at the rear, hitched up the horses, and with bandwagons vying with the elephants to make the greater noise, marched down main street in a spectacular procession, some creatures pacing back and forth in cages now, some walking with the men, the unicorn tiptoeing, golden-tied, a virgin smiling at his side. And not only animals paraded, not only animals had poured forth from the train, but marvels of all kinds: tom-walkers, dwarves, and tattooed men; magnificent tableaux of ancient Egypt and Brazil; a castle made entirely of hair. How many wonders rolled down Main Street on the magic circus wagons? And how many frauds displayed? For the Topekans, fresh from the field and barber shop, the circus must have seemed another world crammed full of miracle and wonder come right into Topeka, and marching down its street. And the Topekans? They were willing to believe.

But winter always came, and in October, when ice just skimmed the milk-pails in the morning and the first flakes fell upon the western prairies and culled-out hayfields not far north, then the Topekans returned to the less exotic comforts of their fires and their churches, and the circus wagons went to Baraboo where throughout the luxury of winter – luxurious in time, if nothing else – the lions stretched and slept, the tumblers rolled to rest at last, and the clowns, unmasked, stared idly at their tubes of whiting and waited for the spring.

But perhaps not everyone waited so idly. Circuses are the great ships of the inland seas; winter grounds are like the ship's homeport. For some of these circus-sailors, port meant a kind of idle and suspended animation between one slapstick voyage and the next, and yet for others – the lion tamers and the trapeze artists, most particularly – port was where life fully and finally began. Thus, we can imagine that great quantities of bars and brothels arose in

Baraboo and on winter nights past midnight the escapades of circus people sometimes kept the native Barabooans fretfully awake and peering from their window sills or quaking in their sheets. Sometimes gunshots fired. Sometimes one heard the snatches of a very bawdy song. And most times, in the last hour before dawn, there emerged from *The Juggler's Inn* the snake charmer who, along with his charmed companion and two painted ladies (one for him, and the other, it was rumored, for the snake), sang an aria from *Turandot* all along the half-lit streets.

The Barabooans drew up ordinances, of course. There was an ordinance against swearing on a street corner, for example, and a leash-law just for tigers, and another one, much tougher, for the apes. When two contortionists were discovered in Mrs. Figgins' hen house, in some position only labeled at the trial as "extreme," the legislature passed the infamous *Three Acts against Contortion in a Barnyard,* which acts however, by the intricate delicacy of their phrasing were themselves so convoluted that even in this day some far-off scholars of such things tie themselves in knots in vain attempts to unravel what these three acts meant.

And perhaps there was another problem with the circus-sailors. Maybe they came, as do all sailors, from very far away. Mr. Bononosetta's hero Ishmael who went whaling tells us that whaling ships were manned by nearly every species of mankind that nature can produce, and thus New England's whaling ports were like the Tower of Babel in the new world where, according to Herman Melville, some foreign sailors were like cannibals who sold shrunken heads by signs and gestures to farm-fresh boys who longed to go to sea. But the circus people were not cannibals. They sold no shrunken heads. Still they were from foreign parts – from China and Malay in many cases, and (as was the case with a chubby set of acrobatic dwarfs) even from the Republic of Peru. Cannibals or not, they all seemed vaguely heathenish to the native Barabooans who overwhelmed, built sixteen churches with the profits from the brothels and the bars.

The modern Barabooans will probably say that none of this is true. And they probably are right. They may say that Baraboo has always been a sober town with a solid chamber of commerce and an ambiance only slightly more alive when these circus people boarded in their midst throughout the winters long ago. They will show you the barber shop, perhaps, or the green grocer's with a sign that really says *Green Grocer*, the policeman on the corner with his whistle, the large, imposing bank. They may even tell you that the circus people were locals mostly, or at least Midwesterners, even farmers sometimes, who when the season ended, stored their capes and wigs inside their trunk and then went home to see how well their wives and children had worked the land while they had been away. And perhaps the Barabooans would be correct in all of that. But truly now, what people ever know the truth about their past? The past slumbers beneath a blanket of dust so thick that no man can ever find it; no trail of documents will lead us to the past, not even those housed in the town hall or in the rectory, nor any voice surviving from those times in some asylum for the very, very old — nothing leads us to the sleeping past, and should we ever get a glimpse of it, we shall not shake it back awake. What isn't known, therefore, must be imagined. Thus, may we imagine Baraboo.

So then, perhaps the circus-sailors came from far away, and so the Barabooans built their sixteen churches. Many foreigners attended mass most Sundays, dressed well for the occasion, and yet retaining in some subtle way (the color of a shirt perhaps, the cocking of a hat) a flavor of their more exotic selves. Sometimes they prayed in foreign tongues. Sometimes, perhaps, they left their foreign coins upon the plate.

Harry Jinx knew nothing about any of this, of course, and when he finally arrived in town where Katie was waiting for him beneath the red and white striped awning of an ice-cream shop, there was really very little to inform him, or to dispel the dull enchantment that had overcome him on the way to Baraboo. The honky-tonks and brothels, if they ever had existed, had been painted over now, and as he peddled into town, he saw a Main Street he was sure he recognized, but to which he had never really been, the Main Street of the picture-books of his childhood: *Make Way for Ducklings*, maybe or *Frosty the Snowman,* complete with a barber pole, a wooden Indian, the green grocer, and the bank. Harry and his coin were safe here, Harry thought; Baraboo is like a storybook and wears a very pleasant face.

Katie, too, had found herself in the pages of a children's storybook when she arrived in Baraboo, but Katie was in search of the McGuffin. True, she had not found the tower, or McGuffin between Blunderbee and Baraboo, but she had no doubt that both existed somewhere, and that in her guise as hero on a quest, she could not afford to be distracted (as Red Crosse had been distracted by Duessa, for example) by the seductive surface of streets that were truly like the pages of a children's storybook. Something lurks, she told herself. Rub out this picture, and there is sure to be a dragon underneath.

And then, as she surveyed the town, another image occurred to her. She must, she told herself, ravel out this emperor's imaginary robe. For what were Blunderbee and Baraboo, she asked herself, if not metaphoric emperors from a storybook, waltzing down a Main Street in well-embroidered robes? Katie could imagine the embroidered robes of emperors: doves flew there, moons and stars sometimes abounded, or secret signs and secret symbols, and along the hem might rise a golden castle with a princess locked up in its tower with a shock of golden hair. Katie knew an emperor's robe would be a thing of beauty with many little stories woven in and out. To Kate, it would resemble the face of Baraboo, and no doubt the maker of the robe would link its story-pictures by a single, magic thread. Her job as quester then was simply this: to find the thread that bound up all the stories, and stitch by stitch to ravel each one out – which unraveling would, if nothing else, reveal the blank white garment underneath.

This last image, had Katie thought of it, might have appalled her – after all it was the blank whiteness of the whale in *Moby Dick* that nearly drove poor Ishmael mad. But Katie didn't think of that. She was seeking the McGuffin, that was all, and not for a moment did she think of what might happen once she had metaphorically unraveled all the pictures on the robes and turned the stories into a useless ball of string. Besides, if a blank white robe remained, she might have decided to unravel that as well. In the famous fairytale, the entire robe is a delusion. Unravel it, Katie might have thought. *Cover not the nakednesse* of emperors. Let us see if the McGuffin lurks beneath the robe, and so beneath the story-streets of Baraboo!

Thus, thinking only of her naked emperor, Katie had poked around Main Street, seeking something hidden, like a tower or a whale, a magic thread that would eventually lead her to the truth. She read the street signs. She checked the interest rates in the window of the bank (not a single three or seven in the lot). She asked the policeman for "the famous tower," and – receiving from him only odd looks and a shrug – asked next for the location of an "inn named something like *The Talking Rooster*, or maybe *The McGuffin Bar and Grill*."

"What's that you said?" asked the policeman. "McFuggin?"

"No. McGuffin. Never mind." Katie turned away, and headed to the ice cream parlor, stopping at the tobacconist to buy the local newspaper and thinking briefly (but only briefly) about how absolutely ridiculous her questions must have seemed. Nothing to do but wait for Harry, she thought, and then after satisfying herself that there were no hidden codes in the twenty-six flavors of ice cream listed at the ice cream shoppe, she ordered herself a double peppermint cone with sprinkles, settled on a bench outside to eat it, glanced down at the headline of the newspaper, and nearly fainted dead away.

It wasn't long after that, that Harry Jinx came along, but by then Katie had recovered enough to answer his inquiries about the ice cream, give him change, and watch him disappear inside the shop. Soon enough, he reemerged with, of course – she could have guessed it – a double-scoop vanilla. Well, that was Harry all over, Katie thought, twenty-six flavors, but sticking to vanilla – but Katie had something far more urgent on her mind.

"Look," she said, when he had finally sat beside her. Katie pointed to the headline of the *Baraboo Gazette.*

Harry stopped licking his cone and leaned toward the paper. "My God," he said, nearly jumping up again, like someone waking from a dream into a nightmare, "Annabel Higgins! What's she doing here in Baraboo?"

"Who? No, not that, that's some obituary. The headline, Harry. The part about the poison, '*POISON PLAGUES THE WELLS OF BARABOO.*'"

Harry was silent, dumbstruck, which Katie thought was normal for the squire who accompanied the knight. She knew that squires were not supposed to be especially brave or especially intelligent, but she nonetheless could not help thinking that this was one of those moments in the quest when Harry, in his role of squire, was supposed to come to her aid, possibly by offering some explanation of the astounding headline, (which explanation she in turn would certainly negate), or else by asking the right questions so that she could expand, delve – plunge even!– into the heart of the matter, knowing that the squire waited nicely on the sidelines with an extra lance or two. That's what Katie hoped for. But Harry, for his part, wasn't thinking of knighthood, or squiredom, or even the headline in the *Baraboo Gazette*. Harry was thinking only of his coin and the old lady from Sag Harbor who had lost it and who was – had been? – named Annabel Higgins. In terror, he licked his cone and didn't speak.

"Well," Katie finally said. "Aren't you going to ask me any questions?"

"Questions?"

"Questions, Harry. About the poison."

"She…died of poison?"

"Who? The cows, I mean. Three in the last two weeks, and a couple of sheep too. No one seems to know what's causing it. The officials come in, they test the water in the wells, nothing shows up, and the next day, there's another Flossy dead."

"What's a flossy?"

"Cow."

Harry was confused, but he had recovered enough to realize that Katie wasn't talking about Mrs. Higgins and her coin at all, and that unless he came back with some acceptable reply, she might begin to get suspicious and ask some questions of her own. "If nothing shows up in the tests, then how do they know it is poison in the wells?" he finally managed.

"I don't know…vapors or something. There are some ghastly vapors rising like steam from the wells, as if…well, look what Polly Pitt says – as if there were a dragon there." Katie stood up suddenly. "Vapors, Harry. Rising from the water."

Harry looked down at his half-eaten ice cream cone. *Homemade* the sign at the ice cream parlor had said. From the cream of local dairies? Local cows? Local milk? Annabel Higgins and her coin were trouble enough, but now, to think that he may have eaten poisoned ice cream without even the benefit of absorbing the twins' weird squabcake to cushion the blow. Harry tossed the cone into the garbage and, seeing that Katie had wandered off, got up to follow her.

Katie, meanwhile, had gone to the end of Main Street, which she now saw ran along a ridge above the Baraboo River. Down below and to the right she could see as far as where the train station nearly met the river bank. From there the river continued forward, passing directly below at the bottom of the hillside, bordering the little town until it disappeared into the woods off to the left. The river, she thought. And all the poisoned wells. Katie had taken an Earth Science class in eighth grade, and in the car on the way to Wisconsin she had seen the local maps. All these rivers – the Fox, the Plover, the Baraboo – they were probably connected in a maze of underground lakes and streams from here to Madison. And all the wells tapped into them of course. The rising vapors, therefore…her hydrodragon, the McGuffin…

Harry came up beside her. "Look, Kate, there's the circus." Katie looked down to where he pointed. In the wide crook of the river's elbow, she now saw what must have been the former wintering grounds of the greatest show on earth, where there still rose a big-top, its flag flapping in the gentle summer breeze. "You think it's a real circus?" Harry asked, all his troubles taking a back seat to the possibilities of a circus that suddenly arose.

"I don't know," Katie said. "It's in the river's grip." She looked at Harry. "I'm going to the library," she said. "You coming?"

"What, to look for books on poison?"

"Of course not, silly. In Baraboo we have delved into a children's storyland, remember? I want to check the *Mother Goose*."

But Harry decided not to join her. He was a coward, Harry Jinx, and Katie did make him feel safe, but Harry needed time to read the story of Mrs. Higgins' death, and given a choice between reading it seated next to Katie in the library, who would ask a load of questions, or escaping for a while to the circus, he chose, quite naturally, the circus, a distraction he had always dearly loved. At the circus, Katie told him once, one viewed the thrill of danger from the safety of one's seat. Maybe. But just to prove he was not merely a coward taking flight, he bought a copy of the *Baraboo Gazette* and took it with him to the circus grounds.

What Harry found when he arrived there was a circus that was not really a circus, but rather the winter grounds of a circus where the great show had hibernated throughout the coldest months. But these were not the winter grounds anymore. Ringling had long since moved its wintering to the pink-flamingoed landscapes of Florida, and the old grounds were now home to *The Baraboo World Circus Museum*, an institution that was something less than a circus, but something more than a museum, acting, as it did, as a kind of holding pen for hopeful trapeze artists and baby elephants who put on shows beneath the big top for an audience drawn mostly from the small surrounding towns. In addition to the big-top, there were two main buildings, one of which housed the memorabilia that a circus leaves behind (historical displays and posters among them, as well as a slice of wedding cake from the three-ring wedding of Lavinia Warren and Tom Thumb). The other building was an enormous hanger where the hand-carved circus wagons, now retired, spent their declining years at rest, though even now, and even for the jaded visitor they still evoked – like the ancient icons of the Virgin Mary brought out of churches, scrubbed clean of candle soot and hung against the white walls of museums – some strange upsurging of the heart through the crude simplicity of their grand designs.

Too much weighed on Harry's heart, however, and neither the wagons nor the intricate displays of the museum could lighten it. The more he wandered among these things (there being no shows beneath the big-top on that day), the more the obituary he was avoiding loomed before him until finally, resigned, he settled down just across from a painted circus wagon, opened up his newspaper, and read of Mrs. Higgins' great demise.

There was no way of telling for certain from the article whether or not the Annabel Higgins who had lost her coin during a break-in at the whaling museum back in Sag Harbor was the same Annabel Higgins, who, as it turned out, had slit her own wrists with a barnyard axe here in Baraboo the night before. Still, there were uncanny correspondences. This Annabel, like the other, had been ninety-six, and like the Annabel of Sag Harbor she had a fondness for philanthropy in the service of adventure – though in this case it wasn't sunken-treasure seekers that she funded, as it had been in New York, but something the papers called "the famous mountain expedition," a phrase that the editors didn't even bother to explain. Finally, there was the matter of her suicide note. Labeled "cryptic" by the paper, the note had said, *Do not doubt that the gods are drunk and laughing, and from their palace, they toss us beggars nothing but loose change.* Loose change, thought Harry. A reference to the coin?

Harry dropped his head into his hands and closed his eyes. Something was definitely going on, and there was no point in pretending that it wasn't. It was as if the ground were opening up beneath his feet, or the sky were parting and something very big was after him. A barnyard axe? He asked himself. What kind of suicide is that? Hadn't Jack the Giant been carrying an axe? Perhaps, he thought, he should give up the thing inside his pocket. Leave it here, right on the step of the wagon, or give it to the twins. He thought to do it, but could not, would not, – he had found it, hadn't he? He lifted his head and stared across the aisle at a wagon carved with half a dozen leering angels, and suddenly he felt a hot breath in his ear.

"What are you reading boy?" it whispered. "'Tis Annabel Higgins, is it not?"

'Tis? Harry swung around and saw an aged face that for one brief second brought to mind his dead grandfather who had always cheated him at chess.

"I…I…didn't," he began to say.

"Didn't what?" the old man whispered. And then, "Of course you didn't. *Some* boys never do. *Some* boys wait for others to."

Wait for others to what? Harry was silent while the old man came around opposite him and sat down on the runner of the wagon infested with the leering angels. His hair was long and white, Harry now saw. His eyes, like Kate's, were blue.

The old man spoke again. "So, what do they say in the paper then? How do they say that Mrs. Higgins died?"

"She slit her wrists with an axe," Harry stammered out.

"Ha! Is that what they say? But the axe 'twas but the agent. 'Twas the coin that killed her. Have no doubt of that."

"The coin. You mean…?"

"I mean the coin, boy! It consumed her, didn't it? Every night for ten years, every night in rooms barely lit by moonlight, lamplight, candlelight – every night she laid it on her palm and examined every hieroglyphic on its face. She looked for clues. Was it real, she asked herself, or only hoax? Had it been there when the ship went down with her great-grandfather? Had it? That's what the divers had told her, but divers lie, and she had paid all their expenses. What harm, they might have said, in such a hoax? Or was it real? Was it a true link between the past and present, between the epiphany of shipwreck and the humdrum shipwreck of her life, for – know thou this, my boy, we seek the past because the past abides eternally, and stories of shipwrecks wherein men are drowned in vast immensities of blue, are eternity's most potent metaphors. So then, something from a shipwreck, coughed up onto shore…you understand? Like a Rosetta Stone. But…real? Or fake, as everybody said, as her own brother, dead five years before had said, told her about the divers, about the people in the town who laughed behind her back. And either answer – real or fake – filled her with more dread than the other, for if real then who dares to riddle out eternity by reading out the hieroglyphics on its face; yet to imbue a hoax with meaning, to live and die by it and suspect that it is nothing but a hoax. My God, Harry Jinx! Wonder ye then, at this consummation by the coin?"

Harry shifted about uncomfortably. What was the old man talking about, he wondered. Nothing seemed quite clear. And how did he know poor Harry's name? And what had happened to the clear blue sky, the emerald hills, the yellow duck that glided on the pond? This old man, did he too want the coin? That last possibility would have been terrifying had not Harry's memory of his beloved grandfather been still too close for unremitting fear. Finally he asked, almost as if it were confession, "But, still, why would she kill herself?"

"Why? Why else?" The old man growled and paused to pull a pipe out of his – what was it, a cloak? – and tap down the tobacco, strike a match and draw tobacco down into his lungs in a single crackling pull. The match went out. "She didn't have that coin anymore," he said, the smoke curling around them as he spoke. "She was like an alcoholic in the last stages of disease who in some foolish moment of resolve locks up the liquor and gives someone else the key. Annabel Higgins gave the coin to a museum. But drunks always want the key back, and so it was with her. She suffered by that separation, Harry, but the museum was robbed, and the coin had disappeared."

So. It was the same Annabel Higgins. He had held out hope that that mention of shipwrecks and coins had been coincidence, but there could be no denying the museum. And yet, the article about the suicide in *The Baraboo Gazette* hadn't mentioned the coin or the robbery at Sag Harbor. Maybe they didn't know about the coin, he thought. And maybe someone else didn't know she didn't have it. Maybe someone… "But…what if someone thought she still had it?" Harry asked now. "What if someone…wanted it?"

"What? Murder?" The old man shrugged. "Murder happens. Even for the acquisition of a hoax." And now he leaned in close to Harry, breathing in his face. When he spoke his voice was terrible, and slow. "Some men are drawn to hoaxes, Harry Jinx, even when they know that it's a hoax. Reality can be tedious, but these ingenuities of man's devising never are. They shadow forth the greater mysteries, the mysteries of the things that are, and of things that are not. A hoax that is acknowledged as a hoax…who would not be drawn?"

Harry didn't understand. He tried to blink and found that he could not.

"Do you like the circus, Harry?"

Harry nodded.

"The sideshow freaks, the man on the trapeze?"

Again, Harry nodded.

"They are hoaxes, Harry, hoaxes, all of it. And would you rather go to church or to the circus?"

"A…circus," Harry stammered turning red.

"Of course a circus," the old man whispered, "what boy would not prefer a circus? Now listen carefully. Hoaxes reach into darkness and draw their audiences in. The circus is acknowledged hoax, and therefore much more loved. The masters of the ring know when to wink, and so the circus binds its faithful in a spell, while the congregation at the temple drums its fingers, checks its watch. Ring masters wink, Harry Jinx, but preachers in their robes up on their altars never do."

"How do you know my name?" Harry whispered, understanding nothing else but that.

But without another word, leaving Harry to flounder there, to wonder if he too were being drawn in by a hoax, or (thinking now of the coin inside his pocket) by a hoax of a hoax, since he did not even know if the coin in his pocket had been Annabel's, let alone whether or not Annabel's coin itself had been a shipwrecked coin or a crafted fake – leaving Harry, the old man walked down the aisle of circus wagons, a staff in one hand, a satchel in the other, a skeleton key dangling loosely down his back.

In the library meanwhile, Katie was having troubles of her own. Amazingly enough, there had been only one book of fairytales and one book of nursery rhymes in the entire Baraboo Public Library, and though at first Katie thought this extreme want might have been arranged by unseen forces friendly to her quest (since it precluded the necessity of her having to find among one hundred books the one through which the threaded code must run), it turned out to be instead the catalyst for yet another trial, the *trial by bureaucracy* as she had dubbed it by the time that she and Harry Jinx were peddling safely home.

"Why call it that?" he asked.

Katie looked over at him. Sweat coursed down his face, she noticed, and it wasn't just from peddling up the hills. There's something in his soul, she thought, remembering *Hamlet*, which, like Hamlet, Harry's melancholy sits and broods. Alas, poor Harry is more likely to break those eggs he broods upon then hatch them. "She wouldn't let me check the books out," she said finally. "The castle gate (by which I mean the door of the library) was guarded by an ogre, Harry Jinx, a female ogre with four hairs coming out the tip of her nose, a wart on her upper lip, and not one tooth in her mouth."

Harry tried to peddle faster. "Sure," he said. "Like I'd believe –"

"Believe it or not, Harry Jinx. She was there nonetheless, trolling about –"

"Ogering about."

"Ogering about by the gateway that lies between the labyrinth of books and the wide plain of freedom, and aided in her onerous task of keeping these poor books locked up by a monstrous weapon that could detect a book escaping–"

"You mean the scanner."

"Yes. The scanner. Exactly. With a nose so well-honed that it could detect a book escaping even if it wore a sheepskin, as several men did to escape the monstrous, one-eyed Cyclops."

"Books couldn't do that, that was –"

"Something like that anyway. There I was. I stood before the ogre. First, merely as an excuse, merely to get the size and shape of her, to see exactly what manner of ogre she was, I asked her where the bathroom was."

"You think I'd believe anything, don't you." Harry shook his head. And then after a pause, "And did she tell you?"

"She did indeed, but in directions so confused – up one hall, and down the next, three staircases to the left, and through the sixth revolving door – all this and more, and the library barely bigger than a single room –"

"As if that would really –"

"I found it, of course. The bathroom. But more important, by asking I learned just what sort of ogre we were dealing with: an ogre who overcame her enemies with befuddlement and obfuscation – befuddlement because that was how the ogre acted, quite befuddled (for this ogre was quite old). And now, knowing this, I knew how to approach. But! Lo! I did not expect the second blow!"

Harry waited. Katie let the tension build.

"Finished with the bathroom, and having returned to my desk, I now gathered up my books and approached her once again. May I check these out now? I asked with both ears straining and my wily brain a whirring, ready to untangle whatever befuddled obfuscation she might hurl, be it obscure procedures, requests for signatures in nineteen places, God knows what – when all she hurled at me was NO!"

"No? Just like that? One word?"

"Just like that. She shouted it. NO! NO! she shouted, and NO! again, as if befuddlement and obfuscation were but a ruse to hide some deeper nastiness."

"Were you…afraid?"

"Afraid? Of course I wasn't afraid. Can Katie of the Eastern Kingdom ever be afraid? WHY NOT? I shouted back – it was a lucky thing, this being a library, that we two were the only creatures stirring in the place. RESIDENCY! she replied, much louder. Oh, well, and as for that, I said, and produced my newly-minted driver's license, Lincoln High I.D. a merit badge I earned as a girl scout, seven years ago, several phone bills of my mothers, a love letter or two –"

"Love letters!"

"Don't worry, Harry. They had not been near my heart. Covered her desk in identifications *and* obfuscations – all to disguise that I did not quite reside in Baraboo."

"So, out-obfuscate the obfuscator."

"It didn't work. Or, it might have worked, we'll never know, for then she asked, *And just what book would you like to borrow, Katherine White?* She saw my name upon the driver's license, and assumed that I was willing to let one of the two books go. I showed her the two books, the *Big Book of Fairy Tales* and the *Big Book of Mother Goose* – and she screamed – NEVER! NEVER!"

"Never?"

"NEVER! NEVER! Just like that. Those are for the children," she said, "not for the likes of you. They are all we have left, and I will never, never-ever let them go."

"My God, Kate. What did you do?"

"What would anybody do? I smiled. gathered up my licenses, the merit badge, the phone bills and the rest, returned to my seat, and ripped the scanner's sensors out."

"My God!"

"I freed the books."

"Oh c'mon."

"It's to serve a higher purpose, isn't it? Besides, my father taught me how when I was young."

Harry found this difficult to believe. "Your father rips out sensors?"

"Well, not all the time." Katie dropped her storytelling voice. "But he's in a very competitive field, Harry, he has to publish theories about books. It's dog eat dog out there." Katie looked at Harry and saw he didn't understand. "Look, it's like this. Let's say he has a theory and some other guy has a similar theory and the key to the other man's theory is in some particular book and there's only one copy of that book (kind of like our McGuffin, you might say), well, then he has to steal it, because then he doesn't have to return it, so the other guy gets delayed and has to get an interlibrary transfer, which can really take a while –"

"Your father, Kate…"

Katie shrugged.

"So, did it work?"

"What work?"

"Ripping out the sensors."

"Oh, that. Of course it worked, what kind of hero do you think I am? I ripped them out and walked right out the door."

They had reached the farm by now and were heading up the driveway. The twins came to greet them, wringing their hands and looking vaguely dismayed.

"It's late!" said one.

"It's almost storytime!"

Chapter Seven

Storytime? Katie and Harry looked at one another and then at the twins. Even Katie hadn't expected that in storyland there would be a storytime. "We didn't know…" she started to explain.

"Didn't *know*?"

"And you even missed the dinner!"

"Jellied hake with hollandaise."

"And curried fish-eggs on the side."

Fish eggs! Harry blanched. And what the heck was hake? He suspected he was in for another long night of it – *it* being things he didn't understand and things he didn't want to eat, and a short time later his suspicion was confirmed when he and Katie arrived in the kitchen where the twins had left them soup, and where indeed a large pot (it's a cauldron, Katie corrected) of something very golden rumbled and boiled, exhaling in its muttering an aroma that Harry couldn't possibly identify, but suspected it to be just like the vapors rising from the wells near Baraboo. Katie didn't even seem to notice. She sat down and ate four bowls.

"How can you eat that?" Harry asked.

"The soup? It's marvelous. Here, fill this up again. Listen, Harry, about this storytime –"

"Katie." Harry stared into the pot, stirring the contents cautiously with a ladle. "Katie, I think there's a stone in this soup."

"Of course there's a stone. Listen, Harry –"

"A stone, Katie in the soup, there's…"

"It's a children's story. Never read *Stone Soup*? Listen, Harry, tonight, you have to listen for the threads in the embroidery."

"What? You sure you want another bowl? Because there's a stone, and my God! Look at this spice rack, will you? Monkshood…Belladonna…"

"So?"

"So? Don't you know what that is? Belladonna? Poison. There's poison in the spice rack, and stones in the soup, and maybe poison in the soup, I mean smell it, it's like –"

"Don't be ridiculous, Harry. The poison's probably, you know… homeopathic."

"Homo…" Harry furrowed his brows.

"Homeopathic, Harry. It means very small doses are very efficacious."

"Yeah, efficacious, sure." Harry had no idea what efficacious meant except that it probably meant she didn't think the poison mattered. "Yeah sure, it is fine unless you found it, right? Unless you saw it on the spice rack, or in the barn or something, then it would be like some big clue."

"Don't start whining, Harry. You ready for storytime?"

"And fish eggs. Squabcakes. My mother never –"

"Jesus, Harry. Of course your mother never." Katie paused and looked at him significantly. "But I'll bet your grandfather did. You ready for the story?"

"What. My grandfather did what? Why do you have to bring him into this?"

"Nothing. Don't get so excited. I'm just saying that a man who put his queen back on the board would have probably tried the soup. C'mon Harry, don't get so upset."

"I'm hungry."

"Here. Have a little bread. The bread's not poisoned."

Harry took the bread and turned it over cautiously in his hand. Then he took a little bite.

"See? Look, all I'm saying is, this poison doesn't matter, and it's not because you found it instead of me. It's just that it's just part of the backdrop is all, you know to add flavor to the scene, so to speak, to give the reader –"

"What reader?"

"Any reader. To add a little background to the quest. To set the tone. You know. Like that. But storytime, that's different. I think the storytime stories are going to be an actual part of the quest. That's why you have to listen. Carefully. In case I miss something, in case there is a clue. Or think of it as a code, Harry. Because the stories are sure to have codes –"

"Toads?" It was the twins. They had whisked into the kitchen unannounced.

"Good gracious, Kate. Did you say toads?"

Katie decided not to answer them. Had they really misunderstood, she wondered? Or had they overheard. Katie didn't trust the twins, and she watched them closely as they began to clear away the dinner things, but for all her one-eyed squinting, she could not tell what they knew and what they didn't know any more than she could tell one from the other. It is as if they are not quite alive, Kate thought. It is as if they are puppets that work for someone else, as if someone had fashioned them out of a few stray lengths of cloth. But that was not quite it, because the way they cleaned – frantically, like second-string ballerinas who knew the steps but were moving too fast for the music – and the way they spoke – the conversation bouncing between them like a ping-pong ball – was not quite puppet-like.

Odd creatures, Katie thought. And what was it they had said earlier that morning – tower? Or was it only town. She wanted to ask them (subtly of course) but it seemed impossible; they were too busy sweeping the floor, wiping off the table, tidying up the dreadful spice rack, and too busy talking to let her slip in a single edgewise word. They spoke as rapidly as they cleaned, not about the toads, which they seemed to have forgotten, but about Jack, asking Harry (who didn't answer) what he thought of Jack the Giant; explaining how Jack had worked for the circus doing the heavy labor; describing Jack driving stakes into the ground; remembering Jack bare-chested in the morning with his mallet in his hand; recounting how even now they sometimes told him 'Jack take off your shirt,' though "Alas, he never does." *Jack, Jack, Jack* buzzing back and forth as they flitted around the kitchen like bees, like ping-pong balls, like puppets, until finally they brought Katie into the conversation, saying:

"And you, Kate? What did *you* think of Jack?"

"Our Jack."

"Our lovely, lovely Jack."

"Well," said Katie, "he seems –"

"Oh, *seems*."

"Seems what Kate? Rather big?"

"I didn't say!"

"Oh, no, of *course* you didn't *say*."

"And us? What, Kate?"

"Like dwarves?"

"Or puppets?"

"Ballerinas?"

"I never –"

"Never?"

"Never ever?"

"Anyway, Jack says."

"Jack says," (and now both twins, who had been cleaning furiously, stopped and turned to stare at Katie, double smiles exposing double teeth), "Jack says you're bothering the rooster."

The rooster? The buzzing ended; the ping pong ball had dropped. For one long silence something terrifying seemed to hang suspended in the air. "I didn't bother the rooster," Katie said carefully. "He didn't seem upset at all."

The tension held for a second or two, and then "Oh well, that's Jack," said one twin, picking up a dishtowel, clattering the spoons.

"But I'd be careful of that rooster."

"You know how roosters are –"

"Really. Worse than geese."

It wasn't long after that (but only after a mouse had made a sudden appearance in the kitchen sending the twins and Harry scurrying onto chairs, hands up beside their cheeks, mouths shaped like O's, and causing Katie to mumble, "There's sure to be two more," as she swept the little creature out the door) that the twins, descending from their chairs along with Harry, smoothing imaginary feathers and finding peace restored, herded Katie and Harry through the hall into the library and the waiting leather chairs, Harry taking one quick look behind.

"Brandy, Kate?" said one of the twins.

"Your mother *loved* our brandy."

"– Knocked her socks off, one might say."

"Now Harry, you're too young. How about a little double-dutch?"

"Meaning cocoa, Harry."

"Right there on the table."

"But as for Kate –"

Katie waved away the brandy. "I'll have cocoa too."

"Well, if you insist…" one said, and then they watched while Katie poured out two cocoas from the china pot on the little table set between them and handed one to Harry. "If you insist, but the brandy is sublime…"

"Is it…local milk…" Harry started to ask, looking into his cocoa mug. Everyone ignored him.

"Anyway, it's storytime."

"Who tells the story?" Katie asked.

"We do!"

"Both of you?"

"Oh no, not together."

"To every story, a single storyteller."

"If two twins tell one story, then it's two."

"I'll tell."

"I'll listen."

And now there came a pause. Now there came that weighty silence that must precede all great storytelling, into which no sound fell except the pouring of brandy and the puffing of pipes, the rest of the day falling quietly away. A hush. And then the twin began.

"Once upon a time there was a stupid boy who stole a splendid coin –"

"Oh, no, not that one," said one twin. "Save that one for some other time."

The telling twin raised one eyebrow, the other menaced with his two, and then the pouring and the puffing began once again. Finally, the telling twin resumed.

"Once, a long, long time ago, an old man came to Baraboo."

"Oh, yes. That one. I like that one much better."

Chapter Eight

"Even now," continued the storytelling twin in a voice entirely different from what had come before, "Even now, I can see him on the road. It is early summer. He hobbles along with a staff, the way that wayfarers do sometimes, and he is barefoot. He stops, adjusts his cloak, and continues on his way.

"He is going to the circus grounds, and that is why we knew him. Because, in the summer, we too went to the circus grounds. We worked there when the main body of the circus was out performing from town to town. We were part of the "skeleton staff," a phrase we never liked much, as if we were a staff of skeletons, nothing but a bag of bones. We used to turn the phrase over in our minds quite a bit in those days when the letters came from Iowa maybe where there had been too much rain: *expect elephants*, they'd say, because too many elephants would turn the circus grounds to mud, and the letters might also say, *send patches for the tent*, or just *send buckets* – and one year from Kansas where a tornado had touched down and swept a whole house off its foundations, sent it whirling into the air to be lost forever in the storm, and not just the house, but our best magician who was swept away. He used to keep a wagon outside the entrance to the big-top where he did tricks and sold elixirs. That year, the letters came: *send book on magic, a hat, a wand, and a large supply of rabbits.* All these letters written in the broad hand of the general manager and addressed to us, the vital skeleton staff.

"Anyway, the traveler. He came in summer. He did not work for the circus, not officially anyway, because I can't remember ever seeing him on the line at payday among the acrobats with sprained ankles and second-rate trapeze artists who were waiting, hoping for some fatal accident in Minnesota to call them up to center ring. They were all on the payroll, these performers, but the old man was not on the payroll so far as we could tell, no contract signed. Still he was always there, working beside us always, nonetheless. Mostly he did woodwork. It was he who carved the wagon for the merman, a carving that was half man, half fish. Did you see it at the circus grounds today? It is the wagon with seven screaming angels, angels that look as if they manifested in themselves the half-drowned soul of the merman that used to live behind the bars. The merman is another story, the merman's dead now; it was a long, long time ago. But the wagon is a thing of art and it eternally abides. Even with those angels – their mouths exposing stark white teeth, their hair flung out behind them so that they seem to swoop down like seven furies in full cry – even with those angels, and because of them, the wagon is a thing of beauty, the old man's masterwork, and not always used for the merman, anyway. In fact, now I remember, he did the carving before the merman had arrived.

"One year, the tigers toured the whole Midwest in it, and maybe that old man carved the angels to terrify the savage little boys who otherwise would throw lit matches in between the bars. He would have done that, carved it like that to save the tigers, because he loved the animals, and wondrous as he was with carving, he was even more wondrous with beasts, and it is not unlikely that he would have sent the tigers forth with a protection of that kind. It was with the animals that he seemed most at ease, and they healed quickly under his care, because remember, this was summertime and only the outcast creatures, too sick, or old, or feeble to meet even the basest standards of an old-time circus would be kept back at Baraboo – these beasts, outcasts, and yet he healed them.

"To us, the old man never spoke at all, nor to any of the workers, and it went on just like that, him coming and carving and caring for the animals summer after summer until the summer of the Death.

"Oh, what a time that was. It had been very hot that year. We had had no rain at all, and the river – low and foul and strewn with refuse from the mining operations just north in the dells – the river brought some kind of pestilence, so that the circus grounds became infested. It was leeches, the infestation was of leeches, the kind that grab a man and suck his blood, but these were bigger than any leeches we had ever seen, and they crawled out of the river and showed up everywhere: between the horns of the giraffe, for instance, or plastered onto the toe of a lion cub, or along the ropes that dangled from the big-top, and even finally, like worms, inside the wood we used to carve the circus cars. We had to take great care not to be attacked by them because once they had burrowed into your skin, they were tenacious, and even if the victim managed to pull them off, or burn them off, the leeches would leave bruises that would grow into boils, and sometimes the victims died.

"But most of the victims were the animals, because they were harder to protect and more likely to pick at the boils once infected. One of the emu's died, I remember, and two of the elephants, and also a young boy who always swept the stalls. For weeks, all of us went about in a kind of pall. Working was difficult. We had to keep our lunch pails covered and even our boot-tops were not safe, and many were the days we came home and had to pick these leeches off our stockings or else out of our hair.

"The old man arrived late that year. There was no set date for his arrival, no contract to hold him, but usually he arrived by early June, and now here it was the first part of July and still no sign of him. Finally, however, there was that evening, just when the sun was setting in its usual burst of primrose behind our apple trees, when we saw him coming, dressed something like a monk, climbing right up the crest of that hill just beyond our farm. Even the rooster saw him (Jack wasn't with us in those days) and crowed three times, right at sunset, which is an unusual time for a rooster to do his crowing. He came on, passed by, and headed toward the town.

"The next day we arrived at the circus grounds, lunch pails covered, wide-brimmed hats clapped down on our heads to keep us safe from leeches that might fall off the trees and down our collars. There was some commotion going on and the old man was at the center. We worked our way to where we could see, and there he stood half smiling, and at his feet rested a sack moving about as if there were something live in it, a baby tiger, maybe, or a bear cub, pawing about just as you'd expect, trying to get out, except it wasn't any baby tiger, because a tail had found its way through the top folds and it looked something like a lizard's. It was long. Big enough that you could see the scales.

" 'Whatcha got in there, Joe?' one of the men asked him, calling him Joe because that was just the local custom in those days, to call a man whose name you didn't know *Joe,* the way in other places they might say Mac or Buddy. 'Is it a lizard? Something for the sideshow? A two headed snake?' He was more curious than scared because in those days we were used to such things, we being the circus's hired hands, and sometimes farmers even brought us two-headed calves and lambs and such, which always died. But then, what with those leeches killing everything, I can't say it was just curiosity, I can't say there wasn't also in those voices some exhausted kind of hope, for we had been losing the fight against those leeches…but maybe that's just a misremembering.

"'Two headed?' said the old man with a kind of challenge in his voice. 'Tis a seven-headed beast I have!' And with that he loosened the top of the sack and out came this…thing…waist high, scales the color of your own father's blood, vermilion-like, and royal, and whether it had one head or seven I couldn't say, none of us could, though there are some around here who still swear to seeing seven, but the thing darted up and out of that sack, tore over the grounds, plunged into the river and swam away. We never saw that thing again.

"'He'll eat your leeches!' cried out old man, laughing – Ha! Ha! Ha! – just like that, three bursts of laughter. 'He'll eat your leeches, guarantee!' We stared at him and then stared back across the river, not speaking, half-amazed.

"And maybe he was right. Because we don't know how it was exactly, if it was the growing heat of summer that killed them, or the beast, but from that day the leeches began to disappear. But not just disappear. Some shriveled into dust right before our eyes, some burst into flame. And there are some around these parts who say they heard those leeches screaming and who say they saw their faces – the faces of the leeches – contorted into the nightmare masks of souls gone into hell. Well, so some people say.

"Within a week, there wasn't a leech anywhere in Baraboo, and as for the beast, we never saw that beast again. But a few years later, in the fall, and just before the harvest, a boy claimed to have dug something up not far from here, a skeleton, and not just a skeleton either. There were bits of flesh still on it, and a claw of sorts nearly intact. The thing had seven heads. It was covered, head to tail, with leech remains.

"That boy took that thing to town, the papers got hold of it, people came from all over Wisconsin just to see it, the boy charging a penny for a peek, until finally he worked out some deal with the circus, and they took that thing up and down the whole Midwest. It drew great crowds until some girl comes in from that university down in Madison and gets a hold of it, and declares the thing a hoax. Most people around here don't believe that, though. We're circus people. You couldn't pull a hoax on us. We had seen it; it was real."

The twin fell silent. Katie and Harry were silent too. In fact, the silence in the room seemed almost palpable.

"What happened to the old man?" Harry finally ventured.

"The old man? He was never seen again. Though some say –"

"Time for bed!"

"Oh, yes. Time for bed."

And the twins would not utter one more word about the story. They gathered up the cups, winked once at Katie.

"Good night, Kate!"

"Good night!"

"Tomorrow night the brandy!"

And off the two twins headed, into the kitchen and then off to bed – two beds, one room, a lamp with moons and stars stuck upon the shade between them, their little bodies tucked right up to the chin and pinned in by the blankets – so much for twins. A good night's sleep, we can imagine, would be had by both.

Harry Jinx was not so lucky. For a second night he lay on his bed unable to sleep, unnerved and hungry. It had been such a difficult day for him and a difficult evening too, what with the twins threatening to tell a story about a boy who stole a coin, and then all this stuff about the old man at the circus. Perhaps, however, the worst of it had been later, when Katie had turned the universe into a big machine. It had happened after storytime, when – thinking that after all it might be better to tell Katie about everything, even if it meant sharing the coin – he had followed her to her room. When he got there, however, he had found it difficult to speak. Katie had barricaded herself behind a wall of books. Ignoring him, she had begun to look things up.

"Boy, some fairytale," he had finally begun, trying to sound as off-hand as he could.

Katie, however, hardly seemed to hear him, and murmuring merely, "Even fairytales are true, Harry," she continued with her reading. When she finally did speak – because he had insisted, asking her point blank what she thought of the story and hoping that somewhere in whatever diatribe was likely to ensue he might find an opening wherein to tell her of the coin – when she finally spoke what she told him only baffled him, for what she said was that stories were, essentially, like bowls of chicken soup. "Ten different cooks might cook their chicken soup a little differently, but at the core of what they make is the essence of the chicken, chicken stock. Stories may seem different, but like a chicken stock that's been boiled in the deepest cauldrons of the mind, there are the same primal patterns. For example. tragedies, comedies, and demonic archetypes into which the storyteller, whether he knows of this or not, will dip his ladle. Patterns, Harry, throughout stories. But, because storytellers were not merely ladle-dippers, but also artists, they added spice to their stock and then poured their stock out into different lovely bowls – the African Folktale Bowl for example, the Brothers Grimm Bowl, the Hollywood Bowl, even the Herman Melville Bowl – in any case, a zillion different bowls, perhaps, but only, and in spite of the spice, the same soups deep inside."

"Of course," said Harry.

"Right, of course. But of course not all soups are based on chicken stock. At the core might be a different essence. There may be a half a dozen different stocks. There's hero soup, for example, coming-of-age soup, love soup (quite a bit of that) – and tonight we had –"

"Stone soup?" he asked. What Katie had been saying, was a mystery to him, and did not make much sense.

But Katie had only laughed at him and said, "Apocalyptic soup. And a legend soup." She went on to say that what he needed to do was to learn to ignore the bowl and taste the soup instead. By doing so, he would see that in this story about the old man, the circus world was really the pre-apocalyptic land of death where people waited for a savior. That, she said, was the universal story behind the story, or the chicken stock before the artist adds the spice. "See, Harry? Apocalyptic soup. What did you think of all that stuff about the skeletons? The skeleton staff, for example in the beginning. Personally, I doubt the circus called them skeletons. It was just part of the story."

But Harry, who still couldn't tell if by soup she meant the dinner or the story (though he suspected it was the story since so far as he could tell, and in spite of the Belladonna, there had been no skeletons in the dinner soup) – Harry had been reluctant to reply. After a hesitant silence, he ventured, "What do you mean, what was the skeleton staff? It wasn't anything. It's just an expression people use, it's just the summer crew."

"Nonsense, Harry, and you know it," she said. "It was the soup and not the bowl, a patterned metaphor for death and an apocalypse. You just have your eye fixed on the bowl is all, you're not looking at the soup. The circus in that story was the Kingdom of Death, a metaphoric skeleton with an hourglass in one hand and a sickle in the other."

But Harry hadn't wanted to hear about death. His grandfather –

"Death, Harry. You got that? Death being, of course, the wages of sin…"

"Wages…?"

"Of sin" she had said. "Do sin, earn death. You know what sin is, don't you, Harry? Stealing, for example? Or lying?" Katie paused, but when Harry didn't answer, she had continued, calmly, to "rip the skin off of the storybeast," as she called it, saying that the circus men and broken acrobats were metaphors for twisted sinners living in a broken world of ruin – a demonic world, she had said – and telling him how the heat of summer was a metaphor for the lust burning in their veins; how they probably…did things with the animals; how if one looked carefully there were images of greed in the story too, and gluttony (the emphasis on lunch pails, for example), saying – inexplicably at least to Harry – "that's three out of seven sins right there, and if we look, we might find four more," until finally sinning was made manifest by the leeches consuming the circus people, their animals, even their excessive lunch. "That's the set-up for an apocalypse, Harry. Apocalypses come to worlds of sin and death. All we're missing now is the messiah."

And then, as if he were following all of this, as if this first mess of gibberish were not enough, she launched into a second mess after only the briefest of pauses, insisting now that the old man was the messiah, and the monster in the bag was the mere agent of the good.

"Good!" Harry burst out, finally understanding something. "Good! It was a monster!"

"A monster that ate the leeches," she retorted. And now, availing herself as she always did of an opportunity to scorn him, she had started almost shouting about how "good" wasn't always just a walk in the park. "Do you think," she ranted, sitting up on the edge of her bed, "do you think, that just because something is good, it has to be all sweetness and light, a bunch of pearly angels strumming on their harps, their mouths like little O's, their fretted brows, the way they are at Ghent?"

Her eyes were glowing, Harry thought, but he had never heard of Ghent. She began to tell him about some apocalyptic painting in a city in Belgium in which angels played on mandolins and Christ looked like a lamb, but she got confused about the artist's name, and then exasperated and said, "Forget Ghent, look at the *Book of Revelations*. There are monsters, and the four horses of the apocalypse. So, the old man comes to town with this good monster of his, cleans things up a bit, redeems the circus people, and returns to them their little storyland where they've been waiting, totally enchanted, ever since."

"What are they waiting for?"

"The final coming. The ending of the story, which, unfortunately, the twins did not provide."

"And the old man?"

"They probably ate him."

"Ate him! Jesus Christ."

"Right. They ate him too. Last supper, Harry. They always eat the savior, or at least they rip him up. *Sparagmos.* Look it up in Northrop Frye."

But Harry didn't believe any of that, it made him sick the way she twisted things around. The story, so far as he could tell, didn't have anything to do with Christ or apocalypse, or anything like that. It was about the old man and the leeches. But Katie mixed things up, and even once she had calmed down a little and, sitting down once more, like a Buddha in the middle of her bed, legs crossed again, one finger raised, eyes lifted vaguely toward the ceiling, she still made him feel sick, preaching about a storybeast and a naked emperor and the truth about some big white hunted whale. She wanted to rip the skin off things, she said. "Rip the skin off a horse," she had said, "and how is it any different from a zebra? It's like the bowls, Harry – different, but the soup is all the same." Swept away by her own rhetoric, she mixed her metaphors: the embroidered beast, she said, the beastly emperor, the naked emperor hiding in a china bowl.

Katie made no sense.

She went on like this for some time, Harry's nausea growing into anger and resentment until finally – when she concluded by saying that if he ever bothered to look beneath the surface of the story, he'd see it was about apocalypse and death, and that the leeches and the old man were mere fabrications (arching her eyebrows, and adding archly, "that means lie") created by the storyteller just like flowers on a soup bowl – after this final arrogance, he had blurted out, "Oh, they are, are they?" wanting more than anything to prove her wrong. "Fabricators? Liars? You don't know anything! I met the old man at the circus today, he was very real, not at all a lie. He even had a sack with him like that!"

But Katie had only shrugged. She had already pointed out, she said, that this was a legend soup, and that in legends real-life occurrences eventually get embroidered into tales. "Of course," she said, "the old man you met might be the loose thread I'm looking for, but even if a thread or two might come from something real, the garment's still a total fantasy."

Loose thread! Embroidered storybeasts! Naked emperors hiding in a china bowl! – and then, suddenly, Harry thought he knew why she insisted that the "surface of the story" wasn't true. "You're scared, aren't you," he accused her. "You think that creature the old man had is your McGuffin."

But if this had unnerved Katie, she didn't show it, and after only a moment's hesitation, she had said, "Don't be silly Harry. I wasn't the one trembling down there, wondering if there was a leech inside my cocoa." And then came the worst part of all, for now she said that even if the creature seemed to have a certain vague resemblance to her water-dragon, clearly, unlike her McGuffin, it was a hoax.

"A hoax? It's *not* a hoax, it's real!" Harry exclaimed, wondering even as he did so why the word hoax had upset him (and realizing later, lying in bed, that he had not been thinking about the monster-hoax but about Mrs. Higgins and her coin). "You know it's real. They, they found the buried skeleton, didn't they? And it had seven heads, not two!"

But once Katie had got hold of something she was not about to let it go. "The skeleton," she said, "primarily reinforces the leitmotif of skeletons" (here she reminded him about the skeleton staff) "creating a veritable *Danse Macabre* waltzing right across the tale." In any case, she claimed, the skeleton too was a hoax, or to be more accurate, the thing in the bag had been a hoax as well. Hadn't he ever heard of the Cardiff Giant? Katie told Harry how in 1868 a cigar manufacturer named George Hull made a giant out of gypsum and buried him on a farm in Cardiff, Iowa. "When the thing was dug up, it fooled everybody," she said, "everyone thinking it was a million years old, even James Draton, some big-time paleontologist, and thousands of people traveled miles just to see it. Eventually, the hoax was unmasked (and Professor Draton, we might imagine, would have been banished from his enviable post at the university) but the interesting thing," Katie added, "was that P.T. Barnum acquired it from Mr. Hull, made a copy, advertised the copy as a fake, a hoax of a hoax, and made a killing on it. People like a hoax, Harry," Katie concluded, "and even hoaxes of a hoax. People like to think there's something there."

Harry turned away. There was no winning with her: hoax of a hoax, that was what he had said himself about his coin. And now, while the nausea rose up in his stomach, she returned once again to all her favorite themes, the emperor's robe, the white whale of meaning, and the apocalyptic bones. "One must find common threads and clues, and then connect the stories," she was saying, opening up her book of fairytales, – "connect the bones of one beast to another and…string them out along a cable – call it a cabal, if you would like – that runs right through all of them…"

"String up the connections…?" His coin, thought Harry, and the old man, and Jack, the twins, and poor, dead Mrs. Higgins, and even Katie talking all about a hoax…

"Then pull the cable, or flip the switch, and…" Katie paused and looked at the pages "…and make all these stories move together, turning, like gears in a machine, and deep within the stories, like soup stock, there exists that commonality that creates the music of truth, Harry Jinx, or as the ancients used to say, the music of the seven rounded spheres."

"My God," he had said, faintly, blanching. "The world, the truth, it's like an engine."

Maybe she hadn't thought of that. In any case, he thought that she blanched too.

So, now, Harry lying in bed, dreaming of a dreamless sleep and frightened that what he heard outside his window was not the wind among the apple trees, but the rising whir of hidden draughts and pistons. Katie had turned the universe into a big machine. It is just the wind, he told himself, straining not to listen. It is the wind and nothing else, just as the coin is just a coin, and if for a minute he had thought differently it was only because of what Katie had said – it was Katie who turned the universe into an engine; one couldn't blame the universe for that.

In fact, one shouldn't blame the universe for anything.

And now that he thought of it, Harry realized that even Katie had not meant to do it. She had been describing something else, music or something, and if she had blanched when he said it was an engine, she had recovered just as quickly, the high red color returning to her brow. Ducking her head into her storybook she was soon offering less dangerous transformations, turning Chicken Little (that high-strung barnyard fowl of storybooks who suffered from delusions) into the apocalyptic Chicken Little. "My God," she had mumbled, "the sky is falling," as Harry slipped out of the door, thinking, not the sky at all; I love her but perhaps she is a nut.

"*No*," she had shouted after him, as if she'd read his mind. "*Not* a nut! Don't you believe that, Harry Jinx. All things stand for other things, like codes, and you and I are on a divinely sanctioned quest. Mr. Bononosetta, Joachim, the flames, the roosters, the towers in the dust upon our car, the hydrodragon, that story that they told – these things link up: Moby Dick has bumped his brow against our ship; the universe is knocking at our door!"

But Harry did not want to think about the universe or Moby Dick, and rolling over he tried hard to think of nothing but the emerald hills, the deep blue sky and the yellow duck floating in perfect circles on the pond. Hadn't it been a beautiful day? he asked himself. Hadn't the sun remained congenially lukewarm while the duck slid back and forth along the surface of the water? How exact its movements were! It was as if there were some kind of conveyor belt beneath him or an unseen track…but this last thought discomfited him; he rolled over, closed his eyes, and tried once more to conjure up the sun.

It was impossible; he couldn't see the sun. Katie had ruined it with all her talk of engines, and now, instead of blue skies and sparkling emerald hills, little girls in snow-white shifts came unaccountably to mind. Who are they? he wondered sitting up, suddenly – and then, remembering who they were, he laid down again, and tried to block the memory out. He and Katie had seen them in a photograph at a museum exhibit in New Hampshire a year or two ago. The exhibit traced the history of the textile industry in nineteenth-century New England, and though the photograph was tinted in sepia and badly faded, the little girls all in a line were clear enough. They were five years old, or maybe six, and dressed in plain white shifts, they stared into the camera in that sad, serious way that children in sepia photos often do. But these children had good reason to be sad. The caption read *Veterans of the Weaving Mill,* and the vast loom of that weaving mill had mutilated these children in its mechanical employ. "Look," Katie had said, leaning a little closer. "Look how neatly someone's pinned their empty sleeves." Harry had felt sick, but Katie had only called the children heroes and then moved on to examine the display of finished cloth.

Heroes! Harry thought now. That was typical of Katie – to twist one thing into another. It was ridiculous for her to call those mangled children heroes – and just as ridiculous for him to call the universe a big machine. Things, he said to himself, just are what they are and nothing else. They don't mean anything. The wind is nothing but the wind, the coin a coin, and the sound of distant thunder just the crash of one blank mass against another, and not the grinding of the gears. Whatever coin-linked worries he might have, they were here on common ground, not out there tangled in the warp and weave of time and space. Katie was deluded to think there was a cable through her books. Apocalypse! That's crazy, he thought. Harry was sure, even as you and I are sure, as the clock strikes eight and the moon slides into place above the pendulum, that nothing threatens, nothing laughs, and nothing pays attention to whatever Katie weaves.

Chapter Nine

Weeks passed. Every night, the twins offered Katie brandy she refused, and every night they told her stories – or non-stories as she called them because after that first promising tale about the old man and the leeches, the ones that followed seemed to have no significance at all, or were very badly told, or lacked a theme. There were stories about cats in love with bats, and little boys who hated all their sisters' toys. There were *once upon a time* stories made up entirely of lists, stories without *e*'s in them, and one story about a town where all the people stuttered, so that the twins tongue-tied themselves to silence before they ever reached the end. In fact, most stories didn't end. Even a story that started well enough was vulnerable to derailment, as was the case, for example, in the tale of Mrs. Finniby and the contest at the fair. The contest had something to do with fruit pies, but whether it had been a pie eating contest or pie baking contest or even a pie throwing contest Katie and Harry never found out because the twins, each disputing the other's memory, began to hurl at one another the odd names of presumably odder berries that were used to fill the pies – *lollyberries*, one hissed, *such as one finds on Diggins hill* – and the other, *Fool, 'twas dingleberries, and there are no lollyberries to be had since Diggins died some forty years ago!* – until Katie finally mumbled to Harry that even a knight fallen down a rabbit hole would not put up with this, and then she slipped away to bed. Many stories ended this way – in the middle and with one twin in a snit – but even the ones that ended at the end were not much better, and most of them were simply dull. Among the dullest was one entitled *The Biography of a Toddler named John Dough*, a saga of sorts, according to the twins, and they dragged it out in twice-weekly segments. Only a mother with no other little Doughs to dote upon might have told this toddler's story, Katie told Harry later, but that didn't stop the twins from building whole episodes about John Dough's toilet training. Nor did it stop them from listing his favorite foods in alphabetical order, or relating verbatim conversations that the boy engaged in with his father, his doctor, or a large stuffed poodle named The Blue Danube. The John Dough stories drove Katie nearly mad. They lacked conflict, meaning, symbol, pattern, and transcendence – all the things that Katie thought made stories, all the things she most enjoyed.

In fact, Katie was fed up altogether with storytime. It was as if the twins were doing it on purpose, she thought, telling lousy tales to test her, or to send her into fits, or maybe to delay from telling her the one tale she was waiting eagerly to hear. She didn't know just what that tale would be, but every night she listened for it, and every night was disappointed when it didn't come.

But perhaps this disappointment would not have been so bad if in other ways the quest had somehow moved forward. It hadn't. In fact, the trail had disappeared, gone underground, as Katie said, and taken the McGuffin with it too. The tower, for example, which the twins sometimes slipped ambiguously into conversation, saying things like, "Harry, eat that kidney aspic or we'll send you to the tower!" – the tower was nowhere to be found. She and Harry had spent several afternoons wandering the hills between Blunderbee and Baraboo in search of it, even trespassing in cow pastures where bovine clusters turned to gaze at them with a look somewhere between quiet terror and a threat. But so far as Katie could tell, there was no tower anywhere.

Then too, Jack the Giant wouldn't speak to her at all – he ran away in fact when she approached to ask about the rooster or about the story he had almost told that first day in the barn. The rooster itself, when Katie managed to get near it, wouldn't talk; and Harry's old man – if he really had met an old man at the circus grounds that day – had disappeared completely; and, finally, Katie couldn't uncover a single thing about the story of the leeches and the seven-headed hoax. This last was especially disappointing, but there was nothing to be done about it. She couldn't look it up at the library for herself (far too dangerous, as she explained to Harry, since she had stolen those two books), and Harry, though he ventured there without her, came back empty-handed saying that there was no account of any leeches in the archives – nothing in the old stacks of the newspapers, no public-service pamphlets, no record of a town meeting where angry farmers pointed fingers, and local big-wigs called for calm. Even when she asked the few villagers she'd see on Main Street about what she called The Summer of the Plague, they only stared at her blankly, or denied the thing, or simply shrugged and walked away.

Finally, like one last nail in the coffin of her quest, articles about the poisoned wells stopped appearing in the newspaper, and when Katie sought information at both the mayor's office and the office of the *Baraboo Gazette*, the responses that she got were one part polite and one part useless: that the vapors had just been dew rising from the sodden fields of morning, or that only Mrs. Finniby had seen it, who just couldn't be trusted, or that the water tested pure enough to be bottled up and sold to restaurants from California to New York, which to Katie's dismay, one enterprising Barabooan seemed inclined to do. As for the dead cows and pigs and sheep, they had simply died, the mayor's secretary regretfully informed her, of old age. "Everyone gets old, don't they?" she had asked Katie. "Even cows and pigs and sheep…" Not on a farm, Katie thought, animals on a farm don't get old, that's what the slaughterhouse is for. One thing piled on another in a heap until Katie was sure that the whole town had been suspended in enchantment somehow, and her whole quest becalmed.

"I'll not be sacrificed," she murmured to herself one hot afternoon remembering the old myth about the virgin Iphigenia, sacrificed on the alter by her father just to bring a breeze to some enchanted sea. Let them find some other virgin, she thought. I've got a quest to do.

Still, all of these disappointments would have meant little to her if only she could have made some progress in her books. After all, that was where the real trail ought to lay, she told herself, and that was where she would track down the McGuffin, in the steadfast world of written words, not this contingent world where Monday's poisoned wells were Tuesday's health springs, and no one could agree about the species of a berry or the outcome of a pie contest at a local fair.

And it had always been like that. When she was younger, Katie had wondered if she might be beautiful. She had sought the answer in the mirror, but the mirror had not answered, or else it told her different things on different days. In *Sleeping Beauty*, on the other hand, the mirror spoke the truth. But in real life, mirrors were not like that, nor other things as well. In real life who could say for sure what was the nature of the twins or the intentions of her father? Who could say there was no tower hereabout? Reality shifted in her world, but in books reality had fixed itself into a pattern and the ending of the story never changed. Thus, it was in books that Katie quested, seeking that loose and magic thread she had imagined that first day in Baraboo. Find that, she thought, and then unravel it through five hundred stories, and the unraveling will reveal the patterns and the truth of all the stories and her world, and perhaps the great hydrodragon-whale-McGuffin of her holy quest.

By loose thread, she meant a thread by which to tie this world to the books, and if the reader does not quite understand this – how one could tie one world to another and then unravel books to find McGuffins in real life, or how McGuffins in a story book could have a single thing to do with things in Baraboo. If the reader does not understand this, he need not be alarmed. Katie herself did not quite understand it. And so she comforted herself in darker moments, telling herself that no quester ever knew the exact shape of his quest. The seeker seeks, and that is all. Thus, she simply sailed across the printed pages, seeking. Here too, however, she encountered difficulties, not because she could not find that loosely threaded end that wove through other books and into life, but because in books loose ends were everywhere.

It was as if every book she opened might be bound up with her quest – even the Bible, even *Horton Hears a Who*. Horton was an elephant and he searched among the dust heaps for a solitary Who, and in this she saw a dim resemblance to her own relentless quest. Clues cropped up everywhere; the trouble came from making them connect.

One day in town, for instance, at the tobacconist's where she bought the daily paper, she was greeted by a boy about her age. The boy was clothed from head to toe in a cloth akin to felt – all forest greens and harvest yellows – and a smallish charm shaped like a long-stemmed pipe dangled from his neck. In spite of the outfit, Katie took no real notice of him, only murmuring a soft "Good morning" as she scanned the headlines of the *Baraboo Gazette*. The boy, however, replied with a rather complicated exegesis of the phrase "good morning," smiling broadly and asking if she meant to wish him a good morning, or if she meant that it *was* a good morning, or if she meant that she felt good this morning, or perhaps that this was a morning upon which to be good.

Katie, who was concentrating on extracting a quarter from her pocket for the paper, was only slightly taken aback, and after she paid, she mumbled distractedly, "Well, all of them, I guess," and turned to go. But as she turned away the boy called after her:

What has roots as nobody sees
Is taller than trees
Up it goes
And yet never grows?

Odd, thought Katie, that he should be calling out a riddle in the middle of the street. Very odd, in fact. And now that she thought about it, there also seemed to be something oddly familiar about what he had said. It wasn't until the next day, however, that she realized, quite out of nowhere, that the answer to the riddle was mountain, and that the riddle itself (along with the exegesis of good morning) came from a novel called *The Hobbit,* a modern quest-romance that was popular with many and also with a certain boy whom she had known in high school, the type of boy that had a strong imagination but had only read one book, and who then plunged in and promptly drowned himself in text. This phenomenon – the complete submersion of generally indifferent readers into a single text – is not unheard of: Katie had a neighbor who never spoke except to quote Ayn Rand, and the same thing sometimes happens with students of the Bible and other sacred texts. But *The Hobbit* is not the Bible (it is, instead, a work of fantasy, in which the miraculous and magical occur on every page) and this boy from school who took the plunge into *The Hobbit* was reborn as a hobbit, adopting hobbit a name, speaking in borrowed hobbit passages and writing out his homework in the cryptic runes inscribed throughout the text.

A hobbit, for those who do not know it, is a little like a gnome though somewhat smarter – shoeless, barely half of human size, and inclined to be a little chubby what with his sedentary habits and his love of tea and cakes. But what did *The Hobbit* have to do with Katie and her quest? True, there were certain vague connections. For one thing, there lurked a dragon at the center of the novel. For another, the hero's mother had the name of Belladonna Took, and Harry had found a jar of belladonna on the spice rack on their second night in Baraboo. But as for the dragon, it was not a hydrodragon, and why would the name of the hero's mother's matter, if the hero himself was Bilbo Baggins? Bilbo was a reluctant quester, induced to search for treasure by a band of restless dwarves, but more inclined, left to his own devices, to stay at home and smoke his pipe. What possible connection could such a worthless hero have to do with Katie and her quest? None, she answered. And besides that, Bilbo had found a magic ring, and she had not.

And that was the problem – not so much that she didn't have some sort of magic ring, but that the hobbit's trail had led in the direction of the ring, while for her (and not the hobbit), the trail had petered out. It was like this: the riddle that the boy had proffered had led her to a *Hobbit* scene in which the magic ring makes its appearance, but even though the riddle-clues had led her to the story's magic ring, there was no way for her to hook this up and find the real-life trail. Her trail had petered out. To move ahead she would need to find a ring or something like it in real life, which in turn might be inscribed with phrases that would lead to the hydrodragon of her quest. But Katie had no ring. In *The Hobbit* was there some other clue besides the ring somewhere in that riddle scene? Was there a different path to take?

The only other major element in the riddle scene was Gollum, a debased creature, vaguely amorphous, troglodytic, obsessive, petty, mean. Gollum lived beside a blackened lake within a hollow mountain, and he lived on fish but he preferred to dine on goblins, or a hobbit, if he could. The hero Bilbo had lost himself in Gollum's mountain lair while on his quest to slay a dragon, and as Bilbo crawled about in the utter darkness of that lake-filled cave, he found the magic ring upon the stony floor, and slipped it in his pocket. The ring belonged to Gollum, a Gollum life eked out upon the barest of essentials – nothing but fish, maybe goblin flesh, and the pitch dark lake. For Gollum the ring had been the only thing that did not stink of decay. But he had lost it now, and Bilbo found it, and only by its powers did Bilbo escape the creature's grasp. When Gollum realized that his ring was gone, that his one transcendency had slipped away onto the cavern floor and found its way to Bilbo – ah, then into what emotional abysses did that wretched creature pitch himself to drown? After all, the ring was more than magic, it was his secret; and at the same time it was what had mastered him and galled him and sucked him dry the way that scotch and vodka might suck dry mortal men.

Gollum seemed familiar. Hadn't Katie met him somewhere else? And suddenly it dawned on her with absolute clarity that she did know Gollum, and he did indeed lead to another text. Gollum was a mirror image of Despaire, a character that Red Crosse meets in Katie's beloved *Fairie Queene*. Like Gollum, Despaire lived in a cave, and with his tangled hair and hollow eyes, and rawboned cheeks that shrunk into his jaws as if "he did never dine," he must have looked, so Katie thought, like Gollum whose pale dark-seeing eyes, according to the author, had grown too big for his emaciated face. This connection fascinated Katie, for hadn't she herself mentioned Red Crosse and *The Fairie Queene* to Harry that first night in Baraboo? Surely that was more than just coincidence; it had to be a hidden thread, a link.

But she couldn't get the thread to go beyond these first two stories: there were no caves in Baraboo so far as she could tell, nor was she in despair – merely frustrated and incredibly confused.

Finally, to add to all her other troubles, the books her father had given her were useless. She would not open *Trithemius Decomposed*, whose cover had reminded her too much of Dante's gates of hell, and as for the other work, *On Grammatology* by Jacques Derrida, it was unreadable, riddled with intriguing phrases – *transcendental signified*, for example, and *exergue* – that fell apart when she tried to figure out exactly what they meant. What, she wondered, was an exergue? At a loss, she called her father on the phone.

She called and Ellie answered, the graduate student, her hello husky, her vowels hanging long and low like udders. Ellie was her father's latest partner. When Katie's father finally got on the line after a delay, a grunt, and muffled laughter, he seemed distracted, hardly listening at all to what Kate had to say. "What, Hitchcock?" he asked inexplicably when she mentioned the McGuffin, and then long pauses, inconclusive comments, and finally a burst of interest when she mentioned Derrida. "Oh, Derrida. The emperor on the throne, Katie. He's turned philosophy and reading on its head."

"Emperor? I didn't…"

"They construct the beast, Katie, and then we deconstruct him. Nothing holds together. I have to go."

"They? Who they? How do I –"

"The artists, the writers. They construct, we deconstruct. Check your Trithemius if you don't understand."

And he was gone. But she wouldn't check Trithemius. She sat down at her desk, opened up the book of nursery rhymes, and quested on.

For his part, Harry too felt as if things were at a standstill, though the mire he was in was fraught with fear. He heard no more about Mrs. Higgins and her suicide, nor any threats or intimations about the coin, but he couldn't help feeling that he wasn't safe, just as the guilty aren't safe, though he could not imagine of just what he might be guilty. What's more, because he fled from any consideration that such palpable anxieties might actually have their source in something vague, or at least unnamable (something that for lack of a better word he might have called McGuffin), he heaped all his suspicions on Jack out in the barn and ran away when the giant seemed too near. Jack followed him, he thought. He was sure of it, and when he left the house with Katie, he would frequently see Jack standing with his axe against the doorframe of the barn, watching him – never Katie, always him – as if he knew that Harry had the coin, and was only waiting for the opportunity to corner him alone.

It was because of Jack that Harry began to stick closer and closer to Katie. Her little shadow, she called him once when she stumbled over him on the landing after a shower, even though Harry was really the taller of the two, and at night – when he knew she was already falling to sleep in the next room – sometimes he couldn't stop himself from calling out. "Kate?" he would call.

"I'm here, Harry," she would mumble back. "It's okay. You go to sleep."

But Harry couldn't sleep. He was frightened. And he couldn't eat well, either; the twins served such strange dishes, and although the poison scare seemed over (meaning the poison in the wells of Baraboo), he still couldn't trust the spices on the rack. To make things worse, and in spite of all the times he shadowed Katie and called to her at night, he couldn't escape the feeling that she was leaving him somehow, going further and further, deep inside her books. He would come upon her seated at the desk in her room, volumes heaped on either side, fairy tales spread out along the carpet, and a book of maps before her ("bona fide delineations," she once explained, "of lands described by Prester John"), or else a huge and ancient volume in which Harry could not read the words, but in which the illustrations were like dreams that he had suffered as a child during a bout of chicken pox. Katie's head would be bowed above the books, and her chin would rest upon one hand. With the other hand she wrote her notes and flipped the pages, or tugged a straying forelock into place, completely lost in thought. The wrinkles in her brow, he thought, were like the cryptic lines upon the maps she studied, and though she rarely spoke to him, she sometimes muttered the single word *McGuffin* and once or twice, *Spring Green*. He couldn't speak to her when she was like this. Instead, he'd stretch out silent on the bed behind her, twisting the coin inside his pocket, or tapping a finger on the table there, wondering when she'd finally be done.

"Stop that tapping," she would say. "You're driving me nuts."

"Oh Kate you're already nuts," he answered once, trying to make her laugh. But Katie's back seemed very still.

"Don't joke, Harry Jinx," she said so softly that he could hardly hear the words. "Where do you think I'll wind up anyway? Someday when you're married with five children, you'll remember your old friend Kate. She'll be in a nuthouse somewhere, attended by twin nurses. At thirty-three she'll kill herself. The inmates there will mourn. *A shame,* they'll say. *She kept us so amused with all her tales.*"

"I'll never marry," Harry murmured fervently before he could keep the words from slipping out. And then, much softer, "not anyone but you."

But it didn't matter, for Katie seemed not to have heard. She had bent her head and lost herself again inside her books.

It was on one of these occasions, sometime after dinner and before the dreaded story time, that Katie finally said, "You know, I can't help thinking that the leeches are the key."

Harry, who had been lying on his stomach on her bed waiting for a chance to speak, rolled over now. "You ever see that marquee, Kate?"

Katie waved the *Book of Beasts* in his direction. "See what it says here? A leech is a water worm that sucks blood."

"It's down all the way at the end of Shady Lane. You ever seen it?"

"You think that's significant?"

"Well, I think, I mean, the theater never looks opened, but the marque –"

"Not that, the leeches. Leeches are water worms, Harry Jinx. And then there's the Hydrodragon. Take that word *hydrodragon* apart and you'll see the connections. Hydro means water. And worm – that's what they used to call dragons back in the days when people really fought them. Ariosto mentions worms I think, and in *The Hobbit*. Bilbo uses the word worm to describe old Smaug the dragon. So the leeches in the story from the twins seem to me to be connected to the hydrodragon in the *Book of Beasts*, and thus they are – though perhaps just metaphorically – the McGuffin, the object of our quest."

Katie got up and started to pace, working her right thumb into her left palm as she always did when she was thinking very hard. "I think we've got the thread here, Harry, I think the emperor –"

"That's what the marquee said until last week. *The Emperor's New Clothes*."

"The marquee says that?"

"Not anymore. They changed it."

"Well, if they changed it, then it's gone."

Back and forth paced Katie White. These leeches, she said to herself, were perhaps the first irrefutable proof of the existence of the McGuffin, the first time the hydrodragon she had discovered in the *Book of Beasts* had found its way into a story and perhaps into her quest. Of course Harry had thought the McGuffin that she sought was the monster in the sack that purged the leeches from the circus. Katie, however, had not believed that, and had called it one big hoax. But now the significance of the story began to come to light. That's how it is on quests, she thought, the answers are all around the hero, but the hero doesn't see.

"You know what it says now?"

"What what says?"

"The marquee."

"What does it say?"

"It says *Thou Shalt Not Miss Our Circus Eve.* Like a commandment. I guess they meant it as a joke."

"Hmmm. Many a truth. Is this a splinter, Harry?" Katie leaned over and showed him her hand. "I think I got a splinter when we climbed that fence looking for the tower behind the neighbor's barn."

Harry wasn't sure.

Katie went back to pacing and dug into the other palm. But if the leeches were the McGuffin-hydrodragon; then why did they suck blood? After all, the hydrodragon in the *Book of Beasts* did not suck blood, and besides that, bloodsucking was a gross and craven thing to do, hardly worthy of the majestic monster-dragons that were the object of a quest. Bloodsucking was for vampires, and the damned maybe, and maybe a mosquito, but…

And then.

Like lightning.

She realized what it meant. She had even mentioned it to Harry that first night after the twins had told the story of the leeches. *Sparagmos*, she had said to Harry, speaking of the triptych on the Altarpiece at Ghent and its beautiful and sacrificial lamb. She had told Harry that the old man was like that sacrificial lamb, that he had saved the Barabooans, and so the Barabooans maybe ate him up. The monster in the sack, she'd said, was but the mere agent of the old man's goodness (and never mind that she had also called it one big hoax). But now she realized that it was the seven-headed monster, not the poor old man, who saved the Barabooans. And then the creature died and the leeches sucked his bones, and so this blood sucking was a metaphor for the sacred ritual of eating the flesh and drinking the blood of our saviors, Northrop Frye's *sparagmos*, the dismembering of the sacrificial lamb.

"Listen," Harry said, "to what it says in this editorial…*circus eve, a holiday uncelebrated beyond Baraboo and celebrated all the more intensely here…a feast of sorts falling midway between spring and fall, between Fertility and Harvest, or life and death, and merging in its orgiastic rituals the devoured lamb of spring and the dead bones of autumn, colored eggs and fallen leaf, the lily's promise and the desperate candle planted in the hollow grin of October's jack-o-lantern's skull.* – Boy, not the kind of writing you'd expect from the *Baraboo Gazette.*"

So the old man was not the savior, Katie realized, digging distractedly at what might have been a splinter in her hand, and not listening to a word that Harry said. Instead, it was the seven-headed monster in the sack who was the agent of the good and saved the Barabooans and was then martyred. And the old man? Clearly, the old man was the prophet who foretells the savior's coming and even sets him on his way, just like Mr. Bononosetta-Joachim had been her prophet and sent her on her way with that stuff about the four gaunt horses and the whale.

"Bring the family, it says. Can you believe it? Bring the family to an orgiastic ritual? It's at the circus grounds." Harry looked up from the page. "Katie, you okay?"

"Why shouldn't I be okay?"

"I don't know…your hand."

And the fact that that was what the seven-headed creature was…a savior…could be confirmed beyond all doubt when one remembered Jack out in the barn who stood in metaphorically for all giants, and therefore probably consumed human flesh just like the beanstalk giant who growled out fee-fi-fo-fum and cooked the flesh of little boys. Maybe there was a connection between these two. True, she had never witnessed this consumption in the barn, and true too that such consumption is not quite sparagmos, but she was sure there must be some connection in some symbolic way. So then this synthesis of the leech legend and the story of *Jack and the Beanstalk* (for Katie relied always upon connections between one thing and the next), it was this synthesis that made the meaning valid. Thus, if Mr. Bononosetta was her prophet, and the leeches were the metaphor for the McGuffin, then she was the seven-headed monster in the sack, which meant she was not just a questing hero, but a special kind of hero, a savior.

"Kate! Your palm is bleeding! Oh, goodness, not one palm but two!"

Katie looked down at her palms. "When did you say that Circus Eve was?"

"I didn't. The paper says it's Friday night."

"My God," said Katie, collapsing on the bed. "Three days – not four, not two – three days away."

Let it be said in the few minutes we have here, as Harry rinses blood off Katie's hands, and they await the call to story time, that Katie's initial assertion that the leeches were a metaphor for the McGuffin did not mean that Katie thought the McGuffin actually was a leech. Nor did she think that the McGuffin was merely a metaphor for sinning even if the leeches might symbolize the sins of Baraboo. At most, sinning was one small piece of the McGuffin. After all, just because a length of spiny dragon-back may rise above the surface of the waters, that doesn't mean that a whole lot more does not lay far beneath. In some vague way Katie thought the McGuffin would embody all creation, sinning, other evils, and something more. She had seen something, yes, when she connected the hydrodragon to the leeches, but she couldn't claim to fully know the nature of the beast.

Still, it was a beginning, and when they finally heard the call to story time, Katie looked down to see how Harry Jinx had bandaged up her hands (a little too elaborately, she thought) and felt a little hopeful. The quest was moving forward again. Tonight, she thought, the story would be different.

Chapter Ten

"A cross-eyed knight was pricking on the plain," one of the twins began.

"*Pricking?*"

"Hush, Harry," Katie murmured. "That's almost how *The Fairie Queene* begins." The twin – who was not used to interruptions – glared once at Harry and then began again:

"A cross-eyed knight was pricking on the plain,
All dressed in well-worn armor head to toe,
Beneath which wound of battle did remain;
Upon his face he wore a brow of woe,
Though from that wound he bore no blood did flow,
And never had; 'twas wound without a pierce,
And neither knight nor dragon was his foe,
But Love for Lady Truth, which was so fierce,
It reduced our cross-eyed knight to steady tears.

"And it was Truth who e'en now beside him rode
Upon a black chimera, dressed in white,
And in her pocket she kept enchanted toad
'Kiss it,' she told him, 'and it's most like to bite.'
''Tis not your prince?' he asked. 'Oh no, not quite,
For you, my cross-eyed knight that captive be.'
And then on maiden brow some dark did light,
But in her heart seemed inner cares to be:
Thoughts of Father's kingdom 'cross the sea.

"In kingdom there where Father once held sway
A Doubtful Dragon wasted all the land
From sea with vaporous breath he darkened day
And turned once-fertile soil to shifting sand.
And though against him brave knights tried their hand,
Armed with the thrusts and parries they had learned,
Yet no knight could the Dragon Doubt withstand:
And hoist by their own swords against them turned,
In breath of foul contagion, quick they burned.

"At last Dame Truth had wandered from that place
To seek a knight who would her vengeance take;
She found in Eastern Lands the comic face
Of cross-eyed knight, who'd perish for her sake.
He begged to kiss her; always she held back
Until he would this journey with her take
Back home to tie the Worm into a sack
And drop it deep in ancient rivers black.

"So now the dragon, questing knight does seek
To find it out and kill it, come what may,
The days are long, the landscape dreadful bleak,
In stinking mire they often find Delay
And though Truth claims she's certain of the road,
He often thinks they might have lost their way.
To comfort him she lets him see her toad,
But keeps her other treasures safely stowed.

"At length upon the way they chanced to meet
An aged sire in crimson cloak beclad,
A wine jug in one hand, bare were his feet,
And wound about his head fair flowers had,
And from his lips came song with no note sad.
So from the fields he came now toward our knight,
Who stopping, asked him, 'How be you so glad,
When sadness seems to be my only plight,
Since 'gainst the dark, for Truth's hand I must fight.'

"'Good sir, my name is Joy,' the old man said,
    'And sadness is a foreign word to me
    What good will sorrows be once I am dead,
    And on my grave will sprout a gloomy cypress tree.
    'Tis best to live a life whereby I'm free
    Of base contriving by those maids of woe
    Who lead us to their lairs across the sea
    Through labyrinths that more confining grow
With every step, until we are laid low.

"'Come with me now, before the dark draws tight
    To splendid palace past this barren plain
    Where songbirds make a mockery of night,
    And with my daughter Love you shall remain.
    She'll not require silly dragons slain,
    But will unburden you of heavy load
    In love and laughter then, wash off your pain,
    And let this lady stay here with her toad
She is not welcome in Joy's fair abode.'

"'Where he goes, I go,' Lady Truth cut in,
    'Besides, I know quite well your loving daughter.
    We bear some passing semblance, though not kin,
    And she has much less interest in Doubt's slaughter.
    Of course, all know to what her ways have brought her
    How many babies has she now, you wise old sire?
    It seems she's versed in every trick Joy's taught her
    Odd, isn't it, she never seems to tire,
Kept squirming always by the fingers of Desire.'

"'Desire is **your** handmaiden, not Love's,
     But have it your way, you may come along,
     And tarry with us while stars shine above
     Since in our house the Truth may do no wrong
     Against my daughter Love, Truth's not too strong.
     And if in morning still wishes cross-eyed knight
     To slay the dragon in whose clutches you belong,
     My daughter shall not put up any fight,
Or claim she'll leap in grief from some great height.'

"The knight spoke not for he was still Truth's thrall
     And followed always at her dread command
     Until they came at last to Joy's bright hall
     Which, Truth claimed, was built upon quicksand.
     And yet Joy laughed, and with a wave of hand:
     'Dear Truth,' said he, 'we built to suit our pleasure.
     Eternity is not what we had planned.
     Gold is immortal, no? And yet, by measure,
'Tis dead weight. To laugh is indeed the greater treasure.'

"Inside the hall, was spread a sumptuous feast
     To which the cross-eyed knight by Joy was led:
     Figs and roasted apples to name the least.
     And by Delight these trifles knight was fed,
     While Fun and Games wound garlands for his head
     And smiled then, and laughed their work to see.
     And then came one ('Is she for real?' Truth said),
     Twas Daughter Love, who with a saunter free
Came straight to Knight, and sat upon his knee.

"She wore no rose, her skin was not like snow,
Nor were her eyes like lakes or limpid pools,
Her lips did not like tempting cherries grow
Such are the ripe imaginings of fools.
Love had broken all the poet's rules
No more lovely in her looks than girls next door:
A simple dress, a coin her only jewel
'But what,' Knight asked of Truth 'is that coin for?'
'Isn't it clear?' scoffed Truth. 'The girl's a whore.'

"Love smiled kindly, and stroked our poor knight's curls.
'Love is a coin,' she said, 'who profit makes
For those who know her value in this world,
Who can divine her in a sideshow full of fakes,
Who give her freely to whomever takes—
But at our back, Time's chariot draws near,
So let's to bed before the sun awakes
And rest where there's no time, no hate, no fear:
Love lets you sleep, or take communion with her there.'

"But Love could not quite sway the cross-eyed Knight,
And as by hand she went to lead him from that place,
His eyes were fixed upon another sight:
His Truth, who drew a veil before her face,
As if his going was to her disgrace,
And thus, in vengeance she had then withdrawn,
A ploy perhaps, to cross-eyed knight displace,
To bring him to her feet to beg and fawn
Where, prostrate he might lay until the dawn.

"And this he did, upon cold marble tile
  Renewing vows to slay the Dragon Doubt
  While Love lay warm in comfort all the while
  And did not whine, or moan, or bitch or pout,
  Or tell him he'd behaved just like a lout
  But slept, a sleeping baby in each arm,
  And dreamed those things that Love can dream about,
  While knight, in urgent state of stiff alarm,
Redoubled vows to bring the dragon harm.

"And so, in morning (Truth still behind her veil)
  The cross-eyed knight did saddle up his horse
  And promised to follow Truth by hill and dale
  While Joy, in laughter, tipped his hat, 'Of course!
  We do not hold our night guests here by force!'
  But deep in castle one baby was unborn
  (Though Knight would never know or feel remorse),
  And as this cupid from Love's breast was torn,
Somewhere another dragon cub took form."

The room was silent.

"That's it?" Harry asked at last.

"That's it, Harry. Time for bed."

"But…how could that be it? I mean, what happens to the knight?"

"Oh, he slays the dragon, but Truth runs off with some old man and the cross-eyed knight goes mad."

"Mad! But that's ridiculous! You never end your stories right, they're always –"

"Really, Harry. What did you expect, a fairy tale?"

"Well, no, but…"

"But?"

"But, why should he go mad. I mean, it's stupid, why should he end up in a nuthouse?"

"We didn't say a nuthouse, Harry."

"Nobody said a nuthouse."

"No, but you, I mean, that's what happens, isn't it when knights go crazy – and you don't even know him, do you? You're just making it up, why should she follow Truth like that –"

"She?" The twins each raised an eyebrow. "Really Harry. It's just a story. And it's time you were in bed."

Harry was upset. He looked to Katie for support but Katie only yawned and shrugged and headed for the stairs. "Kate…!" he called.

But she didn't turn, just called down sleepily, "C'mon Harry Jinx. It's time for bed. If you're good, I'll even tuck you in," – which she did a short time later, pulling the blankets up to his chin for him, kissing his forehead, and smiling softly, as if he had amused her somehow, when he demanded explanations from the twins.

"Just a fairytale, right, Kate?" he asked to keep her from going.

"Red herring, actually."

"Red herring? You mean like one of those dinners that the twins make."

"No, like in a mystery where the author puts in a fake clue to lead you off the track. It's a dead end – planted on purpose one would think – by our darling twins."

"You mean," – Harry sat up a little, – "You mean you didn't believe it? You don't think it matters for the quest? I mean with a knight, and a dragon and the coin and everything –"

Katie pushed him back down gently and tucked the blanket all around him. "Of course it doesn't matter, Harry," she said smiling. "It's got nothing to do with the quest, they just wanted us to think that, to distract us. That's how red herrings work. If red herrings didn't seem to be important, they wouldn't work at all."

Katie turned away, and even though he wanted to call after her, to tell her to come back, that he was not a little boy anymore, that he was Harry Jinx, he was Harry – he was too exhausted. His rebellion against the twins, small as it had been, had worn him out. He fell asleep almost before she left the room.

Still, Harry had been troubled by the story. The next afternoon, stranded in the house with Katie (the twins having taken the bikes themselves that day to go off in search of nettles in the woods), helping her to sift through nursery rhymes and fairytales, he reached out and brushed her hand.

"Jesus, Harry, what are you doing?"

"Nothing. I was just…I thought…"

"What. What did you think?"

"…That story…"

"Forget that story. It was a stupid story. Spenser's rolling over in his grave."

"Spenser?"

"The poet, Harry. Sixteenth century. The poet of the real *Fairie Queene*, not that hoax we heard last night."

Harry pushed his hands into his pockets. He and Katie were in the kitchen. Katie had decided that she was sick of questing in her room. She needed a change of setting, she had said, and so she had brought all her books down to the kitchen where now she was preparing to make lists. She handed Harry a pad of paper and a pen. "Here," she said, "I can't write with this bandage on my hand. We're making a list of nursery rhymes about a rooster. Write down what I tell you." Katie scanned the index of her book of nursery rhymes. "*Cock-A-Doodle-Do*," she said. "Two of them actually, one on page 32, and the other on 64. Interesting numerical correspondence."

Harry wrote the names and pages down. Katie turned to page 64.

"Oh my pretty cock!" read Katie, *"Oh my handsome cock!*
I pray you do not crow before the day,
And your comb shall be made of the very beaten gold
And your wings of the silver so gray."

Harry blushed. "I don't know why they have to use that word…"

"What word?"

"You know, for the rooster."

Katie raised her eyebrows and smirked at him. "Really, Harry. It's a nursery rhyme, that's all it is. I think you need to get out a little more."

"What makes it so stupid, anyway?"

"The nursery rhyme? I didn't say the nursery rhyme was stupid."

"That story last night, the poem. You said that it was stupid."

Katie leaned back and considered. "You ever heard of a story called *Araby*, Harry Jinx?"

Harry looked sullen.

"It's okay if you don't know it, lots of people don't. It's in a book by James Joyce. Anyway, in *Araby*, the little boy –"

"I'm not a little boy."

"I wasn't talking about you. If anything, I was talking about me. The little boy, he bears his chalice through a throng of foes. You understand that? Bearing your chalice through a throng of foes?"

"I don't know. What does that have to do with the story."

"It means," said Katie, taking up the nursery rhymes again, "that last night's story is stupid."

"You're not making sense, Katie, none at all." And then, after a pause, "That part about the coin…"

Katie looked up. Her eyes, to Harry, seemed very, very narrow. "What about the coin?" she asked.

"Nothing, just, you know…" Harry imitated the twins, "*Love is a valued coin among the hoaxes…*"

"Hmmm…making up a line?" Katie resumed her search through the index. "*Cock Robin.* You think that counts for our quest?"

"I guess." Harry wrote down that one too. "Still, that knight, I mean…" suddenly there was a certain amount of pleading in Harry's voice. "Katie, that knight was crazy."

It had been the wrong thing to say. Harry realized it as soon as Katie closed the book of rhymes a little too suddenly and stared at him with one eye squinted almost shut. "Crazy? You think that knight was crazy?"

"Well, what I meant was…"

"You meant that I'm crazy, right? Like that knight, like I'm in love with truth, and so I'm…" Katie paused. "I'll tell you about that knight, you see today's paper? Of course not. Why should I expect Harry Jinx to read the paper?"

"I do read the paper," Harry said, his voice starting to rise and squeak a little on the vowels. "You know I read the paper. It's, the paper's got nothing to do with this! It's just crazy. You think I don't see you out there petting the tire on your bike? You –"

"Petting the tire on my bike!"

"Yes! You pet it. You pretend it's the nose of a horse, like a steed or something and then you pet it. It's – you're obsessed Katie, you pretend it's a steed or something, and then, me, Harry Jinx, your faithful squire, you leave him with a girl's bike, like he's, like he's riding on a donkey…" Harry turned his face away.

"I...I didn't, Harry." Katie's voice was hushed now, and a little bit confused. "I was just, it's just that you're stronger than me, I thought you wouldn't mind if I had the better bike, then..."

"*I'm* stronger than *you!*"

"Of course you are."

For a long time, they were silent. Katie flipped the pages of the nursery rhymes distractedly. Finally she said, "Look. Harry. Maybe there's poison in the wells of Baraboo and all anyone wants to do is go to the circus. Here, look at the paper, look" – Katie picked up the newspaper – "*BARABOO PREPARES FOR CIRCUS EVE. Will Mrs. Finniby bake her famous pie?* Here's a picture of Johnny Blunderbub polishing up his big red fire engine, and here's something about a coin-operated calliope just restored by a bunch of Higgins brothers, town's pride and joy it says, to be unveiled –"

"Let me see that." Harry grabbed the paper. "Is that how you say that, calEYEopee?"

"Some people say CALee-ope, but I prefer the Greek. It's a machine that makes music, all this stuff about Circus Eve, article after article because all anyone ever wants is to be amazed – and then here, finally" – Katie took the paper back and turned to the last page. "This last page is the garden section, of all the crazy things, and listen to what it says: *Four Vaporous Wells Dynamited Shut. 'We shall not cease from exploration,'* says the mayor (quoting from T.S. Eliot, no less!), '*but Circus Eve is just two days away.'* That's it. Dynamite. And weird that they buried this in *Gardening.* As if, cover the nakedness of your fathers with a little dynamite, as if that would stop the McGuffin. That was yesterday."

"CalEYEopee," Harry murmured.

Katie ignored him. "Don't you get it Harry Jinx? You have to hold yourself ready. You have to be inviolate, pure, like a knight – in spite of all the filthy inanities they fling at you, the shiny fire engines and all the lesser, broken threads and splintered dreams, you still, you hold yourself ready. You bear your chalice through a throng of foes." Katie paused and wrinkled up her brow. "You think it's all a game, don't you? Something to keep Harry Jinx amused on his summer vacation. That knight, he was taking the hard way, he wasn't going to sit back on some plush red pillows and let love do her diddling while something evil was ravaging the land. Evil, Harry Jinx. What is Love against a thing like that?"

"Katie..."

"Have you ever met my father?"

"Of course I have. He's very…"

"Yes. Isn't he." Katie paused. "I called him this morning. He's tossed out Ellie. The new one's name is Beth."

"That's got nothing to do with you…with us…"

"Go, Harry. Go play in your room like a good boy. Go play with whatever it is you keep so secret in your pocket."

Harry didn't want to go, but Katie reached for her Derrida, a sure sign that there was nothing more to say. He stood, picked up the newspaper, slunk away.

Chapter Eleven

Later that afternoon, Harry sat alone up in his room. It was early August and a heat wave had settled in, unexpected after the endlessly perfect weather of July. As heat waves go, it was not a bad one – "They've turned it up a notch," was how Katie had put it that morning – but it was bad enough to make the upper rooms seem stiflingly claustrophobic by early afternoon, and Katie had been smart to move her books to the kitchen before the day's research had begun. Now, however, dismissed by Katie and terrified of Jack who might be skulking just outside the farmhouse door, Harry had nowhere else to go. He leaned back on the single wooden chair the room provided, fanned himself with the newspaper, and tried to think.

Well, he thought, putting his feet up against the window sill, he had tried to save her, hadn't he? To pull her from the flaming ramparts, or out of the labyrinth, or away from the cliff's edge beyond which lurked some horrible Medusa. Those were her heroic images, of course, but he saw them differently. What he saw was madness, and he really had tried to save her from it in his own hesitant way, but Katie did not want to be saved even though he was sure she knew she was in danger, either from the fantasies of her own mind, or the hydrodragon she imagined, or maybe from nothing but the grinding of life's gears.

Harry shuddered. He couldn't help it. Since that night that Katie had turned the universe into an engine, life had not been easy. Everything reminded him of turbines, connecting rods and camshafts. The twins, he sometimes thought were robots, and that little yellow duck he had admired that first morning on his way to Baraboo, shuttling back and forth along the surface of the pond – who was to say it wasn't locked into some groove? Since that morning, he had seen it every time they went to Baraboo, the same duck on the same pond, and he had seen the emerald hills, and the clouds against the clear blue velvet sky, but they no longer enchanted him as they had the first morning.

Katie had ruined it, and everything seemed monstrous now, or even worse. It was as if she had torn a hole into the fabric of the sky, and what he saw beyond the blue were motor works – vast and empty, hissing, shifting, black. Was this, he sometimes wondered, her hydrodragon, the object of her quest? But Harry couldn't believe in the hydrodragon, even though it had somehow become far worse to think that there was nothing, to think it wasn't there. Still, if it did exist, it could only be a monstrous machine…and then with all these strange connections that kept arising – not the ones that Katie imagined, but ones linked to his coin – gears fit one into the other: he was scared.

That morning, before the conversation about chalices with Katie in the kitchen something incredible had happened. The twins had sent Harry out to collect eggs from the barn. He had not wanted to go, of course, since Jack would be there, but he could not think of any way out of it. Katie had slipped away to call her father, and he didn't have the nerve to refuse even though she would not be standing by his side. So he went, relieved as he tiptoed through the open doors that Jack was out of sight. He found two hens, and managed after several tries to pull an egg from beneath the ruffled bottom of the first, but when he moved on to the second – a big white fussy bird that Katie called Henny-Penny – the old bird started suddenly to squawk (viciously, it seemed to Harry), and in another second the rooster that had so intrigued Katie that first morning came strutting around the corner out of the coop and flew up in his face in an attack so Harry thought, or else to take the egg back – because, not being a farm boy, Harry had no understanding about hens and roosters and such things. But the rooster didn't actually attack, and then in that one second just before the giant Jack stepped in and pulled the bird away – nearly wringing its neck in the process, red feathers swirling in a cloud around Harry's head – Harry could have sworn that it had whispered something, one word in his ear: calEYEopee. And yet surely he misheard. Roosters do not talk, he told himself, and besides there is a great resemblance, between cock-a-doodle-do and calliope, or maybe Jack had thrown his voice somehow, a kind of circus trick – even the twins had said he once worked for the circus. Besides, so far as Harry could tell, he had never heard the word before. But then he remembered that there in the paper, like answers to a crossword puzzle he didn't want to solve, there were three words that Katie read, words that had wrapped themselves together in a single phrase: *a coin-operated calliope* the paper said, made by *the Higgins brothers*. And Katie had told him that a calliope was a musical machine. The sky, it seemed, had surely opened up.

At this point, it would perhaps be prudent to assure the reader that if the reader knows nothing more about calliopes than Harry does, he can hardly be blamed since calliopes, magnificent though they are, have fallen out of favor nowadays to be replaced by everything. In fact, in our age when even a citizen of very modest means can conjure up full symphonic orchestras in their cars and living rooms, the notion that the lovely tones of a calliope would never satisfy even the most unschooled of ears (though calliopes had been the darling of the nineteenth-century European courts) seems downright silly, and rare indeed are the graduates of our illustrious schools of engineering who would deign to turn their attention to the making of a grand calliope. Still, the fact that calliopes have fallen out of popular taste does not make them any less incredible, and fortunate indeed are those among us who have seen them in the great museums of Europe, or even in the various collections to be found in small towns at the center of America, where they appear from time to time like fantastic roses, and sometimes in cave-like places underground. And this was true in a small town southward, called Spring Green. That town has a marvelous museum, House on the Rock.

But what exactly is a calliope? A Barabooan could tell you that, for in the old days never did the circus leave for its summer tours but that it took a circus wagon fitted out with a calliope, and sometimes two or three. Simply put calliopes are, as Katie said, musical machines, and we will expand on this only a little by adding that these mechanical contraptions generally made their music out of wind. Now, perhaps wind by itself is nothing, but force it through a pipe and you will discover what lovely music this nothing can create, aided by the ingenuity of human beings. An organ is a kind of calliope, for example, which Bach employed to such effect, and at the center of all true carousels it is the magnificent calliope that spins the music and animates the beasts. But sometimes out of this same wind, the craftsmen of calliopes (simple fellows, mind you, who did not need degrees) made miracles of even more amazing kinds. Think of automatons and wind-up toys, or the animated wonder worlds you might gaze on in shop windows at Christmas, and then you'll have some approximation of what a calliope can be. Of course electric drives these modern-day fantastical tableaux, but that only makes the old calliopes more magnificent, to think that only air, and rudimentary springs and catches, could prompt the sculpted heads to nod, or draw the bow against the strings of violins, or animate the wooden soldier boys to strike their sticks against their painted drums.

Air alone would animate the old calliopes, and thus they wrought their magic like a marvelous tableaux: seascapes, perhaps, where the castanetta seashells and flounder-flutists played their siren songs; or little stages filled with dancing bears; or symphonies where full-sized, formal oboists squinted at their music sheets, their waxy foreheads glistening with the effort of interpreting the dark notes written there. These panoramas moved like an extravagance of magic, driven by wind that drove the unseen pistons, rods and levers, cranks.

Harry knew none of this, of course. He only knew – and did not want to know – that calliopes were machines, and that because of the rooster and the name of Higgins in the paper, these calliopes were linked to a maddening set of coincidences that had plagued him ever since he and Katie had left home for Wisconsin. The rooster, after all, had said calliope, and the Higgins brothers had created the calliope for Circus Eve. Higgins. Annabel Higgins was the one who slit her wrists. Why couldn't he and Katie have just gone to Cape Cod again, he wondered now, taking the coin from his pocket and slipping it beneath the corner of his mattress, hoping by this action to break the chain of mysterious connections, or at the very least to prove he didn't need the thing at all no matter what Katie implied about his pocket. On Cape Cod the waves had broken in a satisfying monotony and Katie had lain near him on the beach blanket, scanning the horizon, and telling stories of the sea.

Downstairs meanwhile Katie did battle with an insurance salesman. He had knocked three times in the early afternoon, and Katie, looking up startled from her nursery rhymes and thinking of the big brass knocker had thought, thus knocks the whale like doom upon the door. The character to whom she opened, however, looked more like an actor in a low-end comedy than a harbinger of fate. There he stood, a mix of the inconsequential and absurd: buck-toothed, freckle-faced, and smiling, a briefcase in one hand, business cards in the other, and on his back a red and gray plaid blazer, slightly shiny, with sleeves that did not quite reach his wrists. "Sharpie Shark's the name," he said, "and as for the game…May I come in?" and then did so before she could refuse, pushing his way through to the parlor where he sat down, admired the parlor's color scheme, and smoothed down his sandy hair.

It was a long time before Katie even knew he sold insurance since at first he spoke of almost nothing but himself, as if, Katie thought later, he had just come from one of those motivational sales conferences they probably sponsored down in Madison where he learned that the trick to selling products like insurance is first to sell yourself. Katie wanted him to leave. She could see immediately that he was not part of the quest, that nothing so ridiculous could ever be part of her quest, but Sharpie Shark would not stop talking long enough for her to throw him out. He began with his name – "not my real name, of course. What kind of mother in her right mind…" and then went on from there: explained how Sharpie Shark was just a nickname left over from his days in the circus; how he wasn't Leonardo da Vinci's Dragon, like his circus wagon claimed; how he had never breathed fire, only eaten it, and never gone to Europe either; how his father had been a preacher; how this same father had fallen out of grace with the church after being caught in a strange and compromising position in a chicken coop in Baraboo with the bearded lady from the circus, the result of which being that he – that is, the father – was tossed out of town and clergy in one swoop; how this same father had sold him to the circus but only after years of stuffing butter knives down Sharpie's baby throat when he was two and three, then steak knives, flames, and finally harpoons – *Better to reign in sideshows, than to serve in church,* his father said before he left Sharpie with the ringmaster. Sharpie said too how his father should have read the contract, for Sharpie never reigned as the ringmaster, but only waded in a small glass tank upon a circus wagon festooned with sneering angels, and swallowed flames and swords from the waist up (something of a hoax), and also a sea monster – or at least a merman – down below.

"Two for the price of one, you understand? My father taught me to swallow things, but the circus needed a merman, their original merman having died in a mountain expedition just the week before. So, there I was…are you listening? I was one thing above the water. Another thing below."

"Yes, yes, just like Duessa," Katie said, not terribly impressed by the comparison. Everything in life was like Duessa. If this absurd little man was going to try to work his way into her quest, he'd have to do better than that. Besides, she had a lot of work to do. She wished there was a way to make him go.

But he didn't go. Instead he recited the poem they made him say when he wasn't busy with his flames. "It's a poem, about a merman," he told her. "Do you know it…

"Where great whales come sailing by,
Sail and sail with unshut eye,
Round the world for ever and aye?
When did the music come this way?"

And then looking downward, he added, "I can't remember anymore."

Katie looked annoyed. "It's a Matthew Arnold poem…*Here came a mortal,*" she recited;

"But faithless was she!
And alone dwell forever
The kings of the sea."

"It's not important, you know," she added when she had finished.

"Not important? No, I…"

"To my quest I mean. Just because there's a whale in it, just because it was on Mr. Bononosetta's final exam, just because you know a little poetry and all – a true hero knows the difference between coincidence and significance, or for that matter between counterfeit and real, and you can't just come in here and –"

"I can't?"

"No. Not you. You can't just come in here like that and recite a poem and then think that it's important for my quest. "

"I didn't, I never –"

"Because it's not fair, it's…"

"I never understood the poem, I –"

"It's easy," said Katie. "The faithless one, that's the mortal who became a sea queen. But then she abandons her sea-king, who loves her deeply. She's restless. She wants to return to the dry land from which she had come, because somehow in her mind it had become something special and true, something worth having. It was Eastertime. She wanted to go to church. And so she goes, even though the sea-king loves her and will miss her terribly. But then, she languishes on land. It's really a retelling of a children's story, *The Little Mermaid*, but from the other side."

"The other side? I never…"

"The other side. The perspective of the king of the sea. Usually when they tell that story, it's all about the little mermaid sea-princess and her travails on shore, but in this poem, she doesn't matter. It's the abandoned sea king who matters."

"Well, it's a nice poem anyway."

Katie shrugged. "She should have stayed with the king."

For a minute, neither of them spoke. Katie was annoyed. The poem reminded her of something, but she couldn't think of what. She wished that Sharpie Shark would go.

And still he didn't go.

Instead, he began to ramble on a little about the circus until Katie thought she'd go mad. He was telling her something about the tokens that the circus sold to the patrons who would use them like money to buy their way into the special exhibits like the sideshow tents, or else to buy cotton candy, or peanuts to feed the elephants before the show began. "Fanciful things, those tokens" he concluded. "Rare now, of course. Collector items if you can even find them…"

His voice trailed off. Katie who had hardly been listening, looked up now that he was silent, and felt ashamed. There had been something sad in his voice there at the end, she thought, and now that she looked at him, she saw he was not young anymore, and that he looked exhausted, as if something were driving him, as if he had something that he had to do. She watched him sink his forehead into his hand and rub at it distractedly with a small embroidered handkerchief. How terrible his life has been, she thought. His father should not have done that. Fathers shouldn't shove things down their children's throats.

"Mr. Shark?" she said gently.

"Yes?"

"Would you like some soup?"

"Soup? No. No, thank you, ma'am."

"Coffee maybe? Cocoa? Brandy?"

"No, ma'am, never touch any of it, poison if you ask me. Of course in this business, everything starts to look like a risk, but –"

"Business?"

"Insurance business. What did you think, that I sold vacuum cleaners?"

"Well…I didn't, I mean –"

"Oh, no, not vacuum cleaners." Mr. Shark sat forward eagerly, all trace of his exhaustion vanishing, and whispered, "What good are vacuum cleaners if the end is near?"

The end is near! Who was this Mr. Shark, anyway? A moment ago he had seemed to be a beaten little man on the brink of a collapse, and now – Katie leaned in closer, and stared into his eyes. She couldn't be sure of it, but there seemed to be something – someone! – reflected in his eyes where her own face should have been: an old man with…something…a key? A wine jug was it…in one hand, and something in the other. What was the old man doing lurking there, like a fishtail just beneath the surface of the water? And when Sharpie spoke, it seemed it was the old man in his eye that spoke, a voice out of all time, a slow voice, full of depth. "The end is near?" she whispered.

"The end is always near."

"But how?"

"Death, Miss White." (How did he know her name?) "Dismemberment, accident, casualty, fire. – all things against which the wise are well-insured."

"Fire…?"

"Fire, yes, of course fire. Do you know how many will die in fire just this year alone? We can't stop fires, Miss White, but we can defray the costs." Mr. Shark tapped the leather of his briefcase. "Do you know who God is?"

"No one really knows exactly."

"My analogy is this: God is like a man who likes vacations."

"Like he's far away, you mean," said Kate. "Not available? Like in Frye's demonic archetype?"

"The opposite. He loves us. He vacations on our earth. But even God cannot stop death."

"But shouldn't knights –"

"Oh, night's the worst time. Do you know how many people smoke in bed and fall asleep? Fire, Katie White, death by fire is what we have to fear."

Then, for one long uncomfortable silence, Sharpie Shark stared straight into Katie's eyes, and Katie stared right back. Was the old man still there? She wondered. She couldn't see him now. Trick of the light, she thought. That's what it must have been.

"Mr. Shark?"

"Yes."

"Do you know anything about the vapors?"

"What vapors?"

"In the paper, the vapors rising from the wells."

"Oh, you mean south of Shady Lane where the cows have died."

"Sheep too."

"Of course sheep too, and not a single one insured against that sort of thing. People around here are very suspicious of insurance. Keep their money under mattresses, and such."

"You know what's causing it, those vapors?"

"Oh, who knows what causes a thing like that. Though…if I had to make a bet on it." Mr. Shark leaned toward the coffee table, and knocked a knuckle on its surface. "I'd say it's Rooster Dells."

"Rooster Dells?"

Mr. Shark nodded. "Rooster Dells. That's what it used to say on the side of the boxcars I saw pulling into Spring Green at night when I was just a kid: *Rooster Dells Mining Company*. You ever been up to the dells?"

Katie shook her head, enthralled.

"The dells are not Spring Green. The dells are north of here. Big tourist attraction now, all amusement parks and neon, but in those days, Miss White, the dells were wild places, and Rooster Dells was the wildest of all, caves and grottoes by the river and going far into the hills, and in and out of these caves came the brothers – six of them maybe – with picks and axes, in and out."

"Not seven?"

"Seven what?"

"Brothers. Could there have been seven?"

"Maybe. If you want to make it seven, make it seven. Anyway they had picks and axes, and they claimed they were miners, mining for gold supposedly, but not everyone around these parts believed that. *Who mines for gold in Wisconsin*, people said. *There must be something evil going on* – those brothers came from somewhere else. People said they were building something monstrous and then transporting it piece by piece under the cover of night to the hills outside Spring Green, a town just south of here, and that whatever they were building would rise up one day and devour all of them, the brothers and the people too."

"Devour them?"

"Well, who knows, people have strong imaginations. But there's no question that there was something strange about it all. Those brothers never came to Baraboo except maybe once a year, and even then it was just to buy the oddest things, like empty wire spools and broken kites that they bought with change from little boys, and once (though who knows if this is true) a broken-down piano with half the strings unstrung and the top all hammered in. They didn't always pay with change though. Sometimes they paid with gold dust, I have heard, and more often, with brandy. Maybe they had a liquor still going up there in the dells. Maybe they made moonshine. Anyway, they worked in those Spring Green hills for half-a-dozen years or maybe more, and then they disappeared. And when they shut down, people said that it wasn't lack of gold that ended it any more than it had been finding gold that had begun it. People said something dreadful happened with whatever they were making, or else that they had met with something down there in the caverns that had terrified them, something living, Miss White, something that breathed fire. And now of course, with all those vapors…"

Katie sat still, hardly breathing. "You…believe that?" she whispered.

"Me? Of course not."

"But you said yourself, the vapors…"

Sharpie shrugged. "Mining's a dirty business. Who knows what might have leached into the water."

"*Leached* into the water…? Like a leech? But you said yourself – why doesn't someone just go up to Rooster Dell and look around?"

"Nothing to see. They dynamited the entrances to those rooster grottos all to pieces years ago. They aren't even on the map." Mr. Shark paused. "But even without that, people wouldn't do what you said: go up to Rooster Dell and look around. The citizens of Baraboo are circus thralls, Miss White, for whom the monstrous is nothing but a sideshow act. And if for one blanched moment some stark evil should present itself, if suddenly there is something truly monstrous lurking at the corner of an eye, why then just as quickly…*Ladies and Gents, Your attention please! In the center ring*…the circus dazzles them; they forget what almost made them horrified."

"But the circus, that's just a hoax! While reality –"

"A hoax? No. Reality? The Barabooans cannot bear very much reality. They love the circus. I'll leave my card here, Miss White. If you want insurance for a fire, let me know."

…The Barabooans cannot bear…Katie showed Mr. Shark out and opened up her book of fairytales. He had said so much, she thought, had handed her half-a-dozen loose ends that seemed bound up with her quest – whales and flames, for example, and harpoons, and rooster dells. Even his parting line had been a loose end, his *Barabooans cannot bear*, stolen from T.S. Eliot just as the mayor had stolen from T.S. Eliot the day he shut the poisoned wells. *We shall not cease from exploration*, he had said. But loose ends were only ends, and in the end she still could not find her hydrodragon. She had thought she

might be some kind of savior, but now, with all these other bits and pieces, it all felt like a trap. Circus Eve would begin tomorrow night.

There is a door I haven't opened, Katie thought, there is a place I have as yet refused to go. The hero opens all the doors. Suddenly Katie realized she was crying. Silly, she thought. I am being melodramatic. But the tears were real and they fell for a long time until finally she picked up her fairytales and tried to find the passages between one story and the next.

Chapter Twelve

"Harry?"

"Kate?"

"Storytime!"

"Ah, there's our Harry."

The twins were home. Harry emerged from the cellar where he had gone to look for an old croquet set the twins had told him of a week or two ago. He had always liked croquet, and in summers past he and Katie had spent many a fine afternoon arguing over the placement of hoops and disputed claims of knocking the croquet balls (for it was Harry's secret contention that Katie liked to cheat). They were not heated arguments, however – nothing is ever especially heated about croquet – and Katie always let him win in any case. Remembering this, and hearing that there might be an old croquet set in the cellar, he had gone in search of it, hoping by the brightly colored balls and mallets to lure Katie from her books. It was not to be, however. Like the missing tower and the phantom coin collections that the twins had made such a fuss over on the night of their arrival, the croquet set was nowhere to be found. Disappointed, he gave up the search when he heard the twins and climbed the cellar steps.

"Ah, Harry, going through our cellar closets?"

"Looking for skeletons, no doubt…"

"Skeletons? No. I…just wanted to see –"

"What you could see."

"And have you eaten?"

"I had a little bread."

"Harry you'll be naught but bones if you eat naught but bread. What will your mother say?"

But Harry didn't answer, and he wouldn't eat either, not even when they ushered him into the kitchen, backed him into a chair, tied a napkin round his neck and – laughing, as if it were just one big joke – cut a slice of something gray for him from something on a plate. Katie sat across the table watching. The twins had prepared some kind of roast ("roast beast," Katie had called it) before they'd left that morning, and Katie had finished eating just as they arrived. Now she sat across the table and Harry saw nothing on her plate but a gray, congealing puddle, which Katie mopped up with a bit of bread and popped into her mouth, smiling while he struggled with the twins.

"Open wide!" one twin insisted while the other held a loaded fork before his lips.

"Just the thing for little boys!"

Harry clenched his lips and looked wildly at Katie. The fork came closer, brushed his lips so that he had to jerk his head back – and suddenly a chair scraped, and Katie stood up and stretched, and yawned, and said, "I think tonight I'll have that brandy," and walked past him, out the door.

The twins, like two dogs turning their noses up at doggy kibble in anticipation of a choicer piece of meat, jumped up and followed her – "Brandy, Kate? Did you say brandy?" – leaving Harry to his own devices so that when he had finally freed himself from the napkin, dumped his meal into the garbage and joined them in the library, Katie was already ensconced in her leather chair peering with a look somewhere between fear and fascination at the golden liquid sleeping in a glass.

"Bottoms up!" twittered the twins.

"Yes! Bottoms up!"

Harry moved forward. "Jesus, Kate, don't drink that."

But Katie only raised one eyebrow as if to say, *What right have little boys who keep secrets in their pockets…* and then she put her head back and drank the whole thing down.

Harry sat down, demoralized. It was storytime.

"Once upon a time," one twin began, "there was a talking rooster who lived upon a mountain."

"Mountain," murmured Katie from behind her brandy glass. "That was the answer to that hobbit riddle on one of the days I went to Baraboo."

"It was a high mountain," the twin continued, "and he was a lonely rooster because he lived enchanted beneath a magic spell. As a youngster this rooster had been a problem, a kind of James Dean of the barnyard, if you will, and had often crowed too early and too loud, awakening not just the farmers in the farmhouse but the villagers in the village too, who swore and grumbled and tried to get to sleep again. One morning, however, he woke a sleeping witch, who, still bleary from the vaporous potions she had worked on until dawn, caught him, cursed him, flew him to the mountain, and then, triumphant, let him drop.

"The rooster squawked – or didn't squawk; in fact, he couldn't really tell if he had squawked or not. He had felt the sounds rise up in his throat, was sure his beak had opened, had thought he heard the faintest cock-a-doodle-doo, but at that very moment when he thought he heard it, it died away and the air was very still.

"The old witch laughed. 'Crow all you want,' she said. 'No one will hear you. I have enchanted this whole mountaintop, and just as quickly as you give your breath to squawks and speech, just that quickly shall enchantment take your breath away. You will wake no one anymore; nor can you leave here, and you cannot break the spell. Your only hope is if someone else should break it for you by climbing up the mountain, and there's little chance of that. The only path is strewn with nettles and overgrown with vines as big as tree trunks. Besides, who would want to climb a mountain just to see a mountain top?'

"And then she left.

"And so, the rooster was alone, and though in the distance to the west he could see another mountain, and one more after that, and though these mountains sometimes seemed to shine like burnished gold, alive with promise, yet no one ever came from there to see him, and eventually he never looked at the mountains anymore. Nor did anyone come to see him from Green Springs, the village on whose outskirts he had once done all his crowing, and which lay now in peaceful slumber at the mountain's feet. The rooster could see the village. He could see the steeples and the schoolhouse, the bakery and the bank. But no matter how he tried to cluck and call, he could not hear them calling back, and it seemed to him that Green Springs was inordinately quiet, as if now that he was gone, the villagers spent all their time asleep. Only rarely did he see smoke coming from the chimneys. Only rarely did he hear the echoes of the old gray steeple bell. Still, awake or sleeping they will not come, he thought. The path is steep and overgrown with vines and strewn with nettles, while the village is a very pleasant place. *Here, the air is sweet*, they probably say, *and the bedcovers are cozy. It's always best, when all is said and done, to stay at home.*

"And so the rooster was alone, and each day he woke, and each day he strutted back and forth upon his mountaintop calling out, as roosters will,

'Cock-a-doodle-do!' and as the witch had said, each time his call died out upon the air just as he almost heard it like the echo of an echo drowned out by the wind. 'What shall I do? What shall I do?' he fretted miserably. 'The very essence of my roosterhood lies in strutting and in crowing, two acts designed to make me seen and heard. An unheard cock-a-doodle-do is like the crowing of a lonely god; it is the sound an artist makes when he's been misunderstood. *I* am that god! *I* am that artist! How then shall I call them to me, those sleeping villagers, indifferent – oh no, stone deaf! – to my voice.'

"Well, he was a rooster after all, and prone to all the self-aggrandizements that are the way of all his kind. So then he fretted and he fumed. But, it didn't last forever. One night while he was sleeping (calling out his wordless dreams to Night who could not hear him and was, in any case, quite fast asleep) he had a vision. In this vision he saw a grand calliope.

"The rooster was astounded. The thing he saw – all pipes and whistles, metal cranks, and bells – rose up like majesty into the midnight sky. It played, and when the rooster heard it, he knew, as if he had been blessed, that if he could build this marvelous machine, its music would not die upon the air like his rooster-music did. No. Instead the strident tune, like the raucous harmony of twenty carousels, would float in ribboned staves down to the village, curl around the steeple of the church, drift under doors and into sleeping chambers, wrap itself around the bedposts and the bassinets, and then slip out to draw a circle around the policeman standing at the corner with his whistle, and then the baker in the bakery and the banker in the bank – music would weave itself, in short, throughout the town like a golden thread shot through a nightgown, until all woke, all left off working, all followed those staves back up the mountain, singing in a glorious rejoinder in their own frail voices to the very mountain top, where they would finally arrive (exclaimed the rooster now, ecstatic, rising from his bed of straw) and see him here with his calliope, and worship at his feet.

"Thus motivated, the rooster set out to build his musical machine.

"Now it just so happened that in the building of this calliope, the rooster had some luck. From the long ago and faraway, there had come to the rooster's mountaintop a wild wind king with his full court of breezes, gusts and eddies, whiffs, and gales. This windy season had been passionate but brief, and when with the restlessness of wind courts everywhere these revelers moved on, they left behind the ruins one expects from such a windy, merry band: old kites and flutes, pinwheels and whirligigs and wind chimes, whistles, weather vanes and hollow bones and seashells, bellows embossed with blowing faces – along with shattered glass and tattered sails, and brass bells cracked beyond all mending by the reckless winds who smashed themselves upon the brass bell's heavy claps throughout the windswept hours of howling mountain nights.

"From these heaped things the rooster built his grand calliope, and it took him seven years. He built it through the summer and the winter; he built it all day long and far into the night; he built across the mountaintop and upward to the sky; he connected flutes to seashells and hollow bones to pipes, he made drumsticks for the beaten bells, and stretched the broken skins of old balloons across the skeletons of kites. In the making of his great calliope, he followed no plan and no tradition, for he was apprentice to no master of calliope, but built instead out of his own imaginings wrought somewhere in the labyrinths of his cock-a-doodle mind, or perhaps built out of dreams, or from an inspiration that he never thought to quantify or name – built like a madman would, or a holy man, a craftsman, or a fool, built until he had made a thing beyond describing, built until the thing was done. And then when it was finished, he stood back and smiled to see his work completed, and when he set it going, the sound it made traveled down the mountain into Green Spring, just as he had hoped. It seemed to him to make the music of the seven rounded spheres.

"The rooster was happy.

"The people of the village were appalled. Everyone lived happily ever after."

"What? That's it!"

"Yep! That's it."

"It can't end like that! What happens to the rooster?"

"Really, Harry. Who cares about the stupid rooster?"

"Besides our Kate is fast asleep."

Harry looked at Katie. She was asleep. Short as the story had been, she had grown restless during it. She had sighed a lot and shifted, almost stood up at one point, crossed her legs and then uncrossed them, sat forward, tossed her hair. Then she grew quiet, and Harry had assumed that she had finally settled down, but now he saw she had passed out. Her eyes were closed, her lips were moving and she was shuddering a bit. The empty brandy glass was lying at her feet.

Something is wrong, Harry thought, something is very, very wrong – and now he saw the twins were moving slowly, not toward him, but Katie. What did they want from her, he wondered, and then – thinking in some vague way that he knew what they wanted – how could he stop it?

"But…the story," he said faintly, for lack of something better. "Did the people climb the mountain?"

The twins had squirmed toward her. One of them ran a long, light finger along her sleeping thigh. Now, hearing Harry's voice, they both turned back and stared at him as if they did not think he could possibly be there.

"Mountain?" one of them hissed, turning his face away from Katie. "Of course the people didn't climb the mountain, Harry. Would you?"

"Me? I…"

"Yes, you."

"If you heard something like that, would you climb the mountain? Would you?"

"But I…"

"They banged their fists down, Harry Jinx. At the town hall they banged their fists down on the podium, or else they waved them in the air. At church, they said their prayers. The preacher told the children, who were inclined at first to like this music, that only the devil had a voice like that, and if at first the music seemed celestial, they should remember how their teddy bears turned into monsters once their mothers had kissed their baby cheeks goodnight and left them in the dark. Of course they did not climb the mountain, Harry. They held town meetings; they scratched out letters to the local paper; they added Silence to the curriculum in school. And when the music wouldn't stop, an old philanthropist funded an expedition and sent the great McFuggins to silence it at last."

"McGuffins!" Harry whispered.

"McGuffins? No, Harry. McFuggins. Seven brothers and not a single one was higher than your hips. Monstrous little things. They carried axes, and ate the flesh of little boys. They visited girl virgins in the night."

The room was very dark, and though the fire in the grate burned savagely, it offered up no light, nor even heat. Harry shivered. If only he hadn't left the coin beneath the mattress, Harry thought.

"They say," one twin continued, moving slowly toward him, "that the McFuggins were thralls of the machine."

"Machine…?"

"The musical machine, Harry. The calliope the rooster built."

Now both twins had moved away from Katie, and were very close, and Harry thought he felt their warm, malignant breath against his ears. "I have to go," he whispered faintly, but he could not move, and now, half whispering themselves, the twins told him how the town had sent the McFuggins to destroy whatever made the music, but when they reached the mountain top, the McFuggins found they couldn't do it. The calliope had enchanted them somehow, so that instead of smashing it to bits, they deconstructed it and hauled all the pieces down the mountain to a hiding place in the caves and river-grottos of the dells, where the people from the village would never dare to come. "Then," whispered one twin, "they tried to put it back together, but it was like a flayed man, Harry, sewn back up, and when they put the coin into the slot –"

"Coin? What coin…"

"*The* coin, Harry, is there any other?" The voice was barbed with impatience and contempt. "And when they put the coin into the slot, the resurrected monster let loose a screeching sound that seeped up from the caverns to the village and drove all who heard it mad. The people of the village killed their wives and hung their sons and daughters, and sometimes threw themselves into the river. Perhaps the McFuggins had not intended it. Perhaps they had only wanted to hear it play again, as it had before. But that's what happens when you take a work of art apart. You cannot put it back together, and then it drives you mad. So then they deconstructed and rebuilt, a second time, a third, each time hoping, and each time the shrill howling of the thing getting worse, and worse…and then…"

"And then?"

"And then they lost the coin. The only coin that made it work."

Harry didn't dare to move. Four deep, blank eyes blinked steadily at him in the dark. "But I…I…"

"You?" Four eyes squinted. They seemed to be waiting for something. From somewhere across the room, Katie mumbled sadly in her sleep.

"Although," one twin finally said, "there are some who say the coin's not lost at all, that a young girl, in some great act of daring whisked the coin away."

"And then the dwarves *and* villagers destroyed her, piece by piece."

The twins were far too close. Harry tried to push them both away. "I don't believe it," he murmured. "You're only saying this to frighten me, to make me go away, so you can be alone with – you are dwarves yourselves, you're –"

"They ate the flesh of little boys…"

"You run along, Harry."

"*We'll* take care of Kate."

And Harry, in perhaps the greatest moment of his failing, ran along.

Deep night. Harry was reunited with his coin, but Harry could not sleep. There beneath the staunch white specter of his sheet, he rocked himself shut, but even to this absolute privation of the light, sound traveled: cries and whispers, a wailing that was not quite a wailing, a wailing that transformed itself to laughter, sighs and lamentations, a litany perhaps? Where did they come from, Harry wondered, all these sounds? Did they rise up from within him? Or did they come creeping up the stairs from where he had left Katie with the twins?

Harry pressed his hands against his ears; he didn't want to know. He wanted for these sounds and their attendant questions to weave themselves back into the dull fabric of his everyday world where they and all things like them could be happily ignored. But they would not weave themselves back in. They shrieked and insisted, tangled him inside his bed sheets. Had cries come creeping up the stairs, he wondered, had they – just like the staves of music from the mountain in that story – had they come creeping down? And what had that meant, that phrase the twins had used, *the music of the spheres*?

"It meant Heaven," something whispered in his ear.

"No," he whispered back "It meant machines, not heaven," but what he heard now was not machines, he told himself, and not the twins with Katie in distress; what he heard, he told himself was rats' feet along the floor beneath his bed, nothing more, and nothing less. Still, his imagination would not let it be. His imagination insisted on turning rats' feet into other things, and he heard embraces too, confused refusals and then resignation; a finger seemed to circle at the porches of his ear, confounding sound, caressing like a tongue, and then, at the last moment, pushing home, all sounds expelled into a vacuum: in the morning when he finally awoke, there would be blood upon his trembling fingertip – and in his other hand, a book called *How it Ends*.

And now he and Kate were in the tower.

Yes. The tower. They were on two cots side by side with a small table between them, and Katie was still asleep. What are we doing in a tower, Harry wondered, as the pale stone walls came curving into focus around them, walls broken by nothing but a rough-hewn door and a single window far above their heads. Harry shuddered, wiped the inexplicable blood from his finger, and looked down at the book. It was hardly a book at all, really, more of a pamphlet of some ten or twelve pages made of plain sheets that had been folded in half and sewn together with a thread along the crease. The text was typed, not printed, and the whole of it was enclosed between two cardboard covers, one blank, and the other printed with the title, *How it Ends*.

How what ends? Harry wondered, thinking vaguely about Katie's insistence that she was on an apocalyptic quest. How what ends, the world? He glanced toward her sleeping form, and longed to wake her, but when he remembered the way that he had abandoned her the night before, and what strange things he had heard after that, and when he thought further on the cowardly things of which she might accuse him when she woke, he decided that perhaps she ought to rest a little more. And, in order to be sure that she would not wake, he did not even get up to try the door; instead, he gently rolled over onto his side so that his back faced her, tried to forget the danger that he might be in, and opened up the little book.

Immediately, a slip of paper slithered out.

Harry, it said, *who can say where stories ought to end? Take this story, for example, about the rooster. Some end it one way and some another; some say, as we did last night, that a brave girl finds the coin, but others say there is no girl at all, that she has been entirely made up. We do not believe that, however. To us she is full flesh and blood. In any case, because you are in the tower now, and because you may be there for some time, we thought we'd let you read our favorite ending to the tale, and then decide it for yourself.*

The Twins.

Harry crumpled up the note. Be here for some time? Best not to think of that at all, he thought. He looked down at the first page of the book and began to read.

"So! How did it end?"

Harry froze. "What?" he said, cautiously sliding the book under the pillow where Katie couldn't see.

"I said, how did it end?"

"How did what end?"

"The story, Harry. Last night. I fell asleep. What happens to the rooster?"

"Oh." Harry sat up on the edge of the bed and hesitated. He didn't want to show her the pamphlet; nor did he want to tell her everything the twins had said about the deconstruction and the reconstruction of the calliope down in the caves. If he did, then he might have to tell her about the coin they mentioned too, and about the girl who stole the coin and then got torn to little bits, neither of which prospects especially appealed to him. "The twins didn't know exactly," he finally answered somewhat carefully. "They said the villagers hated the music. The villagers sent the McFuggins up the mountain to destroy it."

"Impossible."

"I know…McFuggins, the name is –"

"Not that," said Katie. "What I meant was it's impossible not to know what happened to the rooster. It's the rooster's story, isn't it? Told from the rooster's point of view? So how could you not know what happens to the rooster? In fact –" Katie too sat up on the edge of her bed, apparently warming to the topic, "from what you're saying, the whole story is impossible. If the villagers hated the music (as villagers are oft inclined to do) they would have destroyed it for themselves, and no need for these McFuggins. That's how it always is with villagers, just look at what they did to poor Emil Nolde, busy painting Christ with a greenish face in the 20th century, right up until the Nazis drove his paintings out."

Katie paused for a minute, and when she resumed, Harry wasn't sure if she was talking about the rooster story, Nolde (whoever that may be), or something else.

"Not love, but fear and hatred motivate most human beings to act," she said. "Only the few will lift a finger out of love, but give a village full of idiots something to destroy and they will find the will to clear the vines and nettles, to climb the mountain and hack to pieces whatever they might find, and they will be driven to it not by any noble prompting like a hero is, and not by curiosity, or by love – not by these, but by the fretful narrowness of their rat-maze minds."

Katie stared directly into Harry's eyes. "Some preach love, Harry Jinx, but they do not let it move them." Katie looked at him significantly and then leaned back against her pillow. "Now that would have been a story, Harry Jinx: the villagers charging up the mountain to destroy the sacred thing. As it is, the McFuggins presence undermines the story's theme, and the twins probably threw it in just to distract us. In fact, the only important thing about the story as it stands is"—Katie suddenly stopped and looked around—"what are we doing in the tower, anyway?"

"Good morning!"

"Morning, Harry!"

"Morning, Katie!"

"Sleep tight?"

It was the twins. In they bustled weighed down by a large cardboard box and a breakfast tray, and then proceeded to whisk around the room, "tidying up a bit," they said, sweeping the stone floor, fluffing the pillows on the beds, and once or twice laying a quick palm on Katie's forehead. Katie didn't shrink from it, Harry noticed, but her face looked strained, he thought, and her skin was very white.

"Is Katie feeling better?"

"Katie, oh, we know that you slept tight –"

"But Harry's looking peaked!"

"Peaked? What's peaked? And what are we doing in the tower?" Harry stood up and tried to look demanding.

"Oh, Harry. It's for Kate's own good."

"Really, Kate, you oughtn't drink."

"That brandy? Far too strong for you."

"What was it you were calling out? Was it…"

"*Cock-a-doodle-do? I think I've lost my –*"

"Or: *Ride a cock-horse to Bayberry Cross*?"

Katie glowered at them but kept her silence. Harry sat back down.

"No matter now, Katie, we're just glad you seem a little calmer."

"We worked like devils to restrain her, Harry."

"In a word –"

"Like devils."

"That's not true," Katie muttered now between her teeth. "I remember –"

"Nothing. Of course you don't. We brought you here, because frankly Katie…"

"We were afraid you'd wander off."

"You threatened to, you know:

I should like to rise and go,
Where the golden apples grow…"

"That's what you said, Katie."

"We can't have that, Kate…"

"You running off, wandering around the countryside –"

"Finding golden apples, God knows what."

"Oh no, we can't have that."

"And as for Harry,"

"He'll keep an eye on you."

"Won't you, Harry?"

"We know you like to watch."

"You can't just…send us to the tower!"

"Don't be silly, Harry."

"Of course we can."

"We tried to call your father, Katie."

"Beth answered."

"We didn't like her voice at all."

"We didn't leave a message."

"Now eat your breakfast!"

The twins pointed to the tray, which was full of food that Harry could not identify, and then they slipped away. Harry got up and tried the door. "They've locked us in," he said, saying what they both already knew.

Katie looked into the cardboard box they'd left behind. "Well," she said. "At least they've brought the books."

Chapter Thirteen

Time passed. Katie read and paced and read some more. Harry stared at the one small window high above their head.

"Now the question, Harry Jinx, is this," said Katie. "Where on God's green earth is the McGuffin?"

"The McGuffin? Jesus Christ, Kate, how can you possibly think about that stupid McGuffin at a time like this?"

"What better time?" Harry didn't answer. "I don't understand, Harry. What exactly do you think is going on?"

"Nothing's going on."

"Nothing at all?" Katie squinted with one eye. "After everything that's happened? After the flames and towers in the dust? After the knocker shaped just like a whale? After the rooster in the story and the calliope in the newspaper, T.S. Eliot, and the angel faces on the wagon, the hoaxes, leeches, and red-herring *Fairie Queene*? After all the threes and sevens, and Circus Eve only one sunset away? After all these terrifying connections slithering around like tangled threads, like…like beanstalk vines and nettles, – after *everything* that's happened, you still believe ol' Yin and Yang? You think I'm nuts?"

"Who's ol' Yin and Yang?"

"Why do you always do that? Instead of giving an answer you – Yin and Yang, Harry Jinx, or Jack and Jill, or look, you know – the twins. Now answer the question: Do you think I'm nuts?"

"Not…nuts, exactly, but maybe a little bit…obsessive."

"Obsessive! Jesus Christ, Harry! They've locked us up!"

"But maybe that's for our own good, maybe. I mean they said you were – you can't just go wandering all over Wisconsin looking for a McGuffin that – I'm sorry, that just cannot exist."

"Why can't it, Harry? Because the possibility's too scary?"

"Because…because it doesn't add up, that's why. There are some strange things, sure, some funny clues, but they don't come from anywhere, they don't lead anywhere, it's like if I picked some word, like machine, let's say, or mermaid, and I wrote it down and gave it to you. Here, I'll do it" – Harry scribbled *mermaid* down on a piece of paper and handed it to her – "and then you heard the word three times that day, you saw a poster with a mermaid maybe, or you – would that mean anything? Would it mean there was a dragon poisoning the wells of Baraboo? Or a white whale in an emperor's robe with patterns in his bones, just like your chicken stock – I'm all mixed up."

Katie shoved the slip of paper in her pocket. "That's just, you're just talking about coincidences, Harry, like people who experience a coincidence in life, not books, and then believe in magic. But stories, Harry, they're not like that. Do you know what stories are?"

"You told me. Bowls of soup. Different bowls, different recipes, but at the core it's all one chicken stock."

"Yes, that too, that's a metaphor, but it is not just that. Do you know what William Blake said? Don't roll your eyes. Just because you've never heard of him doesn't mean he's not worth knowing – he was a poet of the Romantic period. He said, *I myself do nothing. The Holy Spirit accomplishes all through me.* You understand that?"

"I guess."

"No. You don't. You're lying. Mondrian, you know who he was? Mondrian said, *The position of the artist is humble. He is essentially a channel.* Puccini said his operas were dictated to him by God. Blake, Mondrian, Puccini – they all said the same thing, Harry. Artists are merely the vehicle through which God creates great art. *O sing heavenly muse –*"

"Who said that?"

"Everybody, Homer, Milton, everybody."

"Jesus, Katie, where do you get this stuff?"

"You understand it?"

"There's a God in the machine…"

"What?"

Harry shrugged. "You mean that God inspires all these things, all these books and stuff."

"And if he does?"

"If he does, you think there could be a, like a message from beyond, from God, encoded in them somehow and they are all connected up?"

"Is that so crazy?"

"But there are no connections, there is no –"

"Ah, but there is. And I think I've almost found it."

"The hydrodragon? The McGuffin?"

"Getting close in any case."

"Impossible."

"Two places."

"That's fairytales."

"Exactly, Harry. Look, the key leitmotifs of this quest are roosters, towers, flames, and – just lately – calliopes. Roosters, towers, flames, and calliopes, got that? Now. Look at the *Big Book of Fairytales*. First, *Jack and the Beanstalk*. Get the book. Turn to page one hundred, and I'll show you."

Harry got the book reluctantly, and as he scanned the pages of *Jack and the Beanstalk*, Katie explained how the Jack in the story was just like her in that he was a quester in search of a particular McGuffin. "In Jack's case," she said, "the McGuffin was the giant who had slain his father and stolen his father's fortune many years ago. Now, Jack was a bit of a fool," (and in this one aspect of his character, Katie emphasized, he wasn't like her in the least), "selling the family cow for a handful of beans and all, but once he started up that beanstalk and encountered an old woman (a prophet of sorts, like Mr. Bononosetta) who told him about the giant who had killed his father – at that moment, Jack was transformed and assumed the hero's mantel, and stole from the mighty giant three separate times. He went up and down the stalk. The first time it was a hen that laid golden eggs, and that's just like our rooster. The second time it was the bag of golden coins (the significance of which would soon become clear) and the third time, get this," Katie said, "*a harp that plays its music with the touch of no man's hand* – clearly some early form of calliope." Katie paused to let the words sink in, and then went on. "Finally, on that last journey, Jack killed the giant by chopping down the beanstalk so that the giant tumbled out of the clouds and fell down dead."

"Freudian," Harry said, as surprised as Katie was that he had said it.

"How so?"

"I don't know, like you said the other day, I guess. Oedipus. Maybe the giant is his father. Then you chop the beanstalk and kill him, I mean…it's sort of sexy."

"Sexy? Is the beanstalk phallic? Like castration? And then Jack goes off to live happily with his mother. Like Oedipus? But Freud's not what's important in this case. What is important are the connections."

"The hen is the rooster, the harp is the calliope…"

"And don't forget the flames, Harry. The giant's wife locks Jack in the oven to protect him from the giant. The story makes a point of saying that the flames were burning at the time."

"That's ridiculous."

"What's ridiculous?"

"The flames. Flames would have killed him."

"The flames may have been separate from the oven. It's like the storyteller felt compelled to put the flames in, and if Jack was just above those flames, that would 'break the fictive dream,' as my father would say – or make the reader say, *ridiculous.*"

"Yes. Ridiculous."

"But, Harry, storytellers are compelled. Remember Blake? It's just like that. Writers are inspired by forces greater than themselves. And meanwhile, while Jack is in the oven, the giant says, *Wife, I smell fresh meat.* But I do not think it is because he is above the flames. What matters is that the flames are there, and when you put it all together with the story of the rooster on the mountain, and everything that's happened –"

"And the tower? I don't see any towers in the story."

"Oh. The tower is there by negation."

"Negation. What does that mean?"

"It means, Harry Jinx, that it's there because it isn't. At first, I thought the beanstalk was a kind of tower, you know, interchangeably phallic images and all, but then I started to look through the book and I found almost no towers in the whole *Big Book of Fairytales.* Look for yourself. Page 221–222, the miller's daughter, the one from whom Rumpelstiltskin tries to take her first-born child in exchange for spinning wheat into gold. They lock the miller's daughter in a chamber, not a tower, and on page thirteen some giant puts his victim in a 'parlor in the castle' – who ever heard of a parlor in a castle? We expect a tower, not a parlor, and then, when you add that to the fact that *Rapunzel*'s missing. You know *Rapunzel*, right?"

"*Rapunzel, Rapunzel, let down your golden hair?*"

"Rapunzel is almost a retelling of the Saint Barbara legend – Saint Barbara's father locks her up in a tower, and she ends up being martyred. The father chops her head off finally. In *Rapunzel* though, a prince comes along and saves her. That's a fairytale for you. The point is, you *cannot* do Rapunzel's story without a tower, but it's not in the book. Again, the tower is there by negation."

"Oh, come on!" Harry flopped back onto his bed and stared up at the window. Really, he thought, this was just too much.

"Take a look for yourself, Harry Jinx. I did see the word *tower* once or twice in this book of hundreds of pages. But only once or twice in a book of fairytales? There's *Hansel and Grethel*, *Sleeping Beauty*, *Little Red Ridinghood*, even something called *Blanch and Rosalinda*, which is totally obscure. But no *Rapunzel*, really it's incredible. and quite meaningful for us, just as we could not find the tower of Baraboo where we are currently locked up."

"It's incredible alright…"

"So then, it is here by negation. And don't you think it's incredible that the only storybook in the entire downtown Baraboo Public Library is missing Rapunzel – and that so far as I can tell there are hardly any towers in the entire book? You don't think that means anything? I mean look at us, Harry Jinx, here we are locked in a tower that doesn't exist, a tower that we looked for and couldn't find, and that means that all these things, the flames, and roosters and towers and let's not forget the Hobbit riddle, and the gold coins –"

Harry stiffened. "What coins…"

"The giant in the story, remember? *Jack and the Beanstalk.* Jack stole the giant's golden coins – yes, also the hen that laid golden eggs. And then *our* giant Jack out there in the barn was asking which one of us has the coin, and then, listen to this." Katie grabbed a book that was lying open on her bed and turned to a well-worn page. *So this bright coin,* she read:

'*…came from a country planted in the middle of the world…and it had been cast midway up the Andes, in the unwaning clime that knows no autumn. Zoned by those letters you saw the likeness of three Andes' summits: from one a flame; a tower from another; on the third a crowing cock; while arching over all was a segment of the partitioned zodiac, the signs all marked with their usual cabalistics, and the keystone sun entering the equinoctial point at Libra.*'

There you have it, Harry Jinx. Rooster, tower, flames, all up on mountains. It's the coin that crazy Ahab nails up to the main-mast in his quest for Moby-Dick. The gold doubloon. And, again, Harry, Jack asked about a coin. The key to all the clues."

Harry looked up at the window. "What did that last part mean?" he whispered, "about the calibrations."

"Cabalistics, not calibrations. I don't know, exactly, but think about the stars. Astrology. In astrology, the pattern of the stars is tied to our birth (Capricorns and so on), and astrologers believed – mostly in medieval times – that this connection makes us who we are. That the heavens have a meaning. Meanwhile, Ahab wanted to find this whale that ate his leg. He promised the coin to the first sailor who saw it."

"…You…you couldn't find a whale – one particular whale – in a whole big ocean."

"But that's the thing, Harry. He did."

"How does the story end?"

"Shipwreck. Only one survives to tell the tale."

"Only one?"

"Only one."

Katie watched him. Harry was silent. Finally, heaving a great sigh, he reached into his pocket and pulled out the coin. It was, of course, the gold doubloon.

For the first time in her life, Katie White seemed at a loss for words. She turned the coin over and over in her hand. One side displayed the rooster, tower and flames upon the mountain tops; the other side was strangely blank. As she stared at it, dumbfounded, Harry told her how he found the coin in front of her house, how he thought it might be the very same coin that was stolen from the Sag Harbor Whaling Museum, and how that coin had supposedly been found at a shipwreck at the bottom of the sea and given to Annabel Higgins as thanks for her financial sponsorship of the salvage expedition. "But even if this coin is that coin, it's a fake," Harry concluded. "It has to be a fake. Mrs. Higgins gave that expedition a lot of money, so they had to give her something. And she supposed that coin to be her great-grandfather's when the ship went down. It was his lucky coin."

"What was his name – Ahab?"

"How the hell should I know what his name was? God, you're – it's a fake I'm telling you. They, maybe they read the book or something. Didn't you tell me once that *Moby Dick* is famous? So they make it look like that, and meanwhile, they must have been laughing at Annabel Higgins the whole time. *Moby Dick* is a work of fiction, after all. And didn't you tell me there is no truth in the plot, but that maybe beneath the plot there could be truth and patterns underneath?"

"When did I say that?"

"Remember? The story underneath the story, the soup, is truth, but not the pretty bowl, which I imagine is the plot, something like that, anyway."

"Yeah, well, but maybe we've crossed over. Maybe we've become part of someone else's fiction, or –"

"Kate, you're crazy. The coin's a hoax."

"Well, so what if it is then?" Katie exploded. "Would it matter? The clues still led to it. Maybe a hoax can shadow forth –"

"No! It can't! I, it's all coincidence, it's –"

"Coincidence? I just don't get you, Harry Jinx. You showed me the coin, didn't you? Why'd you show it to me then? It's like you don't want to believe, but you want me to believe for you, and then when I do – where's this Annabel Higgins, anyway? Sag Harbor still?"

"No, she…she slit her wrists with an axe…"

"My God, what a –"

"Here in Baraboo."

******

Maybe it was true, what Katie had said. Harry didn't want to believe it, but he wanted her to believe, and then to take an action. Life offers precedent enough for that.

But for Harry, it was not just non-belief that held him back from saying that the coin was genuine. It was also fear. And it was suspicion too. Those suspicions had begun the previous night. Returning to his own room terrified by the story about the rooster, the first thing Harry had done was seek the coin that he had left beneath the corner of the mattress. He had left it because he had wanted to prove to Katie that she was wrong, that he was not at all obsessed with whatever he kept so secret in his pocket. So, he had muddled through the afternoon well enough without it. Later on, however, when the twins got around to the story of the talking rooster and his calliope, and then the coin, our Harry Jinx (just recently assaulted by a talking rooster) had begun to squirm around – in fact, it had been all that he could do to keep from bolting out the door and up the stairs to make sure the coin was safe.

As it turned out, the coin was right where he had left it, but when he lifted up the corner of the mattress, the sight that greeted him nearly drove a stake into his heart. The coin had been flipped. He had left it with its hieroglyphic face staring up into the mattress, but now it was the steady blank that met his cowered eye. Someone had been there; someone had touched it; someone knew. And, someone would be back. Jack with his axe, perhaps? Or the twins, or – who knew? – perhaps even the seven dwarf McFuggins. No wonder then that with these dark terrors brimming over in his soul, Harry had retreated to beneath the sheets and sweated himself into a little ball. *Who?* He wondered. And eventually, *when?* During storytelling? But if that were so, then he would have heard someone walking on the floor above his head. Or, was it earlier, when he had gone downstairs to search the basement for the croquet set, and Katie had been alone, prowling around.

That was it, of course. Katie must have seen the coin, and having seen it with its rooster, flames and all the rest, had known exactly what to look for in her books. Katie had deceived him, rifled through his things, and then pretended that she hadn't. But this was not the worst of it. For leaving aside for the moment the ignoble motives that must have prompted her to search his room – nosiness at best, or even jealousy, or greed – and leaving aside as well, the sniggering dishonesty implicit in her blood-and-thunder presentation at the tower wherein she wove the clues into a great big web – the tower that is not a tower, the hen become a rooster, Rapunzel, and the rest – along with her sham astonishment when he at last revealed the coin; leaving aside all these things, there was yet this: the fairytales had never led her to the gold doubloon; instead the coin that she had seen beneath the mattress had led her to the fairytales and *Moby Dick*.

And that, Harry reasoned, was a different thing indeed. Having seen the coin, and traveled backward to the books, Katie was no different than the faithful who see the bright blue sky and then turn to holy books. Rather than arrive at answers through free thinking and experience, Harry thought, people derive their crazy answers from something they uncover beneath the mattress of someone else's bed.

Whether these ruminations imply that Harry was a becoming a quester himself, ready to take hold of the steering wheel along his road of life, or whether in fact he served merely to remind us of his fondness for critiquing

Kate the quester from the comfortable backseat (in other words, he would be the squire) – this is something the reader must decide for himself. In any case, Harry did not tell Katie everything. She remembered for herself that Jack had mentioned coins, but other things – the way the rooster seemed to say calliope, for example, or the deconstruction and reconstruction of the calliope machine the twins had told him of, or even the *How it Ends* beneath his pillow (which he would never get a chance to read) – these things she didn't know, and he would keep them to himself. No need to feed her mania, he might have told himself, but the more cynical among us might suppose that by his silence he took his little vengeance on her, showing her his coin.

Chapter Fourteen

Throughout the afternoon, Katie paced. Pacing is a dramatic gesture reserved only for the very few (Harry, for example, never paced), and even those few are generally found only in the pages of a novel. For this reason Katie's pacing might have seemed comical to Harry if it were not so frightening as well, and as Harry drifted through the liquid clouds of half-sleep and then half-waking, both of which are likely to descend on anyone stuck in a tower in mid-August with nothing to do. Each time he almost woke he thought Katie paced just a little faster. She is frightened of tonight, he murmured to himself. She is frightened that the twins will come for her.

But if Katie was frightened, she did not say it. In fact, she said very little. And once when he awoke she was standing right over him so that his opened eyes stared right into hers.

"I forgive you," she said.

"Forgive me?"

"I just want you to know that I forgive you."

He fell asleep. By the next time he awoke, she had tied two sheets together. She told him that she had a plan.

"Escape? We can't escape. They'll —"

"They'll what, Harry? Call my father?" Katie tossed the sheets up toward an iron ring protruding from beneath the window fifteen feet above their heads. The sheet drifted shy of it by at least a yard. "Look, Harry, Hansel's getting out. If Grethel wants to stay here and be fodder for the witch's oven…"

"I think Hansel was the boy, Katie. Grethel was a girl."

"So?"

"So then if you meant to say that you were getting out, you should have said Grethel. That's all."

"You think you can throw this sheet up there?"

"What? Through the ring? It isn't possible. And anyway, where would we go?"

"To Baraboo, of course." Katie sat down on the edge of her cot and explained to Harry how it had seemed likely to her for several days that the showdown with the McGuffin would have to come on Circus Eve, and that recent events seemed to confirm it. Hadn't the story been about calliopes? And hadn't the newspaper said there was a bunch of brothers – maybe even seven brothers! – planning to unveil a *reconstructed coin-operated* calliope at the circus grounds right on Circus Eve? A time and place in which coins, calliopes, and seven brothers converged, could not fail but to produce the great McGuffin.

"In ancient times, all roads led to Rome," she said, and continued on, saying that all threads respooled to one great spindle, all rivers flooded back into their genesis and surely some great revelation was at hand.

Harry did not quite understand this (would anyone?), but he still thought maybe this was true because of how the *Baraboo Gazette* had described the festival of Circus Eve, which he had read to her: *Circus Eve…midway between spring and fall, between Fertility and Harvest, or life and death and merging in its orgiastic rituals the devoured lamb of spring and the dead bones of autumn, colored eggs and fallen leaf, the lily's promise and the desperate candle planted in the hollow grin of October's jack-o-lantern's skull.* These phrases were evocative for Harry, and so perhaps Circus Eve was indeed the moment upon which the McGuffin would choose to make its stand.

There were still questions, of course. First, Katie said there seemed to be at least three sets of seven brothers, some perhaps dwarves, some perhaps not, one set mentioned in newspapers, one set mentioned by a stranger knocking on the door, the third set appended to a story about a lonely rooster.

"Did they all exist?" she asked. "Or none? Or were they all the same. And what of the actual McGuffin? Would the calliope itself turn out to be the great McGuffin? Would something horrible reveal itself when the calliope was fed the gold doubloon – or would something wonderful reveal itself instead? What role would the river play, and from where would come a fire? Most important, what were the McGuffin's weaknesses, and what kind of danger are we in?"

She said all of this and this last question especially bothered her, because if a knight did not know the nature of the enemy, how could he gird himself for battle? "Was there a softness in the McGuffin's underbelly," she wondered. "Did he have a tender foot? Or, alternately, would he transform to stone the knight who dared to look him in the face? Anything was possible, and before heading into battle, a knight was often lucky enough to be able to enlist the aid of a wise old sage or sibyl who could advise him or supply the magic weapons, or whisper charms."

"A wise old sage? The old man, maybe?" Harry asked, willing for the moment to play along.

"What old man? I was thinking of the rooster."

"What? Our rooster? Out in the barn?" Harry trembled slightly, but he still wasn't ready to tell her that the rooster talked.

"The rooster talks, Harry. I'm sure of it."

"Like…like a parrot, you mean…"

"No not like a parrot, more than that, you mark my words."

Perhaps Harry should have told her. Perhaps if he said, yes, the rooster talks, the rooster said *calliope* to me, if he had shown that kind of faith in Katie's quest, then maybe everything would have ended differently. But he couldn't bring himself to do it – he still stung from the way she had cheated, peaking beneath the bed to see the coin, and in any case, even if he did come close to speaking, the whole thing seemed pointless a moment later when there came a rattling at the door. The twins arrived, their faces beaming above a steaming tureen filled to the brim with rooster soup.

"Rooster soup!" said Harry blanching.

"Yep, it's rooster soup! Good evening, Kate!"

"Good evening, Harry! Have an appetite?"

The twins set down the tureen, along with one bowl and spoon, on the table between the two beds, and Katie and Harry peered into it from either side. A three-pronged foot floated listlessly upon the surface, and Harry thought he saw a piece of beak. His stomach turned.

"Why only one bowl?" Katie demanded, "Why one spoon?"

"Oh, the soup's for Harry…"

"Such a fussy eater –"

"But we know he'll love cock soup!"

"I could never…" Harry said.

The twins turned to leave. Katie looked into the soup again and then sprang up, dug a grip into each of their little shoulders just as they reached the door and swung the two of them around. "What about me?" she demanded. "What have you got in store for me?"

"Why, Kate…"

"No need to get excited…"

"You see, Harry?"

"You see how she can get?"

"That's why she sometimes needs to be restrained."

"Besides, we have special nourishment for Kate…"

"Later this evening…"

"Down below."

The twins made a gesture. Katie let go of them and backed up slightly, something like horror spreading across her face. For one brief second Harry thought he heard the vacuum rise of engine fans –

– and then he pushed the two twins down the steps.

A long clatter and then silence. Katie looked at Harry and squinted one eye shut. "I think you've killed them, Harry Jinx."

"They – they killed the rooster!"

"Ah…the rooster." Katie sat down on the bed and picked up the ladle. "And shall we split the soup?"

Harry wasn't listening. He turned back to the opened doorway and looked anxiously down the steps. "You don't really think they're dead, do you?"

"They might be dead. You can't see them?"

"The stairs wind around, they're beyond the – Jesus, Kate, how can you *eat* that?"

Katie rolled a little soup along her tongue. "It's pretty good, actually. A little gamey."

"Gamey!"

"Just a little." Then her voice got serious. "Look, Harry, the rooster's dead. The only thing to do is have some soup." She picked up the bowl and walked toward him. "You must," she said. "It will make you – you need your strength." She lifted the spoon up in front of his mouth. A length of rooster foot dangled down the side.

Harry wretched and turned away. "My God, Katie…" But he turned back again, and when he did, he saw her staring at him intently. Slowly, she turned the spoon around and swallowed what was on it. Then she sat down and finished off the rest.

We have to get out of here, Harry thought. We have to get out of here before Kate goes completely mad. Before the twins awake, or don't awake, before Jack came looking with this axe – "Kate, we gotta go."

"Of course we do. The twins are dead. The first phase is over, Harry Jinx. It's time to face the beast."

"The McGuffin?"

"Yep."

"In Baraboo?"

"Maybe in Baraboo. We'll go to the house and get the bikes. We'll travel light –"

"You mean no books? No *Mother Goose*?"

"No *Mother Goose*." But she didn't say no books, and just before he pushed her through the chamber door, Katie grabbed the two books from her father – the Derrida and the book about Trithemius, black-covered with *Trithemius Decomposed* stamped hard upon it in startling relief.

Chapter Fifteen

High up in the tower, standing just beyond the chamber door, Katie and Harry saw the slanted gables of the farmhouse through a narrow window carved into the stone. These gables were not far off, and it seemed impossible to Katie that in spite of all their searches they had never come upon the tower they were in. True, there was an intervening hill and wood, and true again that even from this height nothing of Blunderbee was visible except for the gables, so that perhaps from Blunderbee itself the tower would have been well-hidden from their view. But they had searched, hadn't they? And still it had eluded them. A tower that is there by negation, Katie thought, a tower such as Percival once saw rise up from nothing in the mists along a river bank. She stared with Harry out to where the sun was setting, blood-red this time instead of primrose. Something like a wolf howled in the distance and suddenly a creature with enormous wings flew up, flapped darkly past, and disappeared. They jumped – a vulture, Harry wondered? – and then Katie and Harry fled.

They fled down winding stairs. They fled past the heap of twins and found the bikes the twins had used, fled through the woods and past the barn, imagined rooster blood on the chopping block, and saw Jack (his shadow-self splashed up ten times his size against the wall) whetting the axe. They thought they heard the scrape of axe against the whetting stone, they thought they heard Jack mumble, *Fee, Fi, Fo*, and then they were past him, and gone into the house where they stuffed supplies into their backpacks and headed out again, down the path to what they hoped was safety on the road.

They were on the way to Baraboo. Night had blanched the landscape to a specter of its daytime self, voiding the massive barns, voiding the silos and the farmhouses and even the picket fences that protected cows and sheep – voiding all this now for Katie and Harry who were folded in night's heart. Here in the darkness there was nothing but the sound of rising wind, and the only light was upon the road, though there were no lamp lights, and thus the pale road was laid out like the breaching back of some great monster whose vanished head must lie submerged beneath the circus grounds of Baraboo.

So it seemed to Katie. She was riding hard; Harry was riding close behind. In her pocket was Harry's coin, and she thought she heard the roar of the McGuffin up ahead. Somewhere ground trembled; somewhere a foul contagion rose up, and in a great heaving, vents and portals sighed. It is at the circus grounds, she thought, the circus grounds that are surrounded by the winding river that holds the festival of Circus Eve tight within its grip. But whether all this trembling could be a mechanical calliope or something that would well up from the river, or something else again, Katie had no way of knowing. She only knew that the coin – tossed into its mouth? tied to its tail perhaps? – would defeat it or reveal it, animate the great hydrodragon of her lonely quest, or bring it finally to everlasting death.

And more than that she almost did not want to know. For – and here is irony – just as Katie White hurtled toward the greatest moment of her quest, she felt least prepared to meet it. Something was dreadfully wrong, she suspected. Events had overtaken her somehow, and though she swore the McGuffin was up ahead, she could not shake the feeling that something also was breathing down her neck.

What was it, she wondered, that had compelled her to drink the rooster soup? She had not wanted to. It had revolted her to see among the bits of celery and carrot the eye, the foot, the half-sunken crest of that poor doomed creature that she knew had tried to speak to her that first morning, and who now drifted like the scrambled letters in a bowl of children's soup, a soup wherein the macaroni alphabet had swirled when she was young. No. She had not wanted to eat that rooster soup, and yet she had eaten it, while Harry looked on horrified, and he had watched until she got the whole thing down. And then? At the foot of the tower steps the soup had nearly come back up again. Nearly. The mangled heap of twins lay on the stony ground, their legs twisted at odd angles. Katie had swayed, and the soup inside had heaved as she took in their frozen faces. But when Harry's trembling hand had tried to shove her past them through the door, she had more than kept the rooster down. She had, in fact, turned halfway back, and with one finger raised and one eye squinting slightly, she had instructed, "Well, now, there you have it, Harry Jinx. Our Rosencrantz and Guildenstern might indeed be dead. Alas, 'tis dangerous when the baser nature comes between mighty Kate and the McGuffin! Will we be arrested?" So she had joked, remembering the minor characters of *Hamlet*, and changing slightly Shakespeare's line, but then she had felt her lips stretched back to breaking on her teeth.

But where was Harry now? He had fallen far behind. Katie slowed and looked toward Baraboo, and then retraced her path. Finally, she found him, breathing hard and in a panic, sitting by the road.

"Harry?"

"I can't go on," Harry sobbed. "I killed the twins." He almost laughed, it sounded so absurd.

"No. I don't think they were dead. They –"

"They were! They were! I didn't mean it, and now Jack'll come with his axe and –"

"Listen to me." Katie laid her bike down and then sat beside him on the grass. "They weren't human, Harry, they were zombies, or monsters, they…something without souls."

Harry stared at her. It was what he himself had sometimes thought. "Kate," he said, "they were machines."

"Machines?"

"All of it, it's all machines. The twins, that duck I saw that was like one of those plastic ducks one sees in a shooting gallery at a fair, all your stories fitting into one another like gears and pulleys, the whole thing turning, making that…monster-music, or what you said, the music of the seven rounded spheres…"

Katie didn't understand – maybe she didn't want to understand – and Harry was too hungry and worn out with worry to explain. "You should have had some soup," Katie said to him gently, pushing the hair out of his eyes, as if he were much younger than he was. "I brought you a little bread and butter from the kitchen. You'll eat bread, won't you, Harry Jinx?"

"Bread the twins made?"

"Maybe they bought it. Eat, okay? Do it for me?"

Harry ate, but he was very quiet, and when Katie finally asked him if he was ready to move on, she saw he was asleep. "Harry?" She nudged him softly. He only mumbled little dream sounds and clutched his fist a little tighter around the remainder of the bread.

Katie sighed and stared up at the sky. There was still time, she told herself, no need to wake him yet. Circus Eve festivities would surely last until the dawn. Besides, the moon had set and the sky was filled with stars. She remembered other nights now, also beneath the stars, nights when her father would point skyward and she would follow where he pointed. "Look," he would say, "there is great Orion, disappointed always. In life he was a hunter blinded by a jealous god. In death he forever chases the seven Pleiades whom he loves. Chases them eternally." Katie would look. She could not even read then – she was too young for reading – but she was not too young for stories, and sitting in her father's lap out on the patio at night she listened while he connected stars into the stories that men had told a long, long time ago. She listened and she looked. One little hand reached out to touch her father's finger that pointed to the sky.

Her father had taught her almost everything she knew, and if she no longer had the rooster to arm her for the coming battle, at least she had her father, or at least her father's books. Quietly, so as not to disturb the sleeping Harry, she reached into her backpack and pulled out a flashlight and the two books she had brought. By the scant light, she examined both the covers, put aside the Derrida, which she had tried so often and found impossible to read, and opened up *Trithemius Decomposed.*

Katie's father hadn't known it, perhaps, but as Katie had hinted on that day he gave the books to her, Trithemius was for Katie something of a hero. A sixteenth century monk, historian, cryptographist, and – most important – master of the darker magic arts, Trithemius had come into Katie's life during the period when she toyed with crystal balls and drugstore horoscopes, not too long after her parents were divorced. Trithemius wrote in cryptic codes; he was perhaps a witch. In fact, in the spring of her twelfth year, she had opened almost no book except one by Trithemius. It was his most famous work, the third volume of a trilogy entitled *Stegonographia,* which had been banned by the Roman Catholic Church upon publication and which witches throughout the ages had claimed contained the answers to the universe's riddles, along with spells by which the able necromancer – and maybe even Katie – could conjure spirits and control the earth, the sun, the sky and all its stars. Thus, in Trithemius' third volume, one might find the loose thread, the grand elixir, the elusive treasure-key. The only trouble was that in that third volume Trithemius had written, his black-arts Holy Grail was in a language that neither Katie, nor anyone else, could figure out.

The language of the occult has always been obscure (what, for example, is the meaning of *abracadabra* in average laymen terms?) and the language of the third volume, riddled as it was with rows of numbers and angelic astrological hieroglyphics, was quite obscure indeed. In fact, it was unreadable, and had been for about five hundred years. As that spring of her twelfth year wore on, Katie began to suspect that whatever Trithemius had known had died with him, and that the significance of the third volume would not reveal itself to her or, for that matter, to anyone of merely mortal flesh. Gradually, she gave up hope of ever understanding the infamous third volume and turned her attention to the other two, books steeped in Trithemius' cryptography and codes. These two volumes (best sellers in their day among courtiers and princes) did not interest her as much, but the idea of codes intrigued her nonetheless, and it was these two volumes that helped to turn her thoughts in the direction that her thoughts would ultimately travel, the road on which a quester might find a hydrodragon among the subtle, coded metaphors of books.

But if Katie had abandoned the magical third volume, she had never forgotten it and she had continued to suspect that no other written work had ever come as close as Trithemius' had to expressing the meaning of the world and the hidden springs of the divine. It is not difficult, therefore, to imagine the thrill with which she had received this gift from her father, a thrill, however, that was mixed with trepidation, for this was not a volume written by Trithemius, but a volume about Trithemius – about his third volume, and its title, *Trithemius Decomposed,* had a triumphant ring to it, as if the great Trithemius was found to be a fraud. It was, Katie thought, as if the author of this modern work had taken Trithemius apart, deconstructing the magic patterns people had believed in for the past five hundred years. Trithemius was their hero. For this reason (for no one looks with eagerness upon the deconstruction of their heroes) it took a great screwing up of Katie's courage to open up that book. But the time had come. Therefore, ceremoniously, thinking of the literary precedents of great men at the turning points of their lives – of St. Augustine with his Bible, for example (who randomly placed a finger on a random page), and of Petrarch with his volume of St. Augustine – she allowed *Trithemius Decomposed* to fall open on her lap. Then, placing one finger blindly on the page, she prepared to take the special counsel of whatever words were there.

But what was this? *The bearer of this letter is a rogue and thief,* the sentence said. What letter, Katie asked herself astounded. This does not sound like magic. What had this phrase to do with her Trithemius and the black magic for which he was so famous? Katie turned to another page and read: *the quick brown fox jumps over the dog,* and then on yet another something that sounded like a psalm. Our heroine was at a loss. She turned to the beginning of the book and read the author's preface, and though she did not want to, she began to understand. As it turned out, this modern author had realized a very simple thing about *Stegonographia Volume Three* that neither Katie nor five hundred years of witches and magicians ever had: its great conjurings and spells were one big hoax. Once the code was broken, there was absolutely nothing that made this feel occult.

What volume three revealed was nothing. No black-arts-holy grails existed in this book, no secrets of the universe, or treasure-keys, not even some enigmatic story or fiery diatribe that might at least have been amusing in itself. The magic tables and astrological hieroglyphics were cheats and teases designed to throw the would-be reader off his course. They deciphered into bits of nonsense: Latin aphorisms, axiomatic phrases, and whatever other catchy phrases the hoaxster had at hand. They reminded Katie of the sentences she had had to translate from her Italian text in school – unconnected to each other, and hardly even interesting in themselves.

Some lesser quester might have soon enough convinced herself that the deciphered sentences of Trithemius' code were themselves a code and that were she to crack them open, she might yet discover the great elixir that she sought. But those lesser questers are the sorts of questers dragons swallow, or the sorts that die ensnared in briar bushes on a sleeping beauty's castle walls. Katie was more nimble and she knew enough to shift with shifting winds: *Stegonographia Volume Three* contained no code beneath its code. It was at heart a hoax, another Cardiff Giant, and if she had any doubt of that, there was her father's second gift right there to confirm it: *On Grammatology*, the book by Jacques Derrida.

With vague foreboding Katie opened up the Derrida. She flipped the pages, glanced at phrases that she had tried before and couldn't understand (just as philosophers sometimes wrap themselves in obscure jargons all their own). But then she suddenly saw something she hadn't seen before. On the inside of the front cover, her father had written her a letter, or at least a little note. *Dear Katie,* it said:

> *You see the magical Trithemius? He crumbles into nonsense once we learn to read him right. Katie, all books are just like that. All books say nothing because the code we think we're breaking when we read them is composed, and decomposed, of nothing but mere words. You understand?*

Listen. What guarantees the stability of words, makes cows "cows," bricks "bricks," what is the meaning of "the good"? Nothing.

Meanings change and multiply. There is no firm link between things and the words we use to write them down, no eternal bedrock of inspired meaning on which to build a book, no divinely written plan, no engineer. Books are made of words that rest on no firm ground; thus built on sand, they crumble into nonsense when the reader gives a little push. We call this push "deconstruction." Do you understand? Not all writers intend, like Trithemius did, to write a book that deconstructs to senseless chatter. Nonetheless, it is what happens when most writers write.

Think of a book as a machine that's always breaking down. Or here is something better: consider a book to be just like a map. Books are like the maps of cities that simply don't exist. That's simple, isn't it? Are not all storybooks like maps designed to guide us through imaginary places, universes the author has created, places we can only visit in our minds? Good. Now, open up one of your books, your story maps, read what's written there, journey to that story's city, but this time take along your Derrida. Derrida will show you that this story map you've opened is not at all a map to the city you imagine, and no patterns, Katie, no links to other books. He'll point out too, this Derrida, that your storymap offers no legend, and no scale, and what signs you find as you walk along the story's streets are bound to be misleading, or lead nowhere, or they march you off to destinations that are not even on the map.

And are you scared to read now? Are you scared to go? Are you afraid your threads will tangle in this written labyrinth? Fear not, my Katie, you have no ball of thread, and it will not be a labyrinth you enter, since labyrinths have destinations. If you go, in spite of all of this, congratulations. You have entered into deconstructed realms.

These are the things that Derrida can teach you if you let him. Enjoy your summer in Wisconsin, Katie. I hope you like the book.

Your father,
Harold White

We can criticize this note. It is too long, it is not fatherly, it is certainly not quite comprehensible. But Katie did not criticize it. Nor did she read further in the Derrida. What was the point of reading anything? If she had only witnessed the unmasking of Trithemius without the further explanations from her father, or alternatively, if she had read her father's letter without the illustrative unmasking of Trithemius, she might not have lost all faith in what she once believed. But she had read them both and her father's letter had compounded the lack of meaning in Trithemius. Her hero, her Trithemius, had been unmasked, and it had been her father who had helped unmask him.

And yet her father who, in spite of all his failings as a father, had been the one who taught her how to read. He could not now be wrong, she thought, and she thought this also because she had been feeling doubtful after skimming *Trithemius Decomposed,* and before she read his letter she had suspected somewhere, dimly, that despite all the frenzied links she had forged between one story and the next, that the links were merely forgeries, and the things she linked – *Jack and the Beanstalk, Rapunzel, Moby-Dick* – had no connections, no intrinsic meaning; they were ciphers standing in for nothing, and nothing could not add to nothing; there could be among them no divinely written code. She had doubt when she read about Trithemius, but not conviction yet. And then she read her father's letter. And now she thought that everything had been made up. She now believed that for years she had forged herself hoax, a Cardiff Giant, because she had wanted to believe in patterns, archetypes, and the focus of her quest – the hydrodragon. And she had made up too the secret threads that bound the coin to the calliopes and then the seven brothers and her books. Maybe it was because a world without such forgeries was unbearable, or maybe it was just that she had somehow been compelled. In any case, all that was at an end now. The door was shutting on the world that she had lived in for so long. The door was shutting the way a cover closes on a book, and in the general apocalypse of her crises, she was left alone without a single text to read.

Katie closed the Derrida and looked up at the sky, an ordinary girl now in an ordinary world beneath the stars. What was that story that her father had told her once when she was very young? It was about a boy named Wyatt Gwyon who thought the earth was like a sea where angels fished. Wyatt was in a book by William Gaddis. "Maybe we are fished for," the boy had said, and little Katie had imagined angels with their fishing poles sitting on the stars. How did that story end? The boy had changed his name, Katie knew, but more than that she could not remember anymore. It had been a long time since her father had told her stories like that, and now above her the stars were only stars, bereft of all the ancient pictures of astrology. Whatever angels had once lounged upon them with their fishing poles, had disappeared.

It's all fairytales, she thought to herself now, her eyelids slipping, the strange fish of sleep breaking the surface of her thought and diving down again to haunted depths.

It's all fairytales; man-made, and not divine.

Part III
Return?

Chapter Sixteen

"We are plunged," said Katie, "into the Land of Death."

They were on Main Street in Baraboo looking down at the feast of Circus Eve spread out upon the riverbank below, twenty minutes after Harry had finally managed to wake Katie up, who did not want to wake, who, even as he jostled her, tried to hold tight to the tail of a mighty dream that moved off into the sky, slow and dragging her, indifferent to her weight – until she could not hold the dream's tail anymore, and it disappeared into the vacant interstellar spaces. She woke and saw the sky above her, and then Harry moving in to block it out.

"Kate, we have to go."

Katie had stared at him. Harry's eyes were pleading. What did he want of her, she wondered. Why wouldn't he just let her sleep?

But Harry wouldn't let her sleep. How could he when the twins were coming, and alive or dead they'd bring some kind of vengeance in their wake? "Besides," he said, trying to entice her, "didn't she want to get to Baraboo and the festival of Circus Eve? What about the McGuffin and the quest?"

Katie opened up her mouth to tell him, based on her father's letter, that McGuffins were just fairytales, but then she saw that he was shivering, and so she shut it up again. "Right," she said, "the infamous McGuffin." And so she rose, and so they went to Baraboo where now they stood above the circus feast, above what Katie call the Land of Death.

"Death?" said Harry "It looks more like a circus."

"Death's circus, Harry Jinx."

Harry didn't answer. He didn't know what she was talking about, and Kate was also murmuring a little hope that the quest had not ended in spite of her father's letter, but had instead gone underground, shifted to the next phase of the heroic archetype in which the protagonist descends into the Land of Death, or the wastelands of despair. Hadn't Christ spent forty desperate days wandering in a desert filled with doubt? And what of Jonah in the belly of the whale? Aeneas had gone to hell, as had Odysseus and Dante – why not then, Katie White began to hope, why not then Katie White?

Old habits die hard. Belief dies hard. And, even after belief seems truly dead, yet some small ember may still smolder beneath the ashes of the fires of apostasy and doubt. Thus it was with Katie White. Her loss of faith after reading her father's letter had thrown her into the mazes of despair, but, as Katie knew, no hero finds his journey's end without an episode of despair. So then, if Katie suffered from despair because she doubted the existence of the quest, might not such doubt be proof the quest exists? Odysseus, Aeneas, and all the others – they all had in their quests moments of despair. And if that were true, then perhaps the feast she gazed on now was not just a feast but hell itself, the pit to which all heroes in the dark nights of their harrowed souls eventually descend.

Certainly the festival she gazed on from the hilltop did little to dissuade Katie of such thoughts. Constricted alleys twisted into other alleys lined with gaming booths, and throngs of revelers drifted through their passageways, drunk and overfed, like the damned who gorge themselves to satisfy desire, but feel starvation still. Perhaps all midnight carnivals look like that. And one phrase struck her too – *midnight carnival* – midnight alone evocative enough, but *carnival* the more telling of the two. Katie's father had claimed that words were signs without a meaning, but Katie knew that in her older system of belief *carn* meant flesh and so for Katie, carnivals were feasts of flesh where revelers wallowed in the gross delights like gluttony and lust, fattening themselves unwittingly and then heaped up in hell with all the other carcasses, fodder for the very kind of feast they once had so enjoyed. But for Katie, it was not just that the feasts would fat the sinners up for tables down in hell, but that the feasts themselves were hellish, and if it were true that the feasters would someday be fodder for a devils' banquet, they were also fodder here and now: fodder for the sideshow tents and prostitutes and narrow gaming booths where con men fixed the skillo wheels and broke their laughter in the patsy's face.

Or at least, that's what Katie thought.

Apt metaphors for hell then, midnight carnivals, but there was more. Along one side of the feast below them ran the river black as Styx (Dante's river into hell), and around the other edges skinny silhouettes with pitchforks fed great bonfires that flung their flame and smoke against the sky. Katie knew, of course, that these were merely mortal silhouettes and hardly devils – local farmers, maybe, or perhaps the man who owned the candy shop – and she knew too that whatever it was they flung into the flames, it was surely not the bodies of the damned. She even knew that the tradition behind these fires was not hellish in the least. In fact, these bonfires were – as their name implied – *good* fires (after all, *bon* means good), rooted in the good, for since those dark ages when clog-shorn peasants had danced around them up and down the Swedish fjords, such fires had been lit to celebrate not hell at all but the splendor of the Heavens' summer sun. Katie knew all this, and she explained as much to Harry as they gazed down at the feast. Still, fire was fire, and fires burned in hell; as she and Harry put aside their bikes and descended to the seething circus grounds, she could not help but think of Dante and his city of the damned.

The moon had set, the stars had clouded over. There were six of these great bonfires spaced along the edges of the feast, but they let off little light, and once Katie and Harry passed the ring of fire, the dark was absolute. Sight was useless here, but sight abhors the blank of utter darkness and turns in upon itself to cast up against the blackness whatever images the other senses can produce. Thus, by the bitter stink of drunken revelers, Katie imagined empty, yawning faces grinning desperately at her – bloodshot eyes and hanging chins and twisted lips. At first, this didn't bother her too much. I am in hell, she thought, I really am in hell, and those around me whom I smell but cannot see are indeed among the legions of the damned. She moved forward into the darkness listening for the telltale weeping and the gnashing, and nodded with a certain satisfaction when she thought she heard them close at hand. Close got closer. Hands and limbs pressed in from every side. What had begun as satisfaction for Katie (who believed she was, like other heroes, on the way to hell) now became a slight uneasiness: her stomach twisted; she was not sure if she would keep the rooster down. The damned came closer still. Rough palms brushed against her cheek sometimes or scraped her arms, and when she pushed them off, they returned to touch her in ways more vulgar and more intimate, and one hand pushed hard and steady at her back. She tried to escape, but she could not. She tried not to breathe in the smell of burning flesh or hear the disembodied prayers and lamentations of the damned. She squinted hard to see what badgered her, but either the darkness was too deep, or else these beings around her were made of nothing but their wretched, ghostly desperation. Yet desperation had become palpable. It threatened harm, or perhaps it wanted something from her that she simply did not have. Someone is suffering, she thought. Someone in particular. Someone that I love. But she could not think of who it was and all around the revelers seemed to press in closer just to touch her, and she thought she smelled the cheap wine on their breath. I am Katie White, she murmured, I am Katie White – but something raked her side and a high heel found its way into her foot. Stumbling, aimless, she struggled to go on, but voices overwhelmed her – senseless voices, hurried, furtive, sad – each rising out of nowhere and trailing off again to nowhere – mocking her like grinning carcasses tossed up on an ocean shore, then taken back into the bosom of the waves.

That's what Katie heard; Harry heard much less. When they had plunged into the darkness of the festival, it had been all Harry could do to keep one hand on Katie's back. In the distance he heard the beat of conga drums, and not too far off a conga line snaked through the surging crowd. But Harry wasn't interested in that. It's a crowd of twins, he thought, keeping his hand attached to Katie's back, and if I look left or right, I'll see a million twins with idiotic smiles, mass produced from some machine and every one a threat. *Rooster soup?* they'll say like broken records, *Rooster soup?*

Harry shut his eyes. Katie veered left and Harry veered left too. Everything was Katie's fault, he thought, Katie with her fairytales and brandy and her bike. It was because of her he'd pushed the twins, it was her fault if they were dead; that's what he would swear if they should hunt him down. "Katie did it," he said out loud, "It's all because of Kate."

Katie didn't answer. The back he clung to twisted one way and the other as if Katie were searching for the conga line, and as she twisted, he was twisting too, his mind wrapped up in knots around the twins and then, somehow, around the seven dwarves. Two is a horror, he thought with shock – two is more than I can handle, but two is nothing next to seven, seven dwarf McFuggins is more than three times two, and it will be the seven who come looking, not the two, because the twins are out of it now – dead, or disabled like machines in spite of all their squabcakes and their belladonna, and their *Brandy, Kate? Oh Harry you're too young* – the twins are dead and out of it, and not so much the problem any more.

But the twins had been a piece of something bigger, Harry thought, and the sabotage of these two little screws might shut down the entire universe machine. When someone meddles with the cosmic motor works in the way that Harry had when he pushed the twins, then come the seven, Harry thought, because God sends them, because someone's got to fix the cosmos, because God can't let some kid down there in Baraboo foul up all the works. "Not that

I blame you, God," he said out loud. "Not that I blame you, you've got a universe to run. But I didn't mean to do it; it was Katie's fault, you saw that for yourself that it was Kate, and the McFuggins dine on little boys. And even if I'm not a little boy, will they dine on me?"

But Harry knew He wasn't listening. Who would listen to one little kid against a broken universe, one Harry Jinx against the seven crack mechanics who could fix the universe, the reconstructers, deconstructers of grand calliopes?

"Listen," God would say to the McFuggins, maybe, "some kid..." and then He'd go on to explain. "You think that you can fix it?"

"Oh, sure," they'd say, "and while we're there, mind if we eat the boy?"

And so they'd come. And they wouldn't only eat him. First, they'd torture him for information, because they wouldn't just be hungry. Besides their hunger, they'd be looking for the coin.

Harry felt a tap upon his shoulder and shook from head to toe. "No," he whispered. But the hand gripped down and Harry broke apart. "It wasn't me," he sobbed. "I swear it wasn't me. Besides, Kate has the coin –" Thank God, Kate had the coin. "The one you want is Kate –"

And then a wire shorting out? Or lightning?

A flash of light in any case, like punishment he thought years later because he had been guilty of wanting to betray her, and in that sudden light he saw that he was no longer following Kate at all, and he realized that what he thought had been a tap upon his shoulder, was in truth a steady hand. Katie had disappeared and he had somehow joined the conga line. With his fellow dancers before him and behind he was twisting through the crowd just like a snake, like at my great aunt's wedding Harry thought, the conga line winding on the dance floor, and me a flower boy or something, and when the dancer that he was holding onto turned around to grin at him, he saw something horrific, toothless and hermaphroditic: the bearded lady of the circus, was it? No, its opposite. Something Harry feared a whole lot more.

Harry jumped and ran, and pushed through the alleyways shouting, "Katie! Kate!" – tripped on his untied shoelace; went down.

Katie didn't hear him. Overwhelmed by all the revelers, exhausted by the assault of sound and touch and smell, she had forgotten Harry, had wanted only to stop moving, to squeeze herself into some unguarded corner of the night and disappear. What was the point, she wondered vaguely, of being pushed around like that? Hell had been so different in her books.

Katie was right. In books hell was much different. In books, hell had a plan: in Dante, nine concentric circles, for example, or a plain and rivers corresponding to a mythic map. What's more, although the hero who descends might bear witness to a throng of shriven souls, he himself was not so buffeted about. Separate, inviolate almost, the hero was like a spectator at some private pageant played out just for him, and he'd stand beside his guide and watch old friends and enemies pass by, and even if he wanted to embrace someone among them, as Aeneas had when he saw his poor dead father, he found that he could not. Nonetheless the pageant and the guide would teach the desperate hero something, give him reason to take heart once more in the seeming-hopeless quest. That's how it was with all of them; Dante had met at least a hundred shades like that.

But Katie had no guide. She had met no one but the drunken revelers, and they had not acted with the prophetic wisdom of the dead. Rather, they had clung to her and pushed her, laughed at her and breathed their sour breath into her face. Perhaps this was not hell then, but if not hell, then just a carnival? As unmapped as the story-cities her father's letter had described? If not hell, what then? But then came the blinding light that had revealed the conga line to Harry, and hope, which seems to spring eternal, pounced once again on desperate Katie White. In sudden light two dwarfish clowns swept low bows before her – death-white masks and plastic grins! – and with a flourish pointed toward a sign above their heads. *This way*, it read, *to the Grand Calliope*. Of course, thought Katie White. Just like a guide. And up ahead waits my calliope, McGuffin. Katie hurried, following the direction of the sign.

Perhaps she should have remembered her father's letter, or should have thought of Tantalus in hell, damned and hungry, reaching for his grapes. But now, as Katie hurried in the direction of the grand calliope (the very direction in which the whole crowd flowed), she thought only of the marvel that waited up ahead. She could not hope, of course, that the calliope could be a real McGuffin – her father and his gifts prevented her from going quite that far. Still, there were some curious coincidences, weren't there? Wheels turned inside of wheels, she thought, roosters in roosters, coins in coins, Higgins and McFuggins – and did Annabel Higgins have a Higgins brother, or maybe six or seven? And didn't the papers say the Higgins brothers had made a calliope that could not operate without a coin? Wheels turned in side of wheels, roosters in roosters, until the word *coincidence* seemed stretched to nearly breaking, and who can blame her if she suspected that something was behind it all and about to raise its head? Not mere coincidence. She clutched her coin and hurried toward the tent that housed the grand calliope, and as she hurried, she could have sworn she heard again those earlier fragmented sighs and lamentations now blossoming into rooster-crow, and monster-roar, and HA!, sounds that she could not place but seemed familiar, and she also thought she heard riddles riddled by a gollem in the dark.

******

The crowd thronged thickest near the entrance to the tent, the Big Top glowing from within, so that a shaft of light poured through the entranceway and bathed the multitude in the broad sweep of its path. After the extreme darkness of the rest of the festival, the light seemed nearly blinding, and as Katie moved forward, she saw that a platform had been built before the entrance, presumably for the barker who would tempt the crowd to step right up and see the show. But where she should have seen the barker, Katie looked and saw – my God! Who was that…God?

Of course, it seemed ridiculous to think that God was here, that God, who never made a guest appearance should suddenly show up in hell of all the crazy places, the whole point of hell being that it is the place where God is not. Maybe it wasn't God then, but whomever it was, he – He? – sure looked like God: long beard, aged kindly face, a flowing robe embroidered over with doves and angels and the rest, and eyes, once Katie got close enough to see, that twinkled even though the only light came from the entrance way behind him, which should have left his face sunk deep in shade. But no shade obscured his face. His eyes were twinkling. There was a wine jug in his hand.

The crowd was dense. It pushed her closer to the platform, and Katie saw not only sparkling eyes but moving lips, and then she realized he was speaking, very softly, to the souls right there before him who cupped one hand to their ears to catch his voice.

He's telling stories, Katie thought. Which story would God tell? She struggled closer. Finally she could almost touch the old man's snow-white hem, and then discovered when on arriving, she had been wrong. He wasn't telling stories. In fact, he wasn't telling anything; rather he was asking something, softly, to every upturned face.

"Have you the coin?" he asked, as Santa Claus might ask a child whether he'd been naughty or been nice. "Perhaps for you, the calliope will play." With infinite gentleness he said this; with infinite kindness he told them they needed nothing but the proper coin. Katie saw him lean above the heads of those who congregated there, and sometimes he touched one like a blessing. "Come, your coins," he said, "let's see if they will work." And the crowd – a coin in every hand raised like a host – disappeared into the tent. But they did not reappear, Katie noticed, as if there were some other exit for the sake of crowd control, or else, perhaps…no exit anywhere.

"Have *you* a coin?" The old man's face was in her face.

"A coin? What kind of coin?"

"Even the least shall not be spurned, and for the chosen –"

"Do not believe him," hissed a different voice close beside her ear. "'Tis a lie."

'*Tis*? Katie spun around and saw a reveler dressed in sackcloth like a monk. "You!" she said, thinking he seemed somehow familiar. And then, after a second, looking down, "Where are your shoes?"

"What need have *I* to cover up my feet? The barker, see?" The stranger pointed to the figure on the scaffold who even as he ushered others through the entrance, kept his gaze attentively at Katie. "He is a dwarf in heels. Into those pointed boots he stuffs his cloven hooves, and coiled in his pocket lies a tail."

"A tale?"

"A pointed tail. Do you know who I am?"

But Katie didn't know, though at first she had thought she did. The being before her seemed familiar. Was he an abstraction? Or was he a human being? "I don't know," she finally said. "I…read somewhere…perhaps something from my father maybe, or else…"

"Perhaps your father. Perhaps we've never met."

"Your coin? Have you the coin?" The figure on the platform had come close again and now leaned down and smiled gently in her face. Katie thought he looked magnificent. She clutched the coin inside her pocket and began to pull it out.

"Do not believe him," hissed the other, "he is a liar. All these people, every single one of them, condemned."

Had he really said that? Had he really said *condemned*? Katie wasn't sure, but as she turned again toward the character in sackcloth the crowd began to come between them. Katie grabbed his disappearing hand. "But if…if Derrida were wrong," she pleaded, "It's possible, isn't it? It's just one book, and if I have the means…"

He raised his eyebrows slightly and pulled away. "The means? To what? Do not believe that man upon the stage. All men plant in springtime, and then return to cull the bones in fall."

Had he really said those things? What did it mean? Katie wasn't sure. The crowd pressed in and they were separated, but just before she dropped his hand, before the night had swallowed him completely, Katie saw a cuff of plaid in red and gray beneath the sackcloth hem.

If in some small corner of her great heart Katie White had sheltered – as we know she had – the hope that this evening in hell had brought her back into her quest since questing heroes mostly triumph after descending to the world of death and of despair – but if she had sheltered such a thing within her heart, now even that was gone. The white robe, the sackcloth above the plaid, the weighty words, the dramatic light and dark – it had all been too confusing and one straw was too much, the camel's back was broken, and the quest had fallen in upon itself, or had, she realized, deconstructed, just as her father said it would.

Her father had not quite said that, of course. He had been discussing books in that letter that he had written, but because Katie believed that her quest came out of books that her father seemed to say were meaningless, she now saw these circus grounds that she had entered into as meaningless, no metaphor, no savage wood or barren heath or dark night of the soul from whose ashes heroes would rise and triumph once again. Earlier, thinking of Odysseus and others, she had ignored her father's letter and returned to the pattern of her quest. But now she thought once again that her father was quite right. Thus, as she pushed her way against the crowd to flee the one shade and the other (the one upon the platform and the other who had been closer to her ear), she could only think that they were not, as she would once have hoped, two loose ends connected somewhere. Rather, they were just two guys at a country feast dressed up in costumes, playing games. And now, again, when the crowds pressed in too thick (the very faces she had considered damned and had hoped to save), when the crowd pressed in again, she no longer believed that they were the damned. They were just people. Then as she escaped, she wondered, what had she just lost? But her mind was clouded; she could not remember what.

She came to the river. Smooth and dark the river was; swiftly it flowed. What was it saying? Was it saying something to her? She thought it was, she thought that it was calling Katie White. Well then, she would go wading, and if it were deep enough, she would push off from the river bank and drift down.

But how deep, she wondered, and how deep could a coin in that swift river fall? Deep enough to find a final resting in its depths, like *Moby Dick's* doubloon?

She doubted it. It was a shallow river. Too soon the coin would find itself back on the verges of the current, where even now, she noticed dully, half-a-dozen leeches clung to life upon the rocky bank.

Something was crying not far off. Something was in pain. By instinct, Katie climbed the bank and searched among the undergrowth following the sound. It was coming from a small, dark cave. She entered, and once inside she nearly stumbled on its sobbing source, the trembling body of her old friend, Harry Jinx.

Chapter Seventeen

"Harry?"

Harry didn't answer. He was lying on his side and the sobbing, which had gone suddenly still when she first entered the cave, resumed now, lighter and softer as if now that she were here, the sobbing would not seem to be distress. Katie sat down beside him, rubbed a tentative hand along his shaking shoulder, waited.

Eventually, Harry sat up and pushed himself against the stony wall of the cave. "Kate," he said, "I think we have to kill ourselves."

"Ridiculous," Katie answered, thinking even as she said ridiculous, how ordinary it seemed to her, the voice of Harry Jinx suggesting suicide. Outside, a slow dawn was rising, and in the brief light of the cave, Katie saw how changed Harry seemed from the boy who had come away with her just a few short weeks ago. That Harry had been flushed and roundly healthy, while this one seemed almost starved, with hollow eyes and raw and sunken cheeks. He's right, she thought, we have to kill ourselves, then aloud, "What good could come from self-annihilation?"

"Self-annihilation?"

"Suicide. Why should we kill ourselves?"

For a long time Harry was silent. "I'm so sorry, Kate. I never realized..." Harry looked away. "Because they're coming for us Kate, and they'll find us and when they do, they will kill us for the coin. Slowly. Painfully. They will...and so we have to..."

"No, Harry. No one's coming for us, and there's no McGuffin either."

"Not the calliope?"

"No, Harry. It's all a hoax. Not even. Just something I made up. There is no McGuffinish calliope here in Baraboo."

"But something is coming, and the McGuffin...it isn't here. It's fifteen miles south. It's in Spring Green."

And now he told Katie what had happened to him. However, the negative things he thought of Katie, he did not say out loud. Here is what happened to Harry Jinx.

Sometime earlier, lying on the ground amid the circus crowd, his elbow bleeding, his untied sneaker somewhere out beyond his reach, and all around him different kinds of feet – clown feet, cloven feet, and a few stilts and stilettos – Harry had a revelation: he should have spent the summer with his mother. July and August would have been much more pleasant if he had taken up his mother's offer that first night and gone with her to see that aunt in South Dakota, or else gone back home and spent the summer mowing lawns or delivering newspapers to the neighbors like most boys did, or watching re-runs on TV. What had he gained by staying here with Kate? She didn't love him, she never would, and what was even worse, she had used him to make herself a little bigger, led him around by the nose and made up stories, thinking he'd be stupid enough to believe them – ogre stories and emperor stories – and much worse, she had snooped beneath his mattress and found the coin.

Maybe Katie was a fake, he thought lying there on the pavement, a fake, like someone who looks between their fingers, while they count to twenty in a game of hide-and-seek. Hadn't it been her fault that they wound up in the tower? It was Kate, not he, who drank the brandy even though anyone could see just what the twins were like, and then she had abandoned him in the middle of this Circus Eve.

He got up. He ran away from the festival and then he fell again. And somewhere in the distance he could hear the conga music. If he could figure out which way to go, Harry Jinx was going home.

But just as Harry was about to try to stand, certain voices – unfamiliar, high, and threatening – made him freeze right where he lay.

"You think he's dead?"

"How should I know if he's dead. Do I look like a doctor?"

"Check him. Someone check his pockets."

"I'm not gonna check his pockets. You see how scared he was?"

"He wet his pants."

Whispering ensued. Harry noted with some small relief that, in fact, he had not wet his pants; nonetheless, he was not yet out of danger. He kept his eyes closed and tried not to move. The whispers – and there were many – seemed malicious, and the breath attached to them was rough with whiskey or with beer. They were very near, he realized. Sometimes someone nudged him with a little poke or prod, and once he thought that someone ran a knife right across his cheek. Finally, against his own good judgment he unshut one eye just enough to see what was around him. What he saw now were little feet in little boots. *Seven pairs?* he wondered. But it looked like only five. Where were the other two? And was it the McFuggins? It had to be. Who else would want to look inside his pockets? And what for, if not the coin?

The whispering broke into full voices once again. "Look. I thought I saw an eyelid move."

Harry squeezed his eyelids shut.

"He isn't dead."

"He isn't dead?"

"Maybe we should drag him to an alleyway or something –"

"Safer there."

"Here in the open it wouldn't look too good."

"And check his pockets there."

"Where?"

"In the alleyway, find out who he is at least, and then –"

"You nuts? You remember that other time we got involved with strangers?"

"That was different, that was a girl."

"I didn't mean the girl. I meant the woman."

Mrs. Higgins, Harry thought. That must be who they meant. But why would they attack her? And then he thought if the McFuggins lost their precious coin, and Mrs. Higgins had it…But what was it that the twins had said at the end of that crazy story about the rooster on the mountain top? And then Harry suddenly remembered the little book called *How it Ends*, and regretted that he had left it in the tower.

"Stupid princess. Or maybe a queen."

"Bitch."

"Always pretending she was so pure and everything –"

"Like driven snow."

"And always playing with my axe."

"And we warned her, didn't we?"

"Three times! Always answering the door."

"Should have tied her up."

"Messy business, that."

Mrs. Higgins, thought Harry in a panic now. Though what they said was incomprehensible to him. It must be her, and that meant that the seven dwarves had killed her with an axe. But whether he was right, or whether it had to do with something else he hadn't thought of, he never knew because just then, as one said, "C'mon, grab his wrists!" and as Harry was about to come to life and scream for help or mercy, there came a *Thump, Thump, Thump,* and a scattering of little feet.

"Hey, watcha doin' you big bully! We found him first!" and something giant lifted Harry by the collar and the belt loops and carried him – arms flailing, mouth prepared to whine – into an alleyway behind the sideshow tents and set him gently down.

"What the…"

"Harry?" Something sighed and waited. "Harry, do you want your shoe?"

My God, thought Harry, backing up against the wall, his hands against his face. Who was it? Jack? What good was it to be released from one threat to another so much bigger? What was he supposed to do? "Look, Jack…I haven't got it…I…Kate's got it."

"Got what?" he asked. And then, "You wanna play a game?"

"A game? What game?"

"I don't know. Tag or something."

Tag? Something wasn't making sense at all, and when Harry finally got up enough nerve to peer out from behind his knuckles, he saw with some surprise that Jack's face was not monstrous in the least. In fact it was really very gentle. Gentleness blended there with the kind of unfocused idiocy that he had seen on the faces of certain boys in grammar school who had been even less popular than himself, boys who worked at sums in math class with their pencils at right angles to the page, tongues out, and a knot of concentration scrambling up their broad white brows while other boys threw airplanes and spitballs at their backs. "Jack," he said at last, picking up the sneaker where Jack had dropped it. "Jack, you saved me."

"Saved you?"

"From the seven dwarves. Or maybe five."

But Jack didn't seem too interested in any of that, and instead of responding directly, he offered up a slow tangle of words that Harry couldn't understand. He's thanking me for something, Harry realized as he put his sneaker on and tied the laces with a double knot. For what could he be thanking me?

"If you hadn't done it, Harry, the two of them…"

The two of them? My God, the twins? "Jack, they aren't, you know, the twins are…" he couldn't quite say dead.

"They killed the rooster, Harry. Cut his head right off. That rooster and me, we used to…out in a barn, a man gets awfully lonely. And I saw those twins come limping home from the bottom of the tower, and then going away again. I heard them talking. And if they were not limping, maybe they would have cut my head off as well."

Jesus. What was he trying to say? Harry changed the subject. "What do you think they wanted?"

"The twins?"

"No. The seven dwarves."

"Oh. The dwarves. I don't know, Harry. What do dwarves ever want? I'm scared of them."

"You're scared of the dwarves?" Harry slid his back along the wall and sat down.

"They tease me, Harry. Sometimes they even threaten me."

"How could they threaten you? You're huge!"

"I don't know. They're very fast."

"They wanted to check my pockets," Harry said.

"Have you got something in your pockets?" Harry didn't answer. "Because, I do. You wanna see?" Jack put his hand into his pocket, pulled something out, and sat down next to Harry. When he opened his fist, Harry saw a little stone that, in Jack's giant hand, looked even smaller than it was. The surface was smooth and pink as if it had been worn away by many years in water or simply by the caresses of a hand.

"Where'd you get it?" Harry asked.

"It's my lucky pebble. I found it at the seaside when I was just a boy. Really my father found it. It's very lucky."

"Has it brought you luck?"

"I don't know." Jack stared at the pebble, and then leaned closer, and whispered into Harry's ear. "Don't laugh, okay? I think my father was a king."

"A king? Did he play chess?"

"But you know," Jack continued as if he hadn't heard, "someone stole me away when I was young. Someone beat me. Someone sold me to the circus. Not my father. Someone else."

"That can't be true."

"It is though. You wanna hold it?"

Harry nodded, and Jack tipped the pebble carefully into Harry's hand. For a moment they sat in silence now, each content in the warmth of a growing friendship. Harry rolled the stone between his palms.

"Why would the dwarves want to check my pockets?" Harry asked.

"I don't know. Maybe they wanted to help you. Maybe they wanted to see who you were…Oh. I see. You think they were looking for your coin."

"My coin?" Suspicion rose its hydra-head inside the skull of Harry Jinx. "What coin?"

"You know, that coin you keep in your pocket."

"What coin? I don't have a coin anymore. How did you know I had a coin?"

"I didn't Harry! Don't be mad!"

"How did you know?" Harry demanded again.

"I, I didn't." A great struggle ensued on the brow of Jack the giant. "At first I didn't know that it was in your pocket, but then I saw it, Harry. Don't be mad, okay? Through your bedroom window."

"Through my window? My room at Blunderbee was all the way upstairs! Even you're not big enough for that!"

Jack shrugged. "I had a ladder. I saw you pull it from your pocket, and then you put it under the mattress. After you left, I reached in and took a look myself and flipped it."

"You? You picked up my coin?" The universe snapped in on Harry's skull. "You, not someone else, and not my Kate?"

"I just wanted to look at it, Harry, and you were so scared of me. When that rooster flew at you in the barn, you ran away, and I followed you. I called out, *Don't be afraid, Harry*, but you didn't hear me – and then, you always had your hand inside your pocket just like me, and I thought maybe you had a lucky pebble too – maybe your father was a king. I, I just wanted to be friends is all…"

And so he thought of Katie, his beloved, whom he had falsely accused of sniffing out his coin. But she had not seen the coin, had not peeked beneath the mattress. And when he showed it to her, she said, miraculously, that it was the gold doubloon! And thus, maybe because of *Moby-Dick* and the children's fairy tales that she was always reading here in Baraboo, she had cut through the tangled vines and nettles of her fictions and found the one true golden thread of her great quest. Maybe she was a hero, after all.

He thought, if Kate were right, then that meant that the McGuffin did indeed exist.

These thoughts about Katie he did not say out loud. But then he continued to tell her what had happened with the giant, Jack.

"Listen, Jack, you ever hear of a place called Green Springs?"

"Green Springs? Spring Green you mean." The anxiety that had twisted up Jack's face now smoothed itself into the grateful smile of a friend redeemed. "Sure! I know that place! That's where the collections are!"

"What collections?"

Jack furrowed up his thick black brows and thought. "I don't know exactly. I can't describe it. A collection of collections all collected by one man."

"One man? Who? The twins?"

"Oh, Harry. Even I know that the twins are two. It is a place called *The Rock* or something. The twins took me there just once. There's a magnificent carousel with hundreds of animals on it and maybe not a single one a horse. But you're not allowed to ride it."

Harry's mind was racing. "Did you need coins there? Was there something musical?"

"You put coins in and then you heard the music. Special coins."

But whatever other information Jack might have had for him, Harry Jinx would never know, for even as Jack's lips worked, trying, it seemed to Harry, to get around a word as difficult as calliope, a net fell from above, and seven dwarves armed with ropes and ladders (and cogs and pulleys, Harry thought) swooped down upon the gentle giant, and while Jack put up only the slowest and most tangled of resistances, they snared and gagged him, hooked and pulled him up by blocks and tackles and carried him away.

"The dwarves? They carried Jack away?" Katie asked him now.

Harry gulped and nodded. He had told her what had happened with the dwarves and Jack, but he left out the bad things that he had thought of Kate.

"And then they dragged him up on a stage, and they" – and here Harry's face took on the extreme edges of terror that it had had when she first entered the cave – "like a platform with a wooden block and then with knives and picks and things, they, Kate, they pulled his skin off piece by piece!"

"Jack the Giant was flayed by seven dwarves?"

"Yes! Filleted! Just like a fish!"

"*Flayed*, Harry Jinx. Not filleted, I mean –"

"Ok then flayed!"

"Because *filleted,* well what kind of fish would a giant be, whereas *flayed,* that's what they do to saints and who knows, why not a giant."

"You think this is funny?"

"No, Harry, I was just –"

"You think this is an English lesson, Katie White? It's not. I counted. I counted and I counted. Seven of them, and Jack screaming the whole time, screaming for his father, Kate, he thought his father was a king, and he asked me, he said (I heard it, I'm sure I heard it), he said *Will you take me with you, Harry Jinx?* And the blood, it ran off the stage, and the crowd was going crazy –"

"Maddened by blood sacrifice, no doubt."

"Go ahead. Be sarcastic. Look though, my own hand covered in his blood, you don't believe?" Harry held his hand up in front of her.

"You cut your elbow when you fell, Harry. That's all." The blood ran down his arm. "What's in your hand?"

Harry opened up his fist and Jack's lucky pebble, like a tiny bone, rolled groundward now, as if released at last from a journey that had taken it, and Jack, too far away from home.

Harry's voice dropped low. "They're looking for the coin, Kate. That's why they killed him. They thought he had taken it from me in the alley."

"So they flayed him? Like the goose that laid the golden egg?" Maybe she was still teasing him, but her voice seemed gentler now and less sarcastic. "Look, Harry, it was just a circus trick. Some midsummer ritual, they probably do it every year. You said he knew them, right?" Harry didn't answer. "It's just a circus act, a hoax. This circus…the coin is meaningless,"

"No. It's not. You remember when the twins told that last story about the rooster? You…fell asleep, remember."

"I remember."

"It didn't just end the way I said. I told you that the McFuggins went up the mountain to destroy the calliope, but there was more to it than that, and I didn't tell you because I didn't think it mattered. But they didn't destroy it, Katie. They got to the top of the mountain, and they saw this thing, this beautiful thing made out of kites and flutes and they fell in love with it. But they couldn't just leave it there because the people from Green Spring wanted it destroyed, and the McFuggins had been paid to chop it up.

"But instead, they deconstructed it, and carried it down the mountain to a dell or something just beyond the town and then they rebuilt it underground.

But when they rebuilt it, they rebuilt a monster, because you can't just deconstruct a thing like that and expect it to be beautiful when you put it back together. When it played, it drove all who heard it mad, and I think that soon little girls were hanging themselves in snow white shifts from all the apple trees. Or maybe not. And they kept doing that, they kept taking it apart and putting it together, trying to make it better, but it kept on getting worse, and then the McFuggins lost the coin that made it go." Harry paused, and looked down at the stone. "That's why they want the coin. It's like their souls are all bound up in the calliope or something. They want to hear it play."

"That's quite a story, Harry." Katie paused. "But still, it's just a story."

"But it can't be! – I found the coin, and then I showed it to you, and you connected it up to all those stories that you read – to the gold doubloon in *Moby Dick – Jack and the Beanstalk* and all that stuff about towers of negation."

"I looked for patterns. I wanted to believe."

"And the newspaper? Did you hook that up too? About the Higgins brothers, which sounds just like McFuggins and McGuffins, with a calliope that operates by coin?"

"No," Katie whispered. "I didn't hook that up. Maybe the Higgins brothers did restore some old calliope, but the whole thing turned into a hoax. They must have spent a lot of money restoring that machine. Maybe they even took out loans. And when they got it running, all that came out was some horrible screeching sound no one wanted to hear. So then maybe they dreamed up this stunt. They clipped the wires maybe, pretending someone's got a special coin. They're raking it in up there on the stage, but still the goddamned thing won't play."

"But that's the one that's here – that's this one – the other one, if we go, if we go together. If we destroy it or something, or make it play…"

"And you think it's at Spring Green. Like the village in the rooster story. Green Springs, wasn't it?"

"Green Springs, Spring Green, it's like McGuffin and McFuggin. It's there, Katie. I know it's there, at something called *The Rock.*"

Katie didn't answer. There was nothing for her to say. She now believed that stories weren't true. She knew that they were uninspired, that storytellers left things out by mistake or else on purpose, that misreadings were the only readings possible, and that emperors, clothed or otherwise were better left alone. Even the possibility of a deconstructed calliope redeemed by a gold doubloon from *Moby-Dick* and all the dazzling cabalistic connections that such a tale implied could not possibly persuade her. She simply could not believe it anymore. Her father's letter told her this.

Harry was watching her, silent now. He was scared to speak, but even more scared not to hear her speak, and he suddenly realized that for years now it had been her voice telling stories that had kept his fears at bay. "Kate," he said now, tentatively, when he couldn't stand the silence anymore, "Tell me again about the great McGuffin."

And suddenly Katie flipped back and left her father's letter far behind. Katie decided she would tell him. From depths Katie never knew she had, she dragged the hydrodragon out: the tooth and claw, the tail whose slap could slay a thousand heroes, the hot and smoking blast of breath that obscured a flat blank face.

And then. Kate and Harry fled to Spring Green on their bikes. Their destiny was *House on the Rock*.

Chapter Eighteen

Mr. Bononosetta put down his pen. The summer was over, but how it ended was not as he had planned. What he had planned was a quiet time at home among his books, or at least with one book, or three chapters of that one book. He thought he might review what are sometimes called the pictorial chapters of *Moby Dick*, chapters 55, 56, and 57. These chapters discuss whales in three different ways. First, the statues, paintings, and engravings were made by ancient or medieval artists who had only read of whales in books or perhaps had seen them dead (that was Chapter 55); then whales painted on a blank white canvas captured by men who might have seen them in their living element (in Chapter 56); and finally, in Chapter 57, the scrimshaw of the whaling sailors who carved the whalish likenesses into the ivory bones of whales and ivory teeth.

In particular, Mr. Bononosetta was interested in the theories of Stuart Frank of the Kendall Whaling Museum of Sharon, Massachusetts, who, in the preface to his book, *Herman Melville's Picture Gallery* asserted that the three chapters move "from error toward truth, from inherited tradition to first-hand experience, from superstition to revelation." Mr. Bononosetta liked this idea – that truth reveals itself only through experience, and not through abstract things like books – and he thought perhaps he would study it, comparing for example, Kendall's book to those of the early pragmatists, or to the work of obscure literary theorists like Wolfgang Izer, or perhaps Harold White. And in Wallace Stevens' poem *The Snowman*, what was that line again? He would look that up, and finally, he thought that he might scrutinize the fascinating picture gallery that Mr. Frank had compiled in his book, and which consisted of representations of many of the paintings and other works of art that Mr. Melville had discussed in *Moby Dick*. Perhaps they would reveal something about the meaning of the novel? These, then, were Mr. Bononosetta's summer plans.

Alas, the best laid plans. Sometime in July, strange reports began to reach him from a sister in Wisconsin who sent him letters and newspaper clippings, first about poisoned wells and then about a circus festival, and she told him too about a calamity that had shaken up Spring Green, the small town where she lived. She wrote to him about how a local museum had been broken into, a museum that was a "collection of collections, collected by one man" she had said, a bunch of bric-a-brac, the sort of stuff anyone might find up in their attic, and the museum was like an attic, but mostly underground, acres and acres, big enough to house a whale (the whale is there, she said), and all of it artfully arranged in fantastical landscapes, a kind of Disneyland. Few were the travelers who passed through Wisconsin and didn't add it to their tour. His sister had enclosed some clippings, and the clippings had included pictures, mostly of calliopes. There were many calliopes, these clippings said, musical machines, survivors from the European courts and the heyday of the Midwest circuses, contrivances that still turned out marching tunes and waltzes to the delight of all who heard them play. "Anyway," the sister wrote, "someone set fire to one of the calliopes, a young girl from somewhere else whom police discovered at the scene and locked away."

"She's in jail?" Mr. Bononosetta asked by telephone that night.

"No", his sister answered. "She went mad."

He went to see his sister and her husband on their farm. The husband was a husband, the sister was very thin and sharp-nosed; she tended to a haggard garden, baked mediocre pies, and harbored in her breast a deep-dyed rancor for the county fair officials from whom she'd never won a single ribbon for her pies.

"I spice them special", she often told her brother, "but I'm from the East, have only married in to this midwest Spring Green, and only very recently, and there are certain lines one must not cross. I'm not a native and so I can never win a contest at a fair."

Mr. Bononosetta barely listened; yes, he had come to see this sister, but really, he was thinking only of the girl. What had happened? What had driven that girl mad? According to his sister, the young lady was mumbling psalms and proverbs when they found her and her legs and hands were badly burned. But the story was unclear. Had she burned it down on purpose? Had she been alone? Had anybody tried to pull her out?

He thought about it for a week. In the mornings while his sister and her husband were practicing their pies, he took to driving. He drove down the hills and up. He drove by emerald pastures and neat red barns, past squawking coops and squealing sties, through all the local towns with Main Streets, charming grocery stores, and banks – up the hills and down, and every day he passed the gated entrance to the house-become-museum where the calliopes had been, and to which tourists flocked like pilgrims, not because of the catastrophe (for that story of his sister's did not appear in local newspapers), but to be amazed by the collection of collections that was housed within the house.

He passed by daily. He yearned to see it. He yearned to know the place and the calliope, the fire, that story's full beginning and its end. And what his sister said – was it even true? He passed by, but he could not enter in. Mr. Bononosetta, though he fancied he was Ishmael, or at least in some vague way Ishmaelean, now that he had brought himself to the very doorstep of what might be called a quest, he found that once upon that doorstep, some scruple held him up. There must be signs, he told himself, there must be indications. And so he got back in the car to drive back down the hill and down to town for ham and eggs.

And then. One morning, sitting at a table in a coffee shop he noticed something jammed between the salt and pepper shaker, and he seized it up and stared. It was a brochure for tourists, the kind of brochure that fills the racks in motel lobbies in every town across the country– triple folded, the advertised tourist attraction looking endlessly amusing, and the prices not listed on the back. This brochure was almost of that sort, though for the genre it was really rather odd. *Have you seen House on the Rock?"* it demanded on the cover. And then inside, closely typed, a wall of words with the intensity of typeface broken only by one small and crudely drawn cartoon that seemed to have no relation to what was in the text. *Have you seen House on the Rock,* the cover had demanded. But it was not the question that confounded Mr. Bononosetta. Nor was it the intensity of type. He flipped back to the cover. Beneath the question was a picture of a whale.

Have you seen
House on the Rock?

Turn not – do you hear me?

Turn not your back on butter dishes.

Turn not your back upon kazoos.

Scrimshaw teeth found rotting in an attic.

Road signs.

Clocks and cannonballs.

Calliopes and Junk, you say. You say it is a mess of junk.

You do not know what true collecting is.

Imagine for yourself an uncle, who keeps old kites up in an attic or else another uncle who grows a garden where no seed is turned away. His is not the garden of an ordinary gardener, who prunes and weeds, plans out a color scheme, seeks the rare and beautiful and fences out the rest. Your uncle's garden is not like that at all. It is a mess. It is a garden run to riot, a tangled, weedy, place where ivy climbs the apple trees and tiger lilies, rampant and tenacious, and chokes out the bleeding hearts. You are a fool, you tell your uncle, you need a pair of pruning shears – but your uncle only smiles and tips his watering can into the purple phlox.

This garden of your uncle's, it began with just one seed.

But there is another kind of collector, too. It begins with a stamp, or storybook; it really could be anything at all. The collector sees it in the window of an antiques shop one day, or he comes across it on a garbage heap, or among the boxes down in his father's basement that he has come to clear away. The thing (let's call it a flamuggin, which like the X in algebra can stand for anything), the thing bewitches him, though there's no reason that it should. He has known flamuggins all his life, played with them when as a child, maybe, or kept them in his pocket, or seen them hanging on a neighbor's wall.

But this is not like your uncle, because for this collector his flamuggin is something very special. He becomes crazy and obsessed. It is as if it suddenly occurs to him that written in the fine lines of his flamuggin-artifact is the story of its own creation, as if the thing to be collected were, above all else, a thing created, the final turn on some great potter's wheel. *Who made those wings?* he wonders, if it's a butterfly-flamuggin. *Who carved the perfect terror of this insect face?* But – and here's the crucial thing – in the beginning the collector does not really want to know. He only asks the question, accepts the silence and then allows himself to be amazed.

All well and good, so far, but if the silence comes to irk him, then just like that the quest begins. Just once, he thinks, just once – and he begins to haunt the auction houses and Sunday church bazaars in search of a more eloquent flamuggin, and he finds another one, and then another and another. He brings them home and puts them on a shelf. The collection grows; here are a dozen, then two dozen, and then a hundred. They all need dusting – somewhere in the background a wife raises an eyebrow, and taps her tiny foot – but this collector hardly notices at all. Each new flamuggin intrigues and then dissatisfies, the whole collection is one great dissatisfaction – it is a choir, but it will not sing, he thinks, and only other failed collectors of failed collections of flamuggins understand.

In desperation, he becomes a connoisseur. He eliminates and organizes. He prunes and cultivates. He reads Flamuggin Histories and Aesthetics in three volumes, he learns to quibble beauty, he bores his friends for six full weeks when he finds a reference to flamuggin worship in a book long out of print. And still he is not satisfied.

Arrangements matter more and more, and the quest becomes the quest to find the one flamuggin that will complete the whole collection because (according to the terms of some silent contract he imagines) these others will only open up their mouths to sing once the perfect flamuggin has arrived. Thus, the collector seeks to finish out the scheme he thinks he has begun, but each new acquisition merely breaks the pattern. Beyond all these flamuggins, he suspects there lurks another, a grand flamuggin, something he has only heard about in the backrooms of antiques shops, or seen alluded to in *The Flamuggin Quarterly*, and even then, in only the most obscure of terms. It is the template and the paragon, and perhaps it is the mythical Flamuggin that the mythic dragon guards. What would he not do to get his hands on this flamuggin of flamuggins, whose very name, they say, is written right across its face? My guess is he'd do anything at all.

Thus, the failed collector, who has whittled down his mind to absolutely nothing, or to the finest point required to thread through labyrinths of acquisition ever narrower in scope.

But this is not the true collector. Just the opposite. No search for grand designs, no thoughts of a single, mythic flamuggin lurking behind the others just beyond his reach. The minds of true collectors expand grander, ever grander, to encompass nearly everything the others left behind. Thus your uncle with his tangled garden. Thus the man who built this *House On The Rock*. We find that this collection of collections is the collection of a genius: butter dishes and kazoos, old paperweights and carved up bits of ivory. And the outsized, outdated waterworks of three mid-western towns?

******

For that true pilgrim who comes wandering through these twisted halls and out-sized caverns, hangers – places huge and dark and without windows, seeming underground, or maybe like the belly of a whale – for such a pilgrim, it is not the fineness of each artifact that draws him on (though some are very fine indeed), but rather the overwhelming aggregate of all of it, the pleasure of submersion into a universe where things almost ordinary and only slightly strange (let's say five spoons from Greece) become extraordinary, near miracles, testimonies to the endless impulse of creation, but creations from an ordinary man: the sailor on the ship who carved the bit of bone into a tiny wonderland, the man who poured the opiate elixirs into the colored bottles; the farmer's wife who on a summer afternoon painted the winter sleigh bells royal blue. A true collector finds such things and gives them back to us again – stuffed grizzly bears and teddy bears, far-eastern statues, boiler plates and butterflies and barber poles, and finally the great automatons and grand calliopes – the true collector finds these things and heaps them up into grand unfathomable designs, mixing the semi-sacred and the half-profane in half-lit rooms arranged like dreamscapes – true gardens these – collections more creation than collection through which the true pilgrim wanders, never asking if there is a beginning or an end or guiding thesis, only believing it is a far flung act of love.

NOTE:
This pamphlet is not from *House on the Rock*. I, an anonymous writer, made it up.

"My God, the whale," whispered Mr. Bononosetta, as if he were a worshiper whispering a prayer. "It seems the whale *is* there."

But then, just as he opened up the pamphlet, "Well? And have you gone?"

Mr. Bononosetta looked up, startled. The waitress stood above him with a thick blond hive of hair. A dishrag dangled from one hand; in the other hand she held a half-filled coffeepot.

"Gone where?" he stammered out, embarrassed to be caught red-handed with such a florid interest on his face.

"*House on the Rock*, honey. That's where that whale is." She waved the dishrag vaguely toward the pamphlet. "You haven't gone?"

"No." And then he added, "I'm a teacher," as if that somehow would explain it. "That calliope…"

"Oh, that. Some crazy girl, she lit a match, burned the whole thing down. That's the rumor, anyway."

"Well I…"

"Resurrection's planned they say."

"Resurrection?"

"Restoration, reconstruction." She leaned closer and whispered in his ear, "You know your shoe's untied?"

Mr. Bononosetta ducked and tied his shoe.

But what had happened?

"Katie White," he murmured to himself, and then, as if inspired, "Harry Jinx."

Harry tried to save her, Mr. Bononosetta thought. Harry would have tried to pull her out. They would have gone to find some end to their adventure, paid the entrance fee and entered into a place half funhouse and half haunted, but maybe not a house at all. This house upon the rock was a labyrinth of darkness lit by sudden spotlights, with narrow passages opening into caverns filled with an extravagance of things, collections and collections of collections: a child's seashells in a box, for example, or old keys in a kitchen drawer, small things and also grander ones (a carousel, a whale, and waterworks) and calliopes with all their grand mechanics gracing nearly every room, all of it somewhat amazing, none of it like anything that Kate and Harry had ever seen before.

But once they entered, Katie and Harry did not linger to marvel at these things. Instead, they looked for nothing but a hiding place and finally discovered a tiny little nook behind a mirrored wall. In they slipped and crouched for hours barely breathing until the gloom of half lit rooms had turned darker and the tourists and the guards had all gone home. The outer doors were locked, and Kate and Harry carefully emerged into the vast and cluttered caverns that seemed to whisper now to Harry in the dark.

Air vents hissed.

"Something's breathing. " Harry said. And then, "Perhaps it's, maybe we are in the belly of the beast."

"Nonsense," Katie said. "It's the ventilation." But still it hissed and Harry heard the slow and steady thumping of a heart. Bits and pieces of the vast collections swam out of the darkness as Kate and Harry sallied forth:, a sign that said *Apothecary's Shop* with windows filled with antique jugs and vials, and then beyond that, an Octopus's Garden, aging puppets, and masks, and wolverines.

And then dolls. "Look at these dolls," Kate said when porcelain faces gleamed into stark relief. But something rumbled somewhere, a sound all men associate with menace, and maybe it was only air shifting about in empty airshafts, but Harry thought he heard a whisper and saw two staring eyes, and thought too that he saw the dull glint of an axe. "Dwarves," he mumbled and began to back away, but Katie drew him back. "No Harry. Dolls," and then she pointed out the lace that fringed a bonnet, and showed him too the light blush on their cheeks. "Who placed that little bracelet around her porcelain wrist?" Katie asked him. "Who thought to give her paper dahlias, and in this other hand, a gilded mirror so she may contemplate her face?"

She called them beautiful, but Harry did not think so. "Are their whole bodies made of porcelain," Harry asked her, just to ask her something.

"Maybe not," she told him. "The bodies of a doll can be made of sackcloth and sawdust." Then she turned away.

Something rumbled. Something ticked. *This way to the organ room,* said one sign sunk in shadow. What organs? Harry wondered. Heart and spleen?

Katie meanwhile showed him other things: a lamp from Tiffany's, a collection of old buttons, and then a single, pickled, disembodied hand, suspended in a dusty mason jar. The hand had been mutilated. The jar had been labeled. *Three-fingered Jack,* it said. *Notorious gunman of the wild west.*

"Jack? My Jack?" Somewhere his heart beat faster.

"Your Jack? No, silly. It is the artist's Jack." And then, while Harry tried to block the beating out, Katie spun a story. What humbug-wonderman had made that hand – from what? "A ball of wax?" she asked. "A potter's corpse?" Or was it from the corpse of this humbug's father buried on a hill behind a barn. "He dug his father up by moonlight," Katie said. "He chopped the hand off with an axe, chopped away two fingers so that the hand may never write again, and then enshrined it in this old mason jar and took it around to farmers who would lay down pennies for a glimpse of it, and never think to disbelieve. *Ah,* they'd say, *so that's the gunman's hand.*"

And after that, she told him about relics. "Frederick the Wise of Saxony had over fifteen thousand relics, and in Rome eighty-six unbodied heads had been set up just like miracles four hundred years ago. Relics, Harry," Katie said, and Harry listened, but he also listened to the rumbling and the hissing and the ticking, and then quite suddenly, he found himself alone.

"Katie?" he whispered. "Kate? I think that hand is real," – but Katie had moved on while he had trembled, and hearing no reply besides the hisses and the rumbles, and the echoes of his own voice calling back to him, he stumbled forward, slow at first, and slowly faster, falling and picking himself up again, running down dark corridors that twisted like his own bowels were twisting. "Katie!" he shouted. "Kate!" heedless now of whatever noise he made – crashing into collections of all kinds, little ships and shoes – and sealing wax, he wondered? and cabbages…and other things and then the magnificent calliopes, whole rooms of them including a fantastic carousel and four apocalyptic men riding horses, blue-wigged and satined waxen ladies at their clavichords, marching bands and mannequin trombonists, and one especially that looked like an emperor playing on a flute. His robes were magnificent; he seemed to slide his eyes and raise his eyebrows as Harry stumbled by.

And incredibly, a great big whale.

The slow and steady thump of heart was wild now. It overwhelmed the hiss and rumble, and drowned his own voice out, even as he shouted, "Katie! Kate! I found the emperor…! And the whale!" Yet even as he shouted, he knew just how ridiculous it was, and that when September came and he was back at school, when the world that he had been plunged into had once again receded to safer distances – to within the magic ring of circus acts, or else back behind the covers of his books – that he might laugh at all of this. But that would not be until September, and so for now he flew down the deep dark corridors, crashed into shining armor and struggled to his feet again, ran on, saw something disappear around a corner up ahead – a tail? Could it have been a tail? But when he got there, he saw nothing, ran, and fell again, this time into the wooden arms of wooden Indians, and then into the arms of Katie White.

"And shall we dance, my Harry Jinx?"

Dance? Katie's face seemed like a blur. She pointed vaguely and Harry spun around, caught his breath and then stood back amazed. Before him stood a marvelous calliope. It was not playing. It was called *The Blue Danube.*

This is the one, he thought. This one is it. And then: My God, oh God, how beautiful it is – and it doesn't matter to us what it really looks like. It only mattered that Harry thought that it was beautiful and saw seven smiling mermaids up at the top of it and several full-sized instruments of music down below – a harp, a cello set against its chair, kettledrums and violins, un-mannequinned, yet fully animate somehow, standing patiently before their music sheets, ready to play without performers for the small price of a token, a coin slipped in a small, half-hidden slot.

"…if only we could leave it as it is," Katie said suddenly behind him, wishing perhaps that she could lose thought like a drowned man in an ocean, let herself drift down into herself and disappear like the shipwreck that she maybe was, and be submerged in wonder. But losing one's thoughts would not be possible. Thought is leviathan, too big for this shallow pool of humanity – thought thrashes, wrecks us, dries us up.

She pointed at the vacuum tubes and wires running all along the ground.

She means to wreck it, Harry realized, horrified. She means to dagger it, or lance it, or tear it limb from limb. And quickly, to distract her, he asked her why its name was *Blue Danube.*

Katie shrugged. "The Blue Danube is a river somewhere. And look, your seven dwarves are all turned into angels."

Harry looked above to where she pointed. The carved and silent figures seemed to sing to him. "Mermaids, anyway," he whispered. "Let's leave it Katie. Let's get out of here."

"And if we turn on this calliope, Harry Jinx, then will all hell break loose? Will Baraboo, or perhaps our hydrodragon, be destroyed?" And then she opened up her palm and he thought he saw the doubloon shining there for one brief second before she slipped it in the slot.

And then? Did hell break loose? All Harry heard was music, the expanding *Blue Danube,* filling every corner of the caverns, and all he saw was Katie waltzing, alone at first, and then he realized that he too was waltzing, that Katie had pulled him close to her, her face a blur, her breath now hot against his ear, her cheek upon his cheek. Wide steps she took, and Harry with her, as if they were sailing on the sea, until he realized that her cheek was damp, that there were tears upon her cheek, and when at last he dared to look into her face, her

Blue Danube eyes were shining and there was a thing there he had never seen before, nor would again.

And something grabbed him. Something pulled him back into the bowels of the machine, and though to the end of his life Harry would swear it had reached out for him, that he had not tripped on untied laces, or on the vacuum tubes and wires running along the ground, entangling him even as he struggled to stand up and then fell back – though he would swear the calliope reached out for him, yet he also swore the thing was just a grand machine. And then, when Katie leaped in, perhaps to save him, he strove to stop her, getting out of it himself and then plunging in to pull her out, her Swiss knife already cutting wires, cutting holes into its vacuum lungs, while Harry tried to wrest her from the instruments, even as the notes sagged, and even as he felt a slow and awful heat.

The calliope was on fire. She had shorted something, and now the flames lunged forward, engulfing Katie and the instruments, pushing Harry back against the wall. Somewhere cymbals crashed, somewhere a violin, and as he struggled to reach her, he realized that the coin was in his hand. Had she not used it then? Had she used nothing but a common token such as all the tourists got when they paid the entrance fee? He stared at the gold doubloon and for one mad second he thought that he could save her with it, that if he tossed it to her, it would lift her out somehow like a lifeline thrown to someone who was drowning. But that was madness. He tossed the coin away and plunged toward Katie, and tried to pull her out.

She did not want to be saved. Three times Harry struggled in, and three times she fought against him until he could not withstand the smoke and flames and tumbled back. Rising, turning, he fled back along the caverns and found the emperor-sultan and stripped him of his robe, and then returned to Kate to plunge in once again to wrap her in it, and try to pull her out. And even then she clung to something there, but this time he overpowered her. Harry was the larger of the two.

It had almost been too late. Burned on hands and legs, she monstrous lay beside the wreck, staring at the fire. Like an emperor, Harry thought, naked and protected by his well-embroidered robe.

Mr. Bononosetta could not know all this, but he could make it up. He didn't even know if there was an emperor, a calliope, or mermaids, or a hand with just three fingers. It was all imagination like Stuart Frank's analysis of chapter

55 in *Moby Dick*. He left the diner, and then left Wisconsin and fled all the way back home. At home he locked the door and from the top drawer of his desk he pulled a blank white sheet to write an explanation of his departure to his sister and her husband baking pies and picking berries way back in Spring Green.

And now his pen paused above the bundle of papers he had been fiddling with through July and August. What would become of Harry Jinx? he wondered. He thought that Harry would survive. He would grow up and go to college; he would build himself a nest in the higher reaches of an ivory tower and live in it alone. Harry Jinx would never marry unless the wife was Katie White. And in the summers, he would leave the tower and wander far beyond its walls.

******

Harry Jinx (and maybe Katie White) would spend many years on the trail of the McGuffin, thought Mr. Bononosetta. And who can say they are not looking for it still?

9 7 9 8 8 8 6 9 3 1 3 3 4